GERALDINE MOORKENS BYRNE

Face the Music!

The Music Shop Mysteries Book 2

Contents

Preface   iv
Chapter 1   1
Chapter 2   9
Chapter 3   17
Chapter 4   31
Chapter 5   47
Chapter 6   67
Chapter 7   88
Chapter 8   102
Chapter 9   117
Chapter 10   136
Chapter 11   148
Chapter 12   158
Chapter 13   163
Chapter 14   180
Chapter 15   194
Chapter 16   203
Chapter 17   216
Epilogue   226
About the Author   230
Also by Geraldine Moorkens Byrne   232

Preface

Welcome back to O'Brien's Music Shop, Ireland's oldest music shop and a landmark in the great city of Dublin.

If you don't already know, the fictional music shop is based on my family's real music shop, Charles Byrne Music. For 150 years it served the people of Ireland, and especially Dublin, and four generations of Byrnes served behind that counter, myself included. The Music Shop Mysteries are a labour of love for me, and the wonderful characters I knew through the music shop come to life again in these pages. Irish musicians and music lovers are a special breed, a law unto themselves.

I have included a Cast of Characters below, because although Mrs. O'Brien is of course the heart of the mystery series, this is an ensemble performance. She is ably supported by her friends and neighbours.

Also included is a short glossary of Irish slang, the colourful words that Dubliners especially use in ever more inventive and funny ways.

I hope you enjoy the story.

Geraldine Moorkens Byrne.

The Hibernian Orchestra

PRESENTS

Face the Music!

A MURDER IN SEVERAL PARTS

CAST OF CHARACTERS

O'BRIEN'S MUSIC SHOP
MRS. TERESA O'BRIEN, PROPRIETOR
MR. MICHAEL CLANCY, LUTHIER

THE O'BRIEN IRREGULARS
MAI KHAN, SETANTA KAPOOR
&
CLARE, PEADAIR, EAMONN AND CATHERINE
OF "THE SUPER UKERS"
ALSO
DETECTIVE MALACHY FLYNN
DETECTIVE HARRY DEMPSEY

WEST STEPHEN STREET
MR. AND MRS. KHAN - THE NOODLE PALACE
PADDY - THE BALD BEAR BARBERS
ASHMARA KAPOOR, SETANTA KAPOOR - KAPOORS VINTAGE
AND FASHION EMPORIUM
DENISE AND DAN - FANCIES CAFE

WITH
THE HIBERNIAN ORCHESTRA
ELSA VON STRENG, CONDUCTOR
LISA KENNEDY, FIRST VIOLINIST
OLLESSA OBU, VIOLAS
FINTAN MCLAUGHLIN, MUSICAL DIRECTOR
&
ARNOLDO MESSINI (TENOR)

* * *

Glossary

Citeog - A left-handed person, from the Irish/Gaeilge "Ciotóg" (pronounced *Kit-ogue*)

Craic - Irish slang for "fun" (pro. *Crack*)

Eejit - a very foolish person (pro. eee-jit)

Gobdaw - someone who runs their mouth a lot, also a foolish person (pro *Gob rhymes with blob, Daw rhymes with awe*)

Gurrier - A very rough, ignorant, probably criminal person (pro Gur-ee-urr)

Gwon - Common Dublin saying, a contraction of "Go on!" eg "Gwon outta dat," or "Gwon with yourself…" (pro. *Go'Wan*)

Hipster - Anyone with notions, especially if they've a beard and a flat cap but are under thirty.

Janey Mac - traditional Dublin expression

Perry - Thomas Perry (Irish: Tomás de Poire; c. 1738 – November 1818) Famous Irish Violin maker.

Scalpeen - see Sleeveen, Gurrier

Shook - Irish slang for upset, disturbed, disconcerted

Sleeveen/ *Sliveen* - an untrustworthy, sniveling person

Chapter 1

Lisa Kennedy strolled on stage, looking every inch the soloist violin player she aspired to be. Under her left arm, she had carefully tucked the Perry violin, a treasure that her boyfriend Michael had lovingly restored for her, and in her right hand she held her precious William Hill bow (a gift from Michael's employer, Teresa O'Brien of the famous O'Brien Music Shop.) The Hibernian Orchestra was about to play its first season with a new permanent conductor, the original one now serving a life sentence in Dublin's Mountjoy jail for murdering the first violinist. For the opening series of concerts Lisa was not only first chair but to her delight, had a shot at a solo piece, possibly even Beethoven's Sonata Number 9, the *Kreutzer*.

The new conductor had managed to both delight and upset a lot of people before ever stepping foot in the concert hall. A fearsome reputation preceded them, but that was nothing new when it came to conductors. Lisa had suffered under quite a few tartars over the years and this new appointee certainly had their own way of doing things. First a handwritten list of music had arrived by post, addressed to the Musical Director, and outlining the pieces expected to be ready for rehearsal on the first of August. It was an eclectic list, ranging from reliable classics to obscure modernists. Lisa was excited - at last, the Hibernian might get a chance to try something new!- but many in the ranks were dismayed.

"No clear direction," sniffed Charles McKay, Double Bass player and resident grouch.

"It is a bit all over the place," admitted Ollessa Obu, Lisa's best friend and principal Viola of the orchestra. "But it will stretch us."

Claire Fitzgerald, cellist and general pessimist, shook her red curls and pouted.

"Stretch us - or ruin our brand." Claire had recently discovered the joys of TikTok, and prided herself on her social media knowledge. "We're known for serious, carefully curated concert series. Not - not a *mashup*."

Still, they had obeyed instructions and prepared as best they could for this moment. First up was the Beethoven, which Lisa had practiced until her hands ached. Then the Amy Beach, *"Violin Sonata opus 34"* - the choice the old guard had railed against most. Followed by - and this had sent Fintan McLaughlin, the Music Director, into hysterics - Sean O'Riada's masterpiece of patriotism, *Mise Eireann* followed by an orchestral arrangement of the theme to the latest block buster film, *Men of Action*. The composer of the theme was Irish and had arranged for the Hibernian to perform it before any other orchestra, in advance of the film's debut.

As Lisa took her place centre stage, her colleague Maria Lawless, second violinist, hissed at her. "This is going to be the strangest concert ever."

"It's only a first rehearsal," Lisa soothed. "I'm sure it's just to put us through our paces."

Fingers crossed, she added to herself. While she had championed change, it was hard to imagine what audience would flock to this particular mix of pieces.

Finally, everyone was on stage, and the noisy chatter gave way to the familiar discordant swell of instruments being tuned. When that faded away, silence settled over the musicians. They glanced nervously at each other while the moments ticked by. Lisa felt everyone's eyes on her, as the tension grew. She was just about to suggest that they try out a few sections to get started when the stage echoed to the sound of firm, unhurried footsteps.

From the wings, her tall thin frame dressed from head to toe in scarlet, a military cut jacket over tight pencil skirt, and ankle boots, blonde hair cascading over her shoulders and her trademark black conductor's stick hanging loosely from long, delicate, red-tipped fingers, Elsa Von Streng emerged.

Their new conductor had arrived.

She took her place at the podium and cast a cold blue eye over the orchestra. To Lisa, as first chair, she gave the tiniest of nods but the others were treated only to an impassive appraisal. A sniff and purse of the lips hinted that she wasn't overly impressed with the result but she remained silent. Lisa's heart thumped uncomfortably, as she waited for some word of introduction from Ms. Van Streng, but the older woman seemed perfectly at ease with absolute silence.

"Sod this," Lisa thought suddenly. A lifetime spent under the domineering control of her uncle had left her with a tendency to second guess herself, but now she was First Chair - and possibly soloist - she felt obligated to speak up for her fellows. She stood and smiled warmly at the conductor.

"Ms. Von Streng, on behalf of the Hibernian - *Céad Míle Fáilte*, Welcome!"

The assembled musicians, relieved that someone had finally

broken the ice, applauded loudly and chimed in here and there with "Welcome, *Fáilte.*"

One thinly arched eyebrow raised slightly in response, and in cool dry tones - her German accent barely noticeable - Von Streng murmured, "Indeed."

It was hard to know what that one word meant, but Lisa choose to take it as a good sign. She sat back down and waited. Von Streng took her time, flicking through scores and arranging sheets of music on her lectern but at last, she tapped the wooden frame with her baton and said, "Phrase one, strings only."

The rehearsal got underway and a more nerve wracking, soul searing, two hours was never endured under the hallowed eaves of the Concert Hall. It wasn't that Elsa Von Streng shouted - her voice never raised above conversational tones - or even that she made cutting remarks like so many of her predecessors. It was just the absolute contempt that she managed to convey by a shrug, a twist of her lips, a tap of her baton. Every error, no matter how slight, every questionable choice or not fully realized effort, was noted and corrected. There was no quarter given and nowhere to hide.

She must have hearing like a bat, Lisa thought, battling the urge to tuck her Perry back under her armpit and leg it from the stage.

But it did occur to her, as the day wore on, that Von Streng's choice of pieces was rather ingenious. Every section found themselves in difficult territory in turn, and it certainly revealed some issues - the Double Basses needed to tighten their syncopation, the timpani were really surprisingly good when given their head, and the woodwind section lacked cohesive leadership. Lisa was quietly pleased with the strings

- the violins dug deep and corrected themselves, while the violas under Ollessa's leadership were full bodied. Claire, for all her complaining, pulled the cellos under control quickly and by the time they tackled *Mise Eireann,* earned herself an approving twitch of the head from Von Streng.

Only the film theme remained, and Lisa - now seated back in her customary first chair position - was surprised when the conductor waved the shiny black baton at her.

"Forward!" The stick indicated the soloist chair again. "You will take the solo."

Lisa tried not show her dismay. There was nothing for it but to go through it, as her friend Teresa O'Brien often said. And thanks to the elderly shopkeeper, the violin was in tip-top form and fitted with the best strings available - ones that were normally out of reach of the young violinist. Michael, her boyfriend, was also the shop luthier and made sure the Perry lacked nothing.

"Here we go," she thought, as the music swelled.

The violin solo was only four minutes or so, but it was a piece of ridiculous complexity - the composer had aimed for heightened emotion and overshot by a mile. It was a musical meltdown, and Lisa had to strain every nerve to lean into it. She didn't risk so much as a glance at the conductor, feeling sure any good impression made by the Beethoven would have been eradicated by that performance. All she wanted now was for the torture to end, and to go home to a glass of wine and a nice bit of dinner - and a shoulder to cry on, if Michael was free.

"Very well." Von Streng gave three sharp raps on the podium to indicate that they were to pay attention. "We have much work to do. None of you are where you need to be - but I will admit, some of you rose to the challenge and others did not. You - the red hair with the cello. Not bad. Cellos, not bad overall. Violas - similar. Good leadership. Double Basses - not acceptable. Timpani - continue to work, but quite good. Wind - very mixed, very. Some of you are competent and others are lazy. Violins - Seconds, solid work but you must strive for more. Firsts, I am not displeased. You!" she pointed a scarlet talon at Lisa, "You have done well. You will be our soloist for the Beethoven- and for *Men in Action*."

She glanced at a gold wristwatch. "Dismissed. Rehearsals at 10 am sharp. You will be seated at ten on the dot, I do not wait for anyone. For any reason."

She nodded once more, and then Elsa Von Streng strode off the stage.

"Well. That was fun." Ollessa remarked wryly. lowering her viola and rolling her head to soothe her aching neck.

"The cheek of her!" Charles McKay was red-faced with anger. "The unmitigated cheek."

"You did well," Sally Murphy, the youngest member of Hibernia and one of the second violinists, grinned at Lisa. "That was almost praise she gave you."

Lisa laughed. "We'll see. I suspect she won't give any of us an easy ride. Still, at least we have a permanent conductor again. And a world famous one - it'll be a huge draw."

"How can they afford her?" Charles grumbled. "They tell *us* there's no money for a decent wage."

Lisa and Ollessa exchanged a loaded glance. Charles had a long list of grievances that he liked to air in turn, and one of them was the fact that orchestral members were notoriously underpaid. If left unchecked, he could launch into a solid half hour rant.

"Yes, yes, Charles," Ollessa soothed the portly older man, "but a name like hers will boost ticket sales. And I for one am looking forward to a season that branches out a bit."

"It'll be good, just hang in there." Lisa looked around. Most of her colleagues had already made their way backstage, grumbling among themselves. "And look, the leaders need to set a good example. We have to bring our sections on, Charles. No point in giving out about it. Von Streng is here to stay, and we might as well just make the best of it."

Charles gave her a withering look. "Hmm. We'll see how you feel after a few weeks of Madame. You might change your tune then, heh!"

Lisa rolled her eyes and followed Ollessa to the dressing room they shared. As First Chair, she could have demanded a dressing room for herself but she had shared with Ollessa since they both joined the Hibernian and by continuing to do so, it freed up a room. Claire Fitzgerald and Marion Chang - a flautist, and very easy going - had grabbed the spare room and now all the dressing rooms were a little less overcrowded.

Ollessa grabbed her wool shawl and matching hat, saying "I'm so late, I was supposed to meet Matthew half an hour ago!"

"Your husband is a saint," Lisa grinned. "You are forever turning up late - if at all."

"I know, but it's not my fault. At least I have a good excuse this time - and he'll forgive me once I tell him all about Von Streng."

"Is he still writing an article about the Hibernian?"

"Sort of. He's decided to concentrate on the new regime, so to speak. The start of a new era. He reckons he can sell it to *Classical Ireland Monthly,* with a bit of luck."

"The joys of being a freelance journalist, eh?"

"Ah, be grand. It's only until he gets his book written - these articles keep a roof over our heads." Ollessa paused and in a carefully neutral tone added, "How's it going with Michael?"

Lisa blushed. She had been seeing the young Luthier, Michael Clancy, from O'Brien's music shop, for over a year now but while he was very sweet, and very attentive and said all the right things, she felt as if they were a bit stuck, somehow.

"Great!" she said brightly. "Go on, run. You're already late."

Ollessa looked as if she wanted to say something, but instead smiled, waved and hurried off to meet the long-suffering and patient Matthew.

Lisa put away her precious violin slowly and carefully, wondering if she was being unreasonable, or paranoid. On paper, she and Michael sounded perfect - a shared love of books, a passion for music. But she had an uncomfortable feeling that Michael would be content to amble on like this indefinitely, meeting up several times a week and not demanding too much from each other.

"We're both busy," she chided herself, "and who knows when I might have to travel for work?" She would be better off concentrating on Von Streng and nailing the *Men of Action* solo section. Not to mention making sure the orchestra managed a better effort at the next rehearsal. No time to be mooning over Michael Clancy.

Still though, she admitted, it would be nice to feel their relationship was going *somewhere*.

Chapter 2

Teresa O'Brien waited patiently while the young man on the other side of the old counter tried to make up his mind. On the worn wooden surface was an array of different violin bows, laid out flat so that each tip faced her and each frog faced the customer. He ran his hand across the selection pausing over a Pernambuco wood, octagonal stick with silver-mounted frog, stamped "Karl Hofner."

"This is the one I really liked," he announced, "but it's not the most expensive one. Maybe I should go for the dearer model?"

"Why?" Teresa smiled at his obvious confusion. "Look, it's not an electronic gadget. It doesn't come with extra buttons and special functions if you opt for a dearer model. They're both good bows. They're both German, handmade, with excellent fittings and top quality horsehair. That's what dictates the price range. The only extra value it has for you is whether or not it suits your hand."

"Oh."

"Did the dearer one suit your hand?"

"No. No, this one felt much more comfortable."

"You felt confident playing with it? Perfect. That's your answer. The extra hundred euros would be worth it if the other suited your hand better. But it's pointless if this one is the most comfortable."

The customer now reassured that they weren't missing out by opting for the slightly less expensive bow, Mrs. O'Brien waved them off with a grin. Some of her friends felt she was lacking in business acumen, by not up-selling at every opportunity, but O'Brien's Music Shop had been in existence for over 150 years. This had been achieved by honest dealings and customer service – despite the slightly chaotic and crowded space, and the eccentricities of its owner.

In her husband's time, people had come to him knowing that they could rely on his word and she took pride in upholding that reputation. As a result, O'Brien's was the cornerstone of Stephen Street West, and a landmark in the city of Dublin.

The old shop door swung open and the ancient, battered bell tinkled. Teresa paused in her tidying of the bows back into their cases and looked up to see one of her favourite customers, and good friend, Clara Walsh.

Short and shapely, with a shock of brightly dyed red hair and draped in a brightly coloured scarf adorned with large roses, Claudia was a cheerful, chatty soul who often popped in to see Teresa when she was in town. A devoted member of the Super Ukes, Dublin's premier Ukulele group, she was also mildly addicted to visiting O'Brien's Music Shop's collection of top-quality ukuleles. Four showcases of gleaming four-stringed instruments dominated the tiny shop space, boasting an array of tenors, concerts and sopranos with a few large baritones and even a futuristic-looking electric model.

"Oooh," Claudia exclaimed, not wasting any time on hello, "You have the new Walnut tenor."

"Just unpacked it."

"It's stunning. I really don't need another tenor uke, but if I did…" She stroked the strings and four clear bright notes filled the air. "It's a beauty. But I swore to Peadair that I wouldn't buy any more ukes. Although, he actually needs a new tenor. He lent his to Maggie Dunne at the Hooley and she's gone off to Argentina with it. I wonder now, if I bought him one of these then we could share it, don't you think that's a grand idea? Wouldn't that be a nice surprise for him?"

Teresa shook her head. "Keep me out of this, Claudia. Poor Peadair, I couldn't look him in the eye if you bought that without telling him first."

"I suppose so," Claudia reluctantly returned it to its place in the showcase. "But I'll tell him to come in and look. So, how are you? Any news?"

"All good here. We're busy, with all the kids going back to school soon and music lessons starting up again next month. How about ye? Peadair back lecturing yet?"

"Not until early October. We're enjoying the time off, I can tell you. We went to Kerry for a few weeks in July, my sister has a place in Cahersiveen. How's Michael getting on?"

Teresa knew this seemingly innocuous inquiry after her protegee, Michael Clancy, was in fact a loaded question. What Claudia really meant was, *"How is Michael getting on with his lovely young lady?"* Michael was the darling of all their customers and friends, who were now deeply invested in his relationship with Lisa Kennedy.

Their slow but steady romance was a major topic of gossip not just among the musicians who frequented the shop but the other shopkeepers and businesses on Stephen Street West. Across the street from the music shop, the Khan family ran the Noodle Palace restaurant. Mrs Khan inquired on a near daily basis if there was *"Any news?"* meaning of course, any hint of an engagement. Paddy from the Bald Bear Barbers had bet Teresa a free wash and shampoo that it would happen that coming Christmas. Setanta Kapoor, whose granny owned the boho-chic dress shop, Kapoor's Emporium, was of the opinion that Michael better not drag his feet, or Lisa would be snapped up by some famous musician.

Teresa tried to mind her own business, content with the knowledge that if there ever was any news, she'd be the first to hear.

"He's grand."

Judging by her exasperated sigh, Claudia found this lack of gossip very frustrating, but she tried another tack. "And any word from Denise and Daniel?"

The owners of *Fancies* café next door to the music shop were on an extended holiday, their first trip away as an official couple. They had gone through a difficult time, which saw Dan accused of murder before a joint effort by Mrs. O'Brien, local shopkeepers and the Super Ukers had cleared his name. But it's an ill-wind, as they say, and the experience had led Dan to realize that he was stone mad about his friend and business partner, Denise. Now the couple had taken a two-month long trip to New Zealand to visit Denise's brother - news of an engagement there would be almost as exciting.

"Nothing much." Teresa saw the disappointment on Clara's face and relented a little. "Well, just between us - Denise did text me last week, she says they're getting on brilliantly and Daniel is talking about them getting a place together."

"Oh!" Clara almost danced on the spot. "That's wonderful. I wonder where they'll look? An apartment in town, maybe - or maybe a proper house, especially if they're thinking ahead. Can't rear kids in an apartment."

Teresa blinked. Only Clara could get from "they may be thinking of moving in together," to "married with kids!" in one breath.

"Clara," she said, "I'm warning you, don't get carried away. They are only thinking of it."

"Ah sure, I know. But still - isn't it nice? The next step in their journey. Your Michael could take a leaf out of Dan's book."

"It took Dan ten years to realize he was in love with Denise, Clara. I'm sure Michael won't be that slow."
"Hmm. I don't know. He's awful set in his ways, Teresa, for a young fella. He's mad about the girl, anyone can see that, but he's just too laid-back."

Teresa didn't like to admit it but Clara had a point. Loyalty to Michael made her defend him but she had to admit, there were times when she wanted to shake him. The young luthier had been a godsend after her husband Cathal had died, and they ran the music shop together very happily. He was more like another son to her than a business partner. She couldn't fault his kindness, or his devotion - but he did seem to be a bit complacent about Lisa.

"Young people, Clara, they're in no rush these days." Teresa turned the conversation gently to other topics. "Tell me about the Super Ukers Gala Concert?

The Super Ukers were celebrating their tenth anniversary as a group by doing a charity concert in the Concert Hall, accompanied by the Hibernian Orchestra - a feat made possible by heavy sponsorship and the patronage of the President of Ireland himself. To keep costs down, and maximize profits for the charity, the forty strong members of the club were doing the decorating, marketing, and general organizing on a volunteer basis. The results promised to be interesting.

"Oh yes!" Clara's face lit up. "I've managed to get a load of balloons on the cheap - someone ordered 150 balloons for a birthday party, but when they arrived, they said they were the wrong colour and the print was wrong. Instead of Happy Birthday, they printed "Hippy Birthday" so I said we'd take them. So we changed the theme to Hippies and The Summer of Love, and we're all dressing up like it's the sixties! We'll ask the audience to dress up too, Teresa, so get ready to channel your inner "flower power." Peadair has a wig, hair down to his bum, and he's growing a beard for the occasion. Oh, and young Eamonn's wife has a friend who makes cakes and she's doing one in the shape of a vintage uke for the after party. We'll start rehearsals in the actual Concert Hall in a few weeks, can you believe it?"

Clara regaled Teresa with descriptions of the upcoming festivities, until she noticed the time and squealed.

"Well, I'm desperate late now! I have to run. See you soon, let me know if you hear anything from Denise. Or Michael, ha ha."

When the heavy old door had swung shut behind her with a thud, Teresa stood lost in thought for a while. It might be time to tackle Michael about his slow approach to affairs of the heart. Maybe he'd say they were happy as they were but at least she'd have broached the subject. She hadn't exactly rushed into marriage with her late husband but they had had an understanding from early on, that they were serious about each other. She hoped Michael and Lisa were the same.

The door swung open again but this time a stranger stood there - a tall, thin woman in a startlingly red outfit, and what Teresa privately thought of as a fine mane of blonde hair. She had a long face with strong features, not conventionally pretty but attractive and very glamourous. The newcomer stood in the middle of the small shop floor and looked around slowly. Teresa smiled, but the other woman didn't respond in kind. This didn't faze the shopkeeper at all - she had dealt with artistic temperaments for over fifty years and it would take more than that to rattle her.

"Hello. Can I help you?" she asked sweetly.

"Hmm. Is this it?"

"This?"

"Yes, this. Is this it?"

"Depends what you mean," Teresa replied calmly. "If you mean, in a general sense, I don't know. Some say we are merely fleeting pin pricks of light in the infinite darkness of the universe and some say we are the pinnacle of existence itself, destined to recycle through lives until reaching perfection. If you mean, is this all there is to the shop, then yes - this is all that is available to the public. How may I help you?"

She thought she saw the faintest twitch of a lip in response but couldn't be sure. The other woman waved her hand and said, "It's very small."

"Well now, that depends rather on your perspective."

"Does it? I would have thought it was a statement of fact. Your shop is very small."

"It is indeed. But that's only from the perspective of square footage. If you look at it from the perspective of time, it's entirely different. We've been around one hundred and fifty years, and four - correction, five - generations. That's big."

This time the twitch was almost a smile.

"I will concede that, from that point of view, it is not so small. You only stock stringed instruments?"

"Mainly. We stock some Irish traditional drums - bodhráns - and whistles."

"And you like these...*toys*?" She pointed rather dramatically at the showcase full of Ukuleles. Teresa O'Brien narrowed her eyes and a touch of frost entered her voice.

"You disappoint me. I thought a world-renowned conductor like yourself would have recognized the quality and workmanship on display - not to mention the potential inherent in the small but mighty Uke. I know classical guitarists who can't play like some of the Ukers."

The woman stared at Teresa, her face a mask.

"You know who I am?"

"Elsa Von Streng?" Teresa grinned widely. "Absolutely. I was only reading about you a few days ago. New Principal Conductor of the Hibernian Orchestra, no less."

Elsa took a step closer. When she spoke again, her voice was quite different. Low, soft and with an unmistakable echo of the inner city of Dublin. A Liberties Lilt.

"But - do you *recognize* me?"

Mrs. O'Brien leaned forward and replied quietly -

"Of course I do, Emer Kelly. I'd know you anywhere. Welcome home!"

Chapter 3

"The last time I was here, this was a pub!" Elsa Von Streng - who used to be known as Emer Kelly, before she reinvented herself - looked around Fancies café in wonder. The little coffee shop was a far cry from the dingy public house it had replaced.

"Knocked it all down, well over ten years ago. Built a four-story apartment block with retail space. That's Fancies café, Kapoor's Emporium and the Bald Bear Barbers."

"And the hotel! It's so modern now."

"Yes, it's a very chic place now, quite the hot-spot. The old bakery is still there and the newsagents, beside The Noodle Palace. Lovely people, the Khans. What else was there? Oh, remember the butchers? They've gone mad posh now. Moved to a unit in the Westbury Mall and sell vegan burgers and steaks the size of your head. Michael, the young fella that took over our workrooms after Cathal died, he sometimes shops there. He says it costs an arm and leg but it's worth it."

"Cathal." Elsa looked sad. "I'm so sorry to hear he's gone. He was awfully good to me, so he was. Do you remember when I got my exam results?"

Teresa certainly did. The young girl had been such a regular visitor to the shop, she and Cathal had begun to look on her as family. She was obsessed with music but struggled to find her niche - a fact that tormented her during her college years. The prestigious university course she was on was unforgiving of what they deemed "mediocrity" and Elsa was great at many things but brilliant at none of them. Violin, Cello, Flute, she could turn her hand to each with ease, quickly becoming proficient, but not outstanding.

Her third-year results almost finished her.

"I cried for a week. I was too ashamed to call in to see him, I thought he'd be so disappointed."

"They were perfectly good results, Emer -I mean, Elsa. You were too hard on yourself."

"Maybe. All I remember is, I felt like such a failure. It didn't help that my tutors made me feel like I didn't deserve to be there." She looked at Teresa and for a moment, the vulnerable young student smiled out through the glamourous veneer of the famous conductor. "It was Cathal, and you too - you remember what he said?"

"Try conducting!" Teresa imitated her late husband's bellow. "You're not meant to be a mere player, you're the one they should be following!"

"Yes. I thought he was mad. We'd touched on it of course, and I enjoyed it, but it never occurred to me that being a conductor could be a career for someone like me."

"It was a snobbish profession back then," Teresa agreed.

"It still is! Why do you think I did all this?" Elsa gestured towards herself. "Emer Kelly from Francis Street wasn't good enough, not for the grand high poohbahs of Irish Classical Music. I got the scholarship to study in Lucerne and well, I realized that I didn't *have* to be that person anymore."

Teresa eyed her thoughtfully. "Well, I liked that person. But we all have the right to reinvent ourselves, love."

She thought of Delilah, the receptionist at the Bald Bear Barbers. She'd bet good money that child hadn't started life as a Delilah, but she was an artist and like Elsa, felt she needed the bit of glamour to stand out.

"Once I'd started, I couldn't stop. I got my first gig as Elsa, and then another and another, and by the time I was conductor of the Lucerne Symphony, everyone knew me as Elsa. I could speak fluent German by then, and French. I changed my name legally and put Ireland behind me."

"But you've been home since, surely? To visit family?"

Elsa looked away. "Not really. I write occasionally. My parents are both elderly and living in Foxrock with my brother. He's done very well for himself too. We exchange cards and so on. He thinks I'm working for a music school and don't get much time off. Like, he's never even been to the Concert Hall - he's more a Death Metal type than Beethoven."

Teresa was faintly shocked. If any of her three children had left to live abroad, she would have haunted them with calls and letters. Especially now, when there was video calling and face messaging or whatever the term was. Her eldest, Philomena, had once spent six months travelling the world and had rung home every Sunday night.

"Then, they haven't seen you in a while?"

"No. Look, I know how it sounds. It's awful. I feel bad, honestly. And when I read about Cathal - it was just by chance, I saw an article in the paper - it got me thinking. That's why I took the job with the Hibernian."

"So that you can reconnect with them? That's good."

"Is it?" Suddenly she was one hundred percent Elsa Von Streng again. Teresa could sense the shutters coming down.

"How on earth do I explain to them? I changed my name, avoided contact, and lied about my life."

"You'll find a way," Teresa replied briskly. "You came to see me, didn't you? You wanted to see how I would react. I could have said, 'Sod you,' but I didn't. You disappeared out of our lives too, you know. Cathal never stopped wondering what happened to you. He was afraid he had done something wrong, had hurt your feelings or annoyed you. No, don't apologize. I'm not trying to make you feel bad. But you have to understand, people may well be annoyed, angry even. They'll possibly be hurt - and you'll have to deal with that. Eventually though, it'll be worth it. I'll open Classical Ireland Monthly and see an interview with "Elsa Von Streng, Liberties Girl Made Good" and you'll tell your story."

Elsa stared at the ground. "I am truly sorry. Cathal meant so much to me and so did you. It just got harder and harder to be both Emer and Elsa, you understand?"

"I do understand."

"Thanks and I promise you, if I ever do that interview, it'll mention him. I'll tell the world how much he helped me."

Teresa smiled. "I'll hold you to that. Now, tell me everything. I want to hear the life of Elsa Von Streng, from the moment you left Ireland twenty years ago!"

A cloud passed over Elsa's face again. "It's been mostly good, honestly. But - well, I won't go into it now but there were other reasons I wanted to come home. It's a long story. Let's just say, my last three years in Berlin were a little more than I bargained for." She gave a brittle little laugh. "It's fine now, but I'm glad to be home."

Teresa didn't press her, asking instead about the new job, the Hibernian orchestra members, and how she was getting on with the notoriously fussy musical director - but her curiosity was piqued. She would have to get the Berlin story out of Elsa at a later date.

* * *

Mai Khan hovered at the door of The Noodle Palace, willing her mother to hurry up. Each day, after she left the large secondary convent for girls on the nearby St Stephen's Green, Mai made her way to her parents' restaurant and did her homework at the desk in the tiny office. Then she was expected to put in a couple of hours behind the counter of the takeaway section, until the evening rush started and one of the regular employees relieved her. Usually she didn't mind too much, as it gave her a chance to chat with customers and catch up on local gossip but tonight the sixteen-year-old was burning to leave.

"MA!" She roared up the stairs to the office, causing Lucy, who ran the hot counter, to jump and spill half an order of duck fried noodles on the countertop. "Mam, come on!" Mai added.

"For heavens sake, Mai," Lucy snapped crossly. "Stop shouting."

"Sorry, Luce. But honest to god, she's so slow."

"What has you in such a rush, anyway? You don't usually go home until five."

"I'm going shopping," Mai beamed. "It's my birthday soon. Mam said she'd take me out to get something to wear. We're going to Chez Maurice."

"You're not! Oh wow, Mai. That place is meant to be fabulous. And pricey."

"I know. I can't wait. Niamh Finnegan was there for her sister's 21st, and said it was *amazing*. Honest, Luce, everyone in my class seems to have been there except me."

Luce shook her head. "Mai, you want to watch that. Them girls like to boast a lot, from what I can see. You're always worrying about what they've got and where they've been. It's not worth it. Next week, there'll be something else - they'll spend their lives chasing after something new."

Mai shrugged. "I'm not like that, Lucy. I just want to go to see what it's like."

Lucy looked unconvinced but forbore to reply, as Mrs. Khan finally appeared, looking rather hassled and not at all as if she was looking forward to a shopping spree.

"Mai, I only have an hour. We'll have to hurry."
Mai rolled her eyes. "I've been waiting for you for half an hour, mam. Come on. See ya, Luce!"

Despite her airy words to Lucy, Mai felt a pang of discomfort as she bustled along, trying to get her mother to hurry up a bit. If she was completely honest with herself, it did matter a bit - just a little bit - that her birthday dinner was in Chez Maurice. It really was the hottest spot in town, reputed to be a heady mix of opulent, French decor, reminiscent of Versailles itself and painfully modern menu and service. The food choices were strictly limited and changed daily depending on the whim of Maurice Moray, the famous chef owner. Once you made your selection you had to collect your own plates and cutlery from a table in the centre of the room and lay your own place settings. Mai had carefully omitted these details when she had pleaded with her parents to book the restaurant. Once they were there, she was sure everyone would enter into the spirit of things.

And she could finally wipe the smile off Niamh Finnegan's

face. She was looking forward to just casually dropping it into conversation soon, as if it was an everyday occurrence. Maybe something like, *"Ah we're not doing much for my birthday this year. Popping to Chez Maurice for dinner."* Niamh had made such a production about it, describing every minute detail, so Mai had a shrewd suspicion that the only way to one-up her would be to act as if it was nothing special. Niamh was forever making pointed comments at Mai - little remarks about fast food restaurants and funny foreign food - as well as ostentatiously sniffing the air and asking, *"Can anyone else smell spring rolls?"*

Surely wanting to beat her just this once didn't make Mai shallow?

They soon found themselves in one of the many boutiques on Grafton Street. Her mother handed her a pretty floral dress with a lace collar. It looked like something a seven-year-old would love.

"This is pretty." Mrs. Khan remarked approvingly.

"Mam. No. Just no. You don't pick, okay. I'll look." Mai honed in on a sequined red mini dress, with long bell-shaped sleeves. "This is more like it."

"Mai Khan, put that back. You are not wearing that. Your father would have a heart attack."

Mai ignored her, grabbing the red dress and a slightly longer blue one with a low-cut neckline. "I'll try these on."

Her mother removed them from her hands, gently but firmly. "Mai, I said no. You don't have to try the one I picked, but you are not wearing these. They are too old for you."

"Can I help, ladies?" The shop assistant hovered, perhaps sensing stormy waters.

"Yes, please. My daughter wants a dress for her birthday

party, something quite formal but not too old for her. She's sixteen. Can you suggest something?"

The woman nodded. She cast an eye over the competing selections and smiled.

"I think perhaps something more like these over here. Those sequined ones are more for a Debs ball, than a birthday. You don't want to be overdressed, do you? Look at this - three quarter length, lovely silver thread throughout, excellent embroidery detail..."

Mai had to admit the lady had taste. She found herself trying on three dresses, that managed to look grown up without endangering her father's blood pressure. Her mother nodded approvingly at each but left the final choice to her daughter.

"The green," Mai announced, and her mother paid - with only the smallest of grimaces at the price.

"I'll get plenty of wear out of it," Mai assured her, as they walked back to West Stephen Street. "I'll wear it over Christmas and for Sama's wedding in January. Thanks Mam."

Mrs Khan patted her shoulder. "You are a good girl, Mai, and we do appreciate your help in the restaurant. And I know you don't get as many treats as some of the girls in your class. We do try, though, you know that."

"I do! And I have lots to be grateful for, Mam, I know that. Honestly. It's just ..."

Mai faltered. Impossible to explain without telling her poor mother that the posh school they scrimped and saved for, with its high fees and extra-curricular activities and trips abroad, was a difficult place when you're not the same as everyone else, when you're not blonde and pale, and rich. "It's just this once. I really appreciate it."

Mai hugged her mother's arm and promised herself silently

that after this, she wouldn't care what Niamh and her cronies said or did. She wouldn't ask for anything else. Just this one perfect birthday night out.

* * *

Teresa made her way back to the music shop, feeling a little guilty for having closed up mid afternoon like that. It wasn't every day an old friend returned, though, and she had thoroughly enjoyed catching up with Elsa. It was a little strange to call her that, but she was impressed with all the younger woman had achieved in the interim years. Elsa was an entertaining companion, with a fund of sharply funny stories about well-known musicians and life in the orchestra. Time had flown by, and they had parted company with promises to meet up again very soon. Teresa had avoided any mention of Lisa Kennedy, and her connection to the music shop, for fear it might seem as if she was putting in a word for Michael's girlfriend. And she was unsure how to broach it with Lisa, without telling Elsa's secrets.

Best to leave it all alone for the moment, she thought. But she was interested in hearing Lisa's unbiased opinion of Elsa, and how she got on with the orchestra.

It was a pleasant surprise to find the shutters up and the door unlocked. Michael Clancy, the young Luthier who rented the upstairs workrooms, was behind the counter.

"You're back." He held out one hand. "I hope you brought me something nice from Fancies, and me slaving over a hot counter for you!"

Teresa produced a fruit scone from a paper bag. "Of course I did. Although I didn't expect you to open the shop for me.

Have you no work of your own?"

"Hah! I'm snowed under. But I needed a break. That cello is driving me bonkers, Teresa. No sooner do I get one thing fixed but another gives trouble. Those pegs were jammed in - no attempt to even fit them. I thought I'd split the peg box taking them out..."

"Yes, yes," Teresa said hastily. She had already heard the trials and tribulations of the benighted cello several times over and didn't relish hearing them again. The truth was it was a cheap, badly set-up instrument, hardly worth the effort to repair, but Michael was too soft-hearted to turn away a parent who couldn't afford a better option.

"You know you're working for free, don't you? The few bob you're charging them won't cover the time you're spending."

Michael looked at her guiltily. "I know. But sure, it'll keep them going for a year or so and then when they can get a decent one, won't they come to you? So really, I'm doing you a favour if you think about it."

"Gwon and eat your cake." Teresa couldn't keep a straight face. "Where were you anyway? I came downstairs for a chat and saw your note."

"An old friend called in. I couldn't say no."

"Fair enough." Michael took a huge bite of his scone. "Now that's the ticket. I was wrecked - it's been a long week. Hey, Lisa called to say the rehearsal went quite well. I said I'd take her out to dinner on Thursday to celebrate."

"Oh, I am glad." She hesitated, before adding "I hope it's all going well between ye?"

"Grand. We rub along nicely."

"Ah. Well, that's nice. Of course. Still - Lisa is a very nice young woman, you know. She's a fine catch. I hope you're not taking that for granted."

Michael paused mid-chomp and stared at her.

"For granted? Of course not. But like, it can't be all romance and high drama, you know. Lisa's a very sensible girl, she's very easy-going. She agrees with me, slow and steady is the ticket."

Mrs. O'Brien blinked. "Sensible. Yes, obviously she's a sensible young woman. But she's also - ye are also young, the pair of you. Like, there has to be some romance. Some fireworks."

"Amn't I taking her out to dinner," Michael protested. "That's romantic."

"Where?"

"What?"

"Where are you bringing her? And if you say the local pub, I'll -"

"What's wrong with Lannigans? They do a lovely shepherds pie."

"For the love of - take the girl somewhere nice, Michael. Take her to one of those posh places off Grafton Street or even make her a nice dinner. I know you can cook when you put your mind to it. Do something different, that's the point. Make a wee fuss of her."

Michael tilted his head, considered this for a moment and then laughed.

"Ah, I dunno. I think you're being a bit over the top there, if you don't mind me saying so. I know Lisa. She'd much prefer a nice quiet meal in the local, to one of those hip places"

Teresa gave it up for a bad job. Maybe Michael was right, and Lisa was happy with their rather humdrum romance. Young people were so different nowadays, too. She grinned as she remembered Cathal O'Brien, trussed up in a suit and tie, clutching a bunch of flowers as he knocked on her front door. No matter that the flowers came from the street sellers on Georges Street, or that the suit was second-hand from Coyle's on Aungier street. It was the effort that counted. A man who rarely took off his brown work apron, whose hands were usually covered in varnish, turning up scrubbed and dressed to the nines.

She hoped Michael was right, but she couldn't shake an uneasy feeling.

* * *

Mai popped her head around the door of the music shop.

"Howya, Mrs. O'Brien! I'm off home now. You won't forget about Saturday night, will you?"

"How could I, Mai? You've reminded me every day for a week and twice some days." Teresa smiled at her young neighbour. "There's no danger of me forgetting. I'm really looking forward to it."

"Chez Maurice…how could you not be excited?" Mai said.

"I'm excited about your birthday, silly. I haven't a clue what Chez Whatshisface is like. Far more importantly, what would you like for your birthday?"

"Oh, nothing. Not from you. As long as you come, that's grand."

Teresa shook her head. "Well, I'm honoured but I'm definitely getting you a present. Or maybe you'd prefer cash - I hear it's an expensive business being a teenager these days?"

She had been joking, of course, but Mai flushed at her words.

"Honestly," the teenager said stiffly, "I don't want anything.

That's not why I invited you."

"Mai Khan!" Teresa frowned. "I know that. You're the least greedy person I know."

"Oh, don't mind me," Mai shrugged awkwardly. "I'm just a bit wound up. Lucy - you know her, red hair and freckles? - she said earlier that I'm being a bit of a brat over this birthday. Dragging everyone to Chez Maurice. She says I'm trying to keep up with the posh kids."

"Oh. Are you? I mean, it's okay if you are. It's only human to want to fit in."

"I don't know," Mai confessed. "I do want to show that we go to nice places too, but it's not just that. I really am looking forward to a night out with family, and with you."

"Well, that's the main thing, isn't it? Don't be so hard on yourself. Be aware of the temptation to compete with them and try not to fall into that trap. But you're allowed want nice things, too."

"You're so sensible, Mrs. O'Brien. You do make me feel better. I'm going to enjoy this night out, and then, that's it. I'm not going to mind what Niamh says."

Teresa didn't have to ask who Niamh was, having heard several times about the way she treated Mai.

"Good on you. And let's enjoy Saturday."

She wondered if Mr. and Mrs. Khan were aware of how hard things were for Mai but even if they were, what could they do? The school was ideal in some ways, because Mai was close at hand while both parents worked so hard in the Noodle Palace. She was nearly seventeen and would be doing her exams in another year, so changing schools wasn't really feasible. And sadly, there were bullies everywhere. She could move to another place and find it even worse or struggle to make new friends. And despite the likes of Niamh Finnegan, Mai had some lovely friends in her year.

As Teresa lowered the shutters on the music shop windows, she caught sight of young Lucy, chatting away to customers as she handed over their orders. Maybe the girl had a point, but it was nearly impossible for Mai not to be influenced by what others had. They would just have to help her keep her feet on the ground, despite temptations.

Chapter 4

The week flew by as rehearsals continued at the same intense pace, and Lisa began to get the measure of their new conductor. Elsa Von Streng rapped the podium lightly. The orchestra, already stinging under several sharp rebukes, immediately sat up straighter and paid attention. Less than a week into Von Streng's tenure, they had learned that she rarely raised her voice, never repeated herself and gave no quarter to anyone foolish enough not to listen. She had an ear that was unnaturally acute, every transgression noted and remarked upon.

"The mid section is horrible. A disgrace. Oboes - I have no idea what piece you think you are playing, but if you could bring yourselves to address the music in front of you, we would all be grateful. Violas, why you cannot keep tempo is a mystery to me. Do you need the aid of a metronome? No? Then kindly note the word "*Allegretto*" written above your score."

She turned her eye to the violin section, and Lisa felt her cheeks redden. "That was...adequate." Her eye moved on. "Basses, you are coming in a beat too late. If I have to ask again, it will be your last day with the Hibernian. Again, from the second phrase and remember, for God's sake, *Allegretto!*"

Lisa was exhausted, every day feeling like a boot camp but

she had to admit that something was taking shape within the orchestra. Members who had long coasted, relying on their seniority to protect them, found themselves under scrutiny. Marguerite Lawlor, veteran of the Clarinet section, was red-faced and puffing while Charles, the longest serving bass player, had a sheen of sweat across his brow. Lisa almost felt sorry for them, but there was no denying that they both needed a good shake up. She reserved her sympathy for Ollessa, who looked close to tears. Von Streng had been hard on the viola section all day, which was slightly unfair. If they actually were off tempo, it wasn't apparent to anyone but the conductor.

Ollessa caught her eye and risked a tiny grimace. Lisa smiled reassuringly. She knew her friend was an outstanding musician; it was just a matter of pulling the others along with her. The viola player glared at the other three players under her leadership and hissed, "Follow my lead!"

To everyone's relief, they finally did so. Somehow the orchestra made it through the middle section without interruption and Elsa Von Streng gave a twitch of the lips that could pass as a smile in dim light.

"Much better. *You* …" she waved her baton at Ollessa, "you did well. Keep them under control from now on."

Her clipped German accent added emphasis without her having to raise her voice, Lisa noticed, and even her praise sounded quite forceful. It was a weary bunch who traipsed off stage in the conductor's wake, glad that the day's session was over.

"Holy lord!" Ollessa exclaimed as soon as they were alone in the dressing room. "I really thought she was going to throw her baton at me at one point."

"No, if she was going to throw it at anyone, it would be poor

Marguerite. Or the oboes - that flat note in the Beethoven was awful."

"Honestly, I didn't think we were that bad, before Von Streng came. Now I can't decide if we were mediocre all along or if she's just obsessed and unreasonable."

Lisa took a moment before replying. "I'm not saying we were mediocre…but I don't think Von Streng is unreasonable, either."

"Ah. She has a point, you think?"

"I think we're already a better orchestra and it's only been a wet week."

Ollessa sighed. "Yes, I agree. But it's infuriating. I did not cover myself in glory today."

"It wasn't you, it was the other three goms sitting on their hands and not paying attention."

"But I am the leader," her friend pointed out quietly. "It took me too long to get them into gear, so to speak."

"You did it in the end! And I think that was the point, honestly. I think she wants the section leaders to step up more. I always feel a bit deferential, the likes of Carl and Paudie have been here far longer than I have - but if we're the first chair, then we need to lead."

Ollessa nodded slowly. "You're right. I am far too ready to give in, even when I know they're just being lazy. Or awkward."

"I have a feeling Von Streng will back us up," Lisa pointed out, "unlike her predecessors. And Fintan won't go against the old guard at all. Now with Von Streng in control, maybe things will finally change."

"Fintan McLaughlin is terrified of the likes of Charles or Marguerite!" Ollessa snorted. "But then again, he is more terrified of our conductor…"

Lisa laughed. "She passed him in the corridor yesterday and I swear to God, he ducked into a practice room to avoid her. Every time he speaks to her, he goes red."

"Coward. Well, I'm away home. Tomorrow, I will beat that tempo into them with my bow if I have to. Right now, I've got a husband and kid waiting for me, and a takeaway if I'm lucky. See you tomorrow. Are you meeting Michael tonight?"

"Yes, he's taking me out to dinner," Lisa couldn't keep the smile off her face. "I'm going to nip home and get changed and then meet him at Lannigans. I can't wait to see where we're going."

Ollessa opened her mouth and then clamped it shut again. Behind Lisa's back, she crossed her fingers for luck and hoped fervently that "dinner out" didn't mean pub grub in the local. Knowing Michael, she didn't feel too optimistic. Especially if they were meeting in the local pub.

Lisa took longer than usual to leave the concert hall, taking her time with a bit of makeup and a change of clothes. Her trousers were fine, but her plain navy shirt was far too dowdy for a date night. She changed into a silky red top, a designer label, picked up for half price in the sales and added some sparkly earrings and a bangle to complete the look. A critical look in the mirror revealed an outfit that was not too fancy, but definitely not her usual, practical style - and she was satisfied.

Grabbing her violin case and hurrying, one eye on the bus timetable app on her phone, she was bustling down the narrow backstage corridor when the door to rehearsal room three swung open and Elsa Von Streng's voice could be heard.

"You will regret this!" Her tone was icy. A male voice responded, his German accent more pronounced than Elsa's, who now that Lisa thought about it, sometimes had only a very slight accent at all.

"You will be the one to regret…*Schnucki.*" He managed to make the term of endearment sound like an insult. "You weren't always so high and mighty, were you? I wonder what your precious orchestra would think if they knew the great Elsa Von Streng was -" The door slammed shut, cutting off the end of his sentence. The rehearsal rooms were sound insulated and not a word more could be heard. Lisa stood where she was for a moment, wondering if she should knock on the door and make sure Elsa was okay? The conductor had not sounded afraid or in distress, if anything the man had sounded more upset. After a moment, she reluctantly decided against it, and made her way out of the backstage area. Dinner with Michael was waiting.

* * *

Lannigan's Bar was busy, the noise level increased by a group of young men in expensive suits at the bar, roaring at each other in great good humour.

"This is nice," Michael beamed, looking at the food menu. "I think I'll go for the steak and chips, they do a nice steak. Are you having a starter?"

Lisa glanced at the list of appetizers and tried to muster some enthusiasm.

"Probably not. You get one if you want, though."

"Ah gwon, love. It's a celebration. You're killing it as first chair." He sounded so proud, Lisa felt her disappointment fade. Maybe he wasn't great at the romantic gesture but he was genuinely supportive. That was more important, she told herself, but as another shout of "Whoo Hooo!" came from the bar, where the excitable young businessmen laughingly pushed and shoved each other, she wished they were somewhere quieter. And less crowded, and maybe with a different menu. There were only so many lasagnas or battered chicken pieces a girl could stomach.

Michael seemed oblivious to her inner struggles, chatting away happily. He asked her about Von Streng and told her about Teresa's worries for Mai, and the extravagant birthday dinner in Chez Maurice. Lisa tried to join in, but a combination of tiredness and lingering disappointment made her efforts fall flat.

"I'm sorry," She glanced at her watch as the barmen started to suggest last orders was approaching. "I'm wiped out. I can hardly sit upright. Would you mind if I went home early?"

Michael was of course instantly understanding and ready to see her to a taxi, which of course annoyed her slightly, however irrational it might be. She appreciated him being supportive, she really did - but he could have looked a little put out at her cutting the evening short. Feeling sad and somewhat deflated, she made her way home, arguing with herself about the relative merits of Michael's easy good humour versus his taking her for granted.

Morning failed to resolve it, despite a good night's sleep. Ollessa asked her first thing about the big celebration dinner, and she tried to sound as if it had been a success, but even to her own ears it rang false. Her friend didn't say much, just smiling and nodding as Lisa talked. Somehow, that made Lisa feel a bit worse.

The rehearsal was in full swing and going far better than the previous few days, when it was interrupted mid Sonata by a deep, sonorous voice that seemed to roll across the auditorium like a velvet carpet.

"Where is she? Where is my muse, my *maestra?*"

A tall, well-built man appeared, arms outstretched dramatically. An expensive overcoat hung open to reveal a dark grey waistcoat over a crisp white shirt and dark trousers. He rushed to the conductor's podium, dropped to his knees and raised clasped hands like a supplicant in an old painting.
"My own *Maestra,* I am here, poor fool that I am."

There was the unmistakable lilt of an Italian accent, which made the already luscious voice even more attractive. The stranger started to blow kisses at the podium and to everyone's shock - Elsa Von Streng laughed.

"Up, up. Don't be such a child, Arnoldo. These people aren't used to your antics." She didn't sound a bit annoyed, Lisa thought. In fact, she sounded delighted to see the man. It was hard to imagine the woman with a young suitor, but surely only someone very close to her would dare interrupt her rehearsal? He was terribly good-looking, with that mop of dark hair and boyish good looks, and twinkling brown eyes - not that it mattered, obviously. Glancing at her colleagues, Lisa realised almost every woman present was thinking the same thoughts, and some of the men too.

She grinned across at Damian Maguire, one of the younger members of the orchestra and a fine cello player. He grinned widely and batted his eyelashes then mouthed, *"He's a fine half!"* - the ultimate Irish compliment to a handsome male.

She grinned back and nodded.

Elsa descended from her podium and embraced the interloper. The orchestra watched in fascination.

"When did you arrive?"

"Just now, *amore mio*. I did not waste a moment, not one. I jumped into a taxi and told them to take me to the temple of music, the hallowed grounds where Elsa Von Streng holds court."

Lisa grinned involuntarily, imagining the reaction of the average Dublin taxi driver to directions like that.
"Well, it's good to see you. When is Yvette coming?"

"Ah. I'm afraid the lovely Yvette will not be joining us. She and I, we have parted ways. A slight disagreement, you understand, she mistook my friendliness with a young mezzo-soprano as being more than what it was. You know her jealousy! Alas, she would not believe her Arnoldo, she rejected my protestations of innocence, she - in short, she dumped me." He collapsed dramatically but elegantly into an empty chair, and batted his eyelashes - long, dark eyelashes that framed his startlingly blue eyes and stood out against his pale skin - at Elsa. "You see before you, a broken man."

"*Dummkopf!*" Elsa replied briskly. "Get up, you are frightening the orchestra. Everybody, I promised that I would bring the best of the world's musicians and singers to the Hibernia. Here is the very best, the great tenor Arnoldo Messini."

A murmur ran through the assembled musicians. While not quite as famous a household name as Pavarotti or Bocelli, the music world was already alight with praise for the man Classical Monthly had dubbed "*the shining light of his generation,*" Arnoldo Messini. He had appeared at the Milan Festival, headlined the New York Classical Week and now...

"Arnoldo, as a personal favour, has agreed to sing *Una Furtiva Lagrima* from Donizetti's *L'Elisir D'Amore* at our opening concert. Yes, yes, this is good news. Exciting. Be quiet. We shall be doing a new arrangement. First, as a violin solo then

Arnoldo will sing, then both together." There was a tiny pause, before she continued, "Lisa, you shall be our violin solo. You and Arnoldo must rehearse."

Lisa tried to keep her face from showing either her delight or terror. She had listened to Joshua Bell's 2006 arrangement of the same piece for violin and orchestra hundreds of times. She had practiced it, for no other reason than that she loved it, until it was at her fingertips - quite literally. But to play it as a solo, with the Hibernian, with Arnoldo Messini - her mouth went dry and she was aware that she was blinking rapidly. She managed to nod and twitch her lips into a quick smile, then busied herself arranging the music on her stand as Elsa continued to introduce the orchestra to the tenor.

When she glanced back up, Arnoldo was grinning at her. It was a very charming smile. She resolutely ignored it.

* * *

Michael Clancy frowned at the cello he was tuning and shook his head. It was a catch 22 situation for parents - cellos were expensive, and few music schools had any they could lend out. But cheap instruments gave so much trouble, and sounded so awful, they ended up pouring money into them anyway. And teachers gave out constantly about having to tune them, with pegs that weren't properly fitted and slipped and then stuck. Nightmare.

The same held true for any instrument, but violins and violas were easier to fix up. Cellos were a much bigger undertaking. It had taken a week of solid work but now the bridge was properly shaped, and the pegs held their place. A decent set of strings had improved the tone. Admittedly it would never sound brilliant, but it was pleasant. His one remaining issue with the instrument was the slightly tinny sound on the A string and D string, especially in the higher register. A cello should never sound tinny.

He reached for his soundpost setter, a long thin S shaped metal implement, and with a practiced (but cautious) hand, inserted it through the F-holes into the hollow belly of the instrument. With two sharp taps he shifted the long thin wooden post a tiny amount to the left. Michael swung the cello down from his workbench, picked up the bow and drew it across the strings - success! The cello let out as full and warm a sound as the cheap wood could muster. From a disaster to a quite decent, fully functioning student instrument, that a child could really lean on.

Michael had a guilty moment as he added up the hours spent on it. Teresa was right, it really didn't pay him. He just couldn't turn away a kid, or a desperate parent.
"Ah well, if I wanted to be rich," he consoled himself, "I should have done accountancy, like Cormac."

His brother was a big name in a well-known financial firm with all the trappings that went with it. A lovely semi-detached home in a leafy suburb, and a flashy car with at least two foreign holidays a year and a private school for the kids. Their parents were madly proud of him, and boasted to everyone in their tiny village in Kerry.

"Cormac made partner, Cormac was in the papers talking about the new tax measures," and the pièce de résistance, *"Cormac was on the Evening Show!"* His brother had indeed been in the audience of Ireland's most popular political show, and asked

one question of a junior Minister, but to hear them tell it, he'd be the guest of honour.

Michael didn't mind - it wasn't Cormac's fault and his brother supported him fully in everything he did. Still, it would be nice if for once his parents boasted about him instead. When Teresa had made him a partner in the music shop, he thought it might please them - O'Brien's was world famous, a Dublin institution! - but apart from a "That's nice, dear," it had made no impression on them.

Lisa, he thought fondly, would understand. He could tell her about fixing the cursed cello, and she would be delighted about it. It was one reason he was so fond of her. She really was the easiest, nicest person to be around. He picked up his mobile and texted her,

"Thinking of you just now! Fancy a pint? How were rehearsals?"
She replied quite quickly.

"Sorry, mad busy. Huge day - Arnoldo Messini is our tenor for the opening. I'm solo on a Donizetti. Have to work on it all weekend. But huge opportunity."
Michael replied,

"OMG that's amazing, well done. Delighted for you. Let me know if you fancy a break, or if I can do anything. Talk soon."
"Thanks, will ring later, tell you about it."
Michael sighed. It was fabulous news, and he was pleased for Lisa. Two solos in the opening concert, that was a big development for her. Still, he'd miss her. They were used to spending weekends together, walking on Sandymount beach or taking the dart out to Howth, or curled up watching old movies. He felt at quite a loose end. He wondered what Signor Messini was like. Michael had a hazy idea of opera singers as being large, burly, middle-aged men. Surely, even if he was

as harsh a taskmaster as Elsa Von Streng, an auld fella would want to have some down time over the weekend. Hopefully, he'd be content with a few hours work and then Lisa might be free to meet up.

Whistling softly, he turned back to work. There was a violin with a ragged crack in its rib and a guitar with three or four worn frets that needed to be replaced. Bows to be rehaired and a few new instruments to be set up ready for sale downstairs in the shop. Plenty to keep him occupied. He'd google Arnoldo Messini later so he could talk to Lisa about him. But one Italian tenor was much like another, after all.

* * *

Ollessa and Lisa looked at each other, the moment they were safely in their dressing room with the door fully closed.

"Oh. My. God." Ollessa fanned herself with a folded-up sheet of music. "The last tenor we had didn't look like that."

"Dominic Crowley? No, he did not look like Arnoldo." Lisa recalled the rather elderly, and very cross man who had joined them the year before for the Christmas series of concerts. "I didn't know they *made* tenors who looked like that."

"I thought at first he was Elsa's boyfriend," Ollessa said. "But then he started talking about breaking up with his girlfriend - Yvette? - and Elsa just laughed."

"I think they're just friends."

"How could you be "just friends," with that man? She has ice-water in her veins instead of blood."

"Or she isn't interested in men," Lisa pointed out. "Or there's something wrong with him and we're just so blinded by his charm, we can't see it..."

"Well, yeah. But he's certainly easy on the eye and seems to be a bit of craic. Oh!" Ollessa had been frantically scrolling on her phone and now she pushed the screen towards Lisa. On it was a picture of an incredibly glamourous woman, with flawless makeup wearing a daringly risque red sequined dress, pouting at the camera.

"His ex is Yvette La Monda, the supermodel."

Lisa blinked. "Holy smoke."

"If Yvette La Monda couldn't keep him in line, there's no hope for us," Ollessa giggled. "He must be a "player," as the young folk say."

"I'd say he's a divil, Ollessa."

"Probably. It's nothing to you, anyway, with you happily shackled to Michael, and me an old married woman. I bet Claire is having palpitations right now though. Betcha she comes in dressed to the nines tomorrow..."

Lisa just smiled, listening to her friend's good-natured chatter with half an ear. She had to admit, she too had felt a surge of nervous energy whenever Arnoldo Messini had caught her eye but of course, that was nothing to do with his dark good looks, or flirty charm. It was just because she would be playing such an important - and intimate - solo piece with him, her violin echoing his rich voice...no wonder it made her pulse quicken. No, he was too obviously a ladies' man for her to be interested in - and of course, Michael Clancy was far nicer. Far, far nicer. Obviously.

"I have to run," Ollessa exclaimed suddenly, breaking Lisa's chain of thought. "I promised I'd leave here as early as possible. We've been rehearsing so late every day, Mathew is exhausted with the kids. Take care, see you tomorrow."

Ollessa made a point of getting home before dinner whenever their schedule allowed. Life in the orchestra meant reasonably flexible hours in one way, but some long hard days when necessary.

"See you, missus!" Lisa called after her. Gathering her bits - violin case, backpack, scarf and gloves - she was about to follow suit when the tall, trim figure of Elsa Von Streng suddenly appeared at the dressing room door.

"Ah!" Lisa jumped.

Von Streng rolled her eyes. "*Donnerwetter!* Are you Irish all mice, that you jump when a person walks in?"

"No. I mean - well, you startled me. You just appeared out of nowhere." The woman walks like a cat, Lisa thought. I didn't even hear her footsteps in the corridor.

"Hmm. Anyway, I have come to ask you a favour." Elsa said it as if she were graciously conferring a gift, rather than requesting something. "You will come to dinner on Saturday, with Arnoldo and me. We will discuss the orchestra. I have plans I wish to discuss, and Arnoldo wants to chit-chat with you about the Donizetti piece."

"Oh." Lisa didn't quite know how to respond. "I'm not sure what my plans are for Saturday."

Elsa raised one impeccably shaped eyebrow and stared at her with cool, blue eyes.

"If you have no solid plans, then there can be no objection. I require your presence, as first chair."

It would have taken a much tougher woman than Lisa to ignore the conductor's imperious tone. It would in fact have taken Teresa O'Brien, or maybe Mai Khan with her irrepressible cheekiness. But Lisa Kennedy, gentle leader of the violin section, was unequal to the task.

"Okay then. Um, where and when?"

"Chez Maurice, dinner at 7 pm. You will be there at six thirty, and we will have drinks at the bar. Wear something suitable, not these hippie clothes. It is a very chic place."

"And can I ask, who else is going?" Lisa tried to ignore the dig at her fashion sense.

Von Streng fixed her with an icy glare.

"If you're going to discuss the orchestra's season, shouldn't Fintan McLaughlin be there too?"

Von Streng sighed. "McLaughlin. I forgot about him. Yes, he is coming too."

People did have a tendency to overlook Fintan, Lisa had to admit to herself. He was a constant presence around the National Concert Hall, in the way that furniture was a constant presence in your home. Useful, and you needed it but you didn't often think much about it.

"He'll appreciate being included," Lisa ventured.

If she was feeling braver, she could have pointed out to the other woman that Fintan was actually the one with the final say over the season's programme and that any discussion should definitely include him. She doubted the conductor would appreciate having that pointed out and probably would just ignore it anyway. Lisa had a momentary vision of Fintan telling Elsa that she couldn't do something and had to stifle a laugh. The poor man would die of fright first.

"So, it is arranged then. Saturday at six thirty." Elsa's tone made it clear that no further discussion was necessary.

Despite a slight resentment of the conductor's high-handed style, Lisa was excited. As she made her way home through the rush hour commuters and Dublin city traffic, her mind was fully occupied. Flattery at being included in Elsa Von Streng's plans, a frisson of excitement at the prospect of spending more time with the Italian tenor and awe at the thought of dinner in the infamous Chez Maurice whirled together in her head for the rest of the evening.

"If nothing else," she thought, as she drifted off to sleep that night, "I'll have a nice night out in a posh restaurant. Sure, what could go wrong?"

Chapter 5

Saturday did not start well.

Lisa, already tired from a long week of rehearsals and the additional pressure of preparing to duet with Arnoldo Messini, found herself increasingly exasperated by Michael Clancy's response to her news. He had seemed delighted for her at first, both for the new solo piece and the invitation to dinner. By Saturday morning, when she popped into the music shop carrying a latte and a bun from Fancies for him, Michael had changed his tune.

When she mentioned difficulties with her solo part, he was uncharacteristically silent. When she mentioned how anxious she was to impress Arnoldo on Monday, there was a distinct lack of sympathy. Her final attempt to engage him in conversation - bemoaning her lack of anything chic enough to wear that evening to Chez Maurice - elicited a sound suspiciously like a snort and a sudden recollection that he had an urgent repair waiting for him upstairs.

Rather hurt, Lisa turned to Mrs. O'Brien and shrugged.

"I suppose I'm interrupting his work," she said with an attempt at nonchalance.
"He's in a tizzy over a buzzing fret on a banjo. You know how much he hates that kind of repair," Mrs. O'Brien said.

"Yeah. Well, see you soon."

"You'll possibly see me later," Teresa grinned. "You're not the only one with an invitation to Chez Maurice."

Lisa looked surprised, then remembered Mai Khan's birthday plan.

"Of course! You're going with the Khan's."

"Indeed. A big occasion, and I'm very grateful to be invited."

"Me too. Of course, I wish Michael was coming. Do you - do you think he's a bit put out that I'm going without him?"

"It's possible," Teresa conceded, hiding a grin. "I mean, he's delighted for you and all that - but he did google Signor Messini. If I had to be honest, I'd say the man is about thirty years younger and a lot fitter than Michael was expecting."

If this was the answer Lisa wanted, she hid it well. Her only response was a noncommittal shrug and a change of subject.

* * *

Despite her annoyance with Michael, morning rehearsals had gone well, and Lisa was looking forward to tackling the *Men of Action* theme again after a nice lunch. The deli was busy, and it took longer than usual to get served, so she was cutting it fine as she hurried back to the Concert Hall.

Her head full of the trickier passages, Lisa had all but forgotten the argument she had overheard between the conductor and the man with the German accent. As she turned into the narrow laneway that led to the stage door of the Concert Hall, there was a man standing to one side. She might have dismissed that as nothing odd - there were always delivery men waiting around, not to mention the lads from the nearby offices using the laneway as a smoking area, out of sight of the windows of their bosses. However, the person was staring at a mobile phone with an angry expression, and she heard him mutter something rude sounding and distinctly Germanic.

Lisa had a good ear for both music and voices. If she had been asked to pick him out of a line-up, she would have had to think carefully. The sound of his voice, however, was a different matter. Without a doubt, this was the man arguing with Elsa the previous day.

He was standing with his back almost turned to her, his shoulders hunched, but as she passed he straightened up and turned. His eyes locked with hers for a moment, and he forced a smile, one that didn't reach his eyes.

"Apologies, miss."

He had a heavyset face, with thick eyebrows and ruddy cheeks. He struck Lisa as someone who had been handsome when younger and in better shape. His nose and cheeks had the broken veins of a habitual drinker and he could have done with a shave. At odds with this however, were his clothes. His overcoat was warm and expensive looking, and his scarf and gloves were new and elegant. It seemed like an odd combination, as if someone rather rough and ready had dressed themselves up.

"That's okay." She flashed a polite smile and made for the stage door. The man quickly stepped in front of her.
"Ah, you are a violinist!" He pointed to her case. "I too, once upon a time - but that is a long story. You work here?"

"The concert hall? Yes. Sorry, I'm actually running late -"

"Yes, yes. Of course. I am here to see an old friend, she also works here. She was to let me in. I have texted her but no reply. I can enter with you, *ja?*"

Lisa eyed him doubtfully.

"Eh, no. I don't think so. We're not allowed to let people in." His smile dropped and the scowl returned.

"Come now, you can oblige me." It was a statement rather than a request.

"No, I don't think I can. Look, please step aside."

He bunched his fists, but shuffled aside, never breaking eye contact. Lisa went to punch in the code on the keypad that secured the stage door but realised she couldn't without him seeing it. She paused and turned her shoulder pointedly, obscuring his view. An angry hiss told her that her instinct had been correct.

As soon as she had inputted the code, the door catch released, and she pushed it open. Like a snake, the man's hand struck out and grasped the handle of the door before it could fully close behind her. Lisa felt a sudden panic, grabbed the door and tried to push it shut but he was too strong. He had almost pushed the door open when a security guard appeared at the end of the corridor.

"Hey!" She waved frantically. "Someone is trying to push in…"

The guard, a young man she vaguely recognised, started to run towards her. Much to her relief, the pressure from the other side of the door disappeared abruptly.

"Are you all right?" The security guard wrenched the door open to check the alley. It was empty.

"I'm okay. Just a bit shaken."

"Did you know him?" The young man frowned. "We've had stalkers and all sorts here, don't be embarrassed to tell me. I've had husbands and boyfriends try to push in, we've no bother putting them on a blacklist."

Lisa smiled. "You're very good. No, he was a stranger. He said he knew someone here, but I told him he couldn't just waltz in."

"Right. I'll make sure to check the CCTV camera, and I'll warn the lads to keep an eye out. Do you know who he came to see?"

"He didn't say," Lisa said, truthfully. She thought it might be better to tell Elsa privately of her suspicion, rather than spread her business through the entire Concert Hall.

"Okay. Well, I'm Anto - if you need someone to walk you out after rehearsal, you come down to the security room. One of us will go with you, okay?"

Lisa thanked him again, before hurrying to her dressing room. She was perilously close to being late for rehearsal and that was far scarier than any encounter with a intruder. She made it into her seat seconds before Elsa appeared, and pushing aside all thoughts of the unpleasant encounter, applied herself to the music. It was only as the rehearsal ended and the orchestra members made their way backstage, that she was able to speak to Elsa without being overheard. The conductor was for once slow to leave the stage, sorting through music at her podium and marking it with her pencil.

"Elsa, can I just have a quick word?" Lisa hovered anxiously.

Elsa gave her a surprised look but nodded.

"Thanks. It's just - there was a man outside the Hall when i got back from lunch. I was last in, and he - he tried to push in when I opened the door. I wouldn't bother you with it but he may have been here to see you."

Elsa gave her a long, cool look. The silence seemed endless to Lisa. Finally, the conductor tilted her head to one side and asked, "He asked for me? By name?"

"Not exactly. I - I overheard you talking to him, yesterday. After rehearsal. I recognised his voice. I think he was pushing in because he wanted to see you."

Elsa raised one eyebrow. In a tone that brooked no argument, she said, "Me? You are mistaken."

Lisa could feel her cheeks redden. "I am certain it's the same man. Look, I'm not trying to be nosey or anything. Just wanted to warn you, okay?"

"Warn me?" Elsa gave a brittle laugh. "But I have no idea about this man. None."

"I thought I heard you arguing with him," Lisa blurted out.

"You must be mistaken. But thank you for the warning. I trust you informed security?"

"I did." Lisa devoutly wished she had not bothered to broach the subject at all. However, she *knew* it was the same man. That voice was unmistakable.

"Good. I will see you at dinner tonight, Lisa. Don't be late."

Lisa nodded and walked away with as much dignity as she could muster.

"Ah well, I did my best," she told herself. "If she won't heed a warning, there's nothing much more I can do."

But it bugged her a little all the same. Why did Elsa deny knowing the man, and why lie about their argument?

* * *

Privately, Teresa was of the opinion that it was no harm to shake Michael up a bit - he was far too complacent about his relationship with the talented young violinist. He was in rotten humour all day and her suspicions were confirmed when she overheard him muttering to himself about good looking singers, and how much he hated opera.

She did feel a bit sorry for him, especially as he swallowed his bad mood long enough to wish her a nice night out, before he headed off home. Still, it was a problem for another day and tonight was all about her young friend, Mai.

The Khans had decided to meet up in the St Stephen Hotel, the very popular boutique hotel at the end of Stephen Street West. The music shop sat on a narrow, curved street that led from the junction of Aungier Street and Georges Street towards the top of Grafton Street and St Stephen's Green. O'Brien's music shop was the oldest music shop in Ireland, but the Khan's had run the Noodle Palace for almost twenty years. Kapoor's Clothes Emporium had been there over ten years while Fancies Café and The Bald Bear Barber were the babies of the group at only five years. The cake shop at the far end, Patricia's Bites, was at least fifteen years old but had changed hands several times, leading to much debate over whether seniority passed from individuals or by the length of time the business name existed.

The St Stephen Hotel was similarly both an institution in the area and under relatively new management. An enterprising couple had bought it in the early noughties and transformed the slightly dowdy but venerable hostelry into something both modern and charming.

Mrs. O'Brien had brought her outfit for the night into work with her, a pale green shift dress embellished with tiny pearls around the collar and hem and a matching bolero jacket similarly adorned. It was simple but well tailored and elegant. She wouldn't let Mai down, she reflected, catching sight of herself in one of the many mirrors in the bathroom of the Hotel. A little light makeup, and she was ready for anything.

She found the Khan family, including Mai's cousins Izz and

Haruum, and her Aunty Farah, sitting at a table in the lounge. Everyone had scrubbed up well, in Teresa's opinion but Mai in particular looked like a princess. A princess with slight leanings towards punk rock, perhaps, but still a knockout.

Mr Khan leapt to his feet and greeted Teresa warmly.

"You look amazing! Well, we are all here now. Let me get you a drink…" He bustled off, as if glad to have something to do. The two younger boys looked up from their phones and grinned at her by way of greeting, and Mai kissed her cheek.

"Aunty! You remember Mrs. O'Brien?"

Farah smiled. "Of course."

"Teresa, please. Well, Mai, are you excited?"

Mai burst into a stream of chat, while Teresa sipped the white win Mr Khan had bought her, and listened with half an ear. She could tell Mai was a little nervous, especially as she then fell silent on the short walk afterwards to Wicklow Street and Chez Maurice. As they entered through the rather gaudy exterior, a riot of faux marble and gilt that looked very out of place among the older shops and cafés, Mai gave Teresa a worried glance.

"Mrs. O'Brien," she hissed, letting her family go slightly ahead. "It's just that, well, this place is a bit *different*."

Before Teresa could reply, a gasp from Aunt Farah made her look around - and up, down, left and right. "Different" was one way of describing it.

The restaurant was housed in one of the old, red-bricked buildings on Wicklow Street, three stories in a rather narrow frame with long sash windows on each floor. From the outside it looked reasonably like its neighbours on either side, albeit with the garish frontage. Inside, however, there was nothing left of the old layout. The first floor had been removed making the ground floor twice the height, with a balcony mezzanine opposite the front door, overlooking the dining area below.

It was decorated as if someone had taken the idea of the Royal Court of Versailles and mashed it up with an attempt at Industrial chic. A huge chandelier was suspended in the centre of the space, but on either side hung long fluorescent lighting tubes. Around the main floor were crammed tables - literally, crammed in tight, with people squeezed into their seats uncomfortably close to the strangers at the next table. The chairs were spindly legged, gilded and ornate, with velvet seats. The walls were painted bright white. Everything, from tablecloths to uniforms, was white, adding to the sensation of being eye-scalded, except for the sudden and jarring splashes of dark purple - a blotch on one wall, stripes down the leg of the uniforms, a weird looking piece of netting suspended over the reception desk. The overall effect would have been strange enough, without the purple and orange neon bulbs that flashed on and off at intervals, reflected off the many gold-painted accents on the fake Louis Quatorze furniture. It made the place both too bright and too dark by turn. Full length portraits of Marie Antoinette and her court adorned the walls, alternating with purple-themed abstracts - a splodge, dab or streak of paint on plain, unframed canvas.

It felt to Teresa as if two very different individuals had decorated the space while blindfolded. And possibly inebriated.

The balcony section boasted a bar and was crammed with young people, obviously enjoying themselves, many looking down at the diners below. At least half the ear-splitting noise level came from that area, despite the extra high ceilings. In the very centre of the room, Teresa could see a long buffet style table, except there was no food on it. Instead, there was a mound of plates, cutlery, and glassware the length of the white and purple tablecloth. Guests were lined up, moving slowly down the length of the table, choosing tableware. She cast a suspicious glance at Mai, who avoided eye contact.

Mr Khan stood blinking at the scene for a moment, but rallied well, making his way to the reception desk. A tall young woman wearing a white tee-shirt emblazoned with a purple monogram of "C.M" and sporting a white powdered wig over a foot high on her head, stared at him in a decidedly unfriendly way.

"You're looking for the Maple Tree, next door," she drawled, her accent the mangled twist of vowels that denoted a certain affluent Dublin suburb.

"I'm not," Mr. Khan smiled. "We are the Khans, table for seven."

She raised an eyebrow. "Really? Oh well. Your lookout, I suppose. You haven't been here before."

It was a statement, not a question.

"First time," Mai's father seemed oblivious to her rudeness. "What do we need to know?"

"Hmm. Your table is over there, by the wall. It's marked "Khan" - please *only* sit at your designated table. It makes things difficult for us if you don't. You can scan the Q-code at the table to read the menu. When you've chosen, press send and your order will go to the kitchen. Then go up and get your plates and stuff from the table behind me - do not queue for tableware until you've ordered!" She eyed the group sternly. "And only take what you're going to use - no stockpiling anything."

Teresa could feel Mrs. Khan stiffen beside her. Mai's mother was a hardworking, no-nonsense person, the type who would jump to her feet to help out if she was sitting in your kitchen.

But when she went out to dinner, she expected a few things. Politeness, for a start, not to mention the restaurant setting the table for their diners. Mai looked at her mother, her face a picture of anxiety.

"It'll be different," Teresa said quietly, smiling at Mrs. Khan. "This is fierce modern, isn't it?"

"It's *something,* all right," her friend muttered in reply, but she didn't make any objection as her husband guided them across the packed floor space to their table. It was quite the journey, as they squeezed between the tables, apologizing to the other diners as they went. Some just nodded in a resigned way, some tutted at them and many exchanged sympathetic and long-suffering glances with them. Teresa didn't need to work hard to deduce they weren't the only ones dragged to the painfully fashionable restaurant under duress!

Having seated herself finally, with a great deal of effort, on an uncomfortable and spindly chair, Teresa sighed at the thought of getting up again to retrieve her place setting. Mai produced her mobile phone, scanned a Q-code that was embedded into the surface of the table and produced a menu.

"Oh." She bit her lip and looked around the table.

"What now?" Mrs. Khan said sharply.

"Um, the menu is quite…short."

Teresa whipped out her own phone and scanned for the menu. A list of four dishes appeared - Horseradish and Broccoli soup or Poached egg salad to start, Beef lollipops with sweet potato fries or Tea Infused Salmon with beans as a main course and a final choice between something called "Maurice's Mess," and a cheeseboard.

"Dear lord, there really isn't much choice." She saw Mai flush and regretted her comment immediately. "I mean, it's very modern. I'd say if they only do a few dishes, they must do them very well though. Let me see, I assume the soup is a starter? And the beef is the main course?"

Mai gave a wobbly smile, obviously avoiding making eye contact with her mother.

Her cousin Haruum sat up and scowled at Mai. "I don't like beef…"

"Then have the salmon," his mother, Farah, snapped. "I'll have the same, with salad, and Izz will have soup and beef. You order for us, Mai."

Mrs. Khan sniffed but took her sister's lead. "Beef for me, and your father. Teresa?"

"Oh, beef, definitely."

"Which dessert?" Mai asked.

"I assume the 'Maurice Mess' is something like an Eton Mess," Farah suggested. "So meringue, whipped cream, fruit - I'll risk that."

Almost everyone followed suit except for Mr. Khan, who opted for the cheese.

"Fine." Farah beamed around the table. "Now we have ordered. Boys, get up and help Mai bring the plates and stuff. Up, Harri, it won't kill you to help. Izz, make sure you bring over some water and glasses as well."

Teresa nodded approvingly. Farah was a woman after her own heart, determined to make the best of the situation.

"Thank you, boys, that's very kind of you. This is very exciting, Farah, we're definitely in the hippest joint in town."

Mai and her cousins groaned but laughed.

"Hippest joint!" Haruum scoffed but he got up with good grace. Mai flashed a grateful smile at her aunt and Teresa and risked a glance at her parents. Mr. Khan was his usual placid self, but her mother had a glint in her eye that did not bode well for Mai later on. Still, at least they had all ordered and were prepared to enjoy their meal.

It looked at first as if that would be rather difficult.

First, a surly young man pushed his way through the throng, and bellowed across another table at them, "Get your soups!" He pointed at a small tureen set on a rickety stand two tables away. "I can't get any closer." Before they could object, he was gone.

"Oh my…" Mrs. Khan muttered, but Izz jumped to his feet.

"Hang on, I'll get it."

Balancing a stack of bowls, he made his way to the soup, with another round of apologies to their neighbouring diners. Filling a bowl with a small amount of red liquid, he tapped the person nearest to him on the shoulder and asked him,

"Howya. Could you do me a favour and pass that over to my Ma? She's the one in the blue dress."

The man stared for a moment, then grinned. "Okay." He took the bowl and passed it to his companion, who in turn passed it on to the next person.

"Great stuff!" the youngster exclaimed. "Now, could you pass this to my Aunty, ta!"

Bowl by bowl, they received their soups - even Mrs. Khan had to laugh as the diners around them joined in.

"It's mad stuff, isn't it?" A cheerful looking chap beside them winked at Mai's mother. "I can't believe we're all paying good money for this lark."

"Hah. I could be at home serving myself and at least be comfortable."

"But you'd have missed all this," he laughed. "And sure, isn't it gas to see how the other half lives?"

Teresa could see Mai's mother relax a little, despite her annoyance. They might be tightly packed, hot and hungry, but there was an air of camaraderie among the guests. If they were stuck with this ridiculous version of a restaurant, they might as well enjoy it. It was definitely the Irish way.

The soup smelled nice, despite its alarming colour but before anyone could taste it, a different but no less surly waiter brought thinly sliced beef on a metal tray, dropped it on the table and retreated. A salad appeared, then some plates loaded with salmon, and finally bowls with the Maurice Mess and a large platter of cheese with flatbread and crackers were squeezed into the remaining space. This ensured that the main courses went cold while they ate their starters and that no one had enough room to eat without elbowing the person to their right in the ribs.

The two boys found this hilarious and their good humour infected the adults. Somehow they managed to serve each other, and despite the bizarre set-up, the food was really delicious. Chef Maurice might be a pretentious prat, Teresa mused, but the man could certainly cook. She enjoyed the meal, the company and the way her fellow Dubliners rose to the occasion, knocking as much fun as possible out of the absurd restaurant.

When it came time to tackle the cheese board and desserts, Mai and the boys cleared away the plates and at least they could spread out a bit. The crowd was thinning out, and Teresa could finally see more than the back of the heads at the next table. She looked around with interest, picking out some well-known faces from Irish television, and a famous musician with his latest girlfriend. Finally, in the far corner opposite them, she spotted the blonde head of Elsa Von Streng and the dark brunette of Lisa.

She slipped on her glasses discreetly. It wasn't as if she really needed them, but admittedly they were handy when trying to see across a crowded room. Yes, that was Lisa, smiling and nodding. Elsa looked amused, listening with her head tilted to one side. Teresa recognised one other of the guests at the table as Fintan McLaughlin. He looked bored, and slightly irritated, Teresa thought. The fourth member of the party was a stranger to her, a handsome man with dark hair and an animated air. He was speaking, gesticulating as he did so, and from the laughter he provoked, seemed to be a most entertaining companion. Teresa watched as he patted Lisa's arm, in a very familiar way indeed. A faint prick of unease stirred as she continued to observe.

This must be the famous Arnoldo Messini. No wonder Michael had been so surly about the dinner invitation. She was quite relieved to see Lisa extract her arm and lean a little further away from the tenor.

"Mrs. O'Brien?" Mai touched her arm.

"Sorry, Mai, I was miles away." Teresa stuffed her glasses back into her handbag.

"I was asking, would you like a coffee or anything?"

"No, I'm fine, thanks." Teresa caught Mr. Khan's eye and he nodded slightly. "Actually, I have something for you."

She handed Mai an envelope. The teen ripped it open eagerly, revealing a brightly coloured birthday card and a gift voucher for one of Dublin's best clothes shops.

"Oh!" Mai hugged her. "I didn't expect anything, honestly. But this is absolute *gift!*"

Teresa's grandchildren had taught her that the highest praise for a present was to exclaim "gift!" in that tone of voice. Farah handed Mai her own envelope, containing a different card and a gift voucher for the same shop.

"We coordinated," Farah said proudly. "Now you can put both together and get something really nice."

Mrs. Khan shook her head. "You spoil her." But she handed Mai yet another envelope.

"This is brilliant," her daughter said. "I'll be buying the place out at this rate. Oh! This isn't a voucher for clothes…"
"No. It's for LearnRite Driving School," her father beamed around the table. "It's time you learned to drive. You can book yourself in for weekend lessons."
Mai looked as if she might faint.

"Ah here," she managed to say. "This is - I thought my present was coming here. But I've been dying to take lessons."

Her cousins snatched the card from her hand and poured over the details, assuring Mai they could literally die of jealousy. Teresa thought Mai couldn't look happier if she tried. Between finally getting to see Chez Maurice and her presents, this was her dream birthday.
"Let's finish up," Mai's father said. "They wouldn't let us have a birthday cake here, I rang and asked during the week. But I have one back at the restaurant. Shall we go light some candles, so Mai can make a wish?"

A general chorus of approval met the suggestion, everyone being thoroughly sick of the cramped seating. Teresa stood and pointed to Lisa's table.

"I'm just going to say goodnight to Lisa, she's over there. I won't be a minute."
That was optimistic, she admitted as she squeezed her way through the throng. A fresh wave of diners had arrived and the noise was nearing unbearable levels. She managed to reach

the others but before she could catch their attention, someone else beat her to it. A figure lurched past her, almost knocking her into the lap of a young man at the neighbouring table. A loud, very slurred voice, cut across even the hideous din of the crowded room.

"Elsa!"

It was a bellow. Everyone at the table turned to face the interloper. Elsa's face paled. She looked horrified.

"Hah," the man continued, swaying slightly. "You thought you would ignore me? Me? You ungrateful cow. Too high and mighty, eh? Too fancy now, for an old friend."

He stuck his red, sweaty face close to Elsa's. "More than a friend, too. We were more than that, weren't we, *liebling?*"

Elsa looked as if she might get sick. The restaurant was now almost silent, all eyes on the commotion at their table. Even the drinkers at the bar above them leaned over the balcony to see the show. The drunk continued, unmoved by her obvious distress.

"So, I must follow you like a dog. A dog. That's what you've done to me. While you play the great conductor, the famous Elsa Von Streng. I wonder what all your nice friends would say if they knew the truth, eh?"

Elsa made as if to stand, saying quietly, "Friedrich, please..."

"Sit down," he roared at her, "I'm going to have my say!"

Before anyone could stop him, the man Elsa called Friedrich grabbed the conductor by her shoulders and shook her, hard. Elsa's hands pushed against his chest but his brute strength was too much. She couldn't break free. Lisa moved instinctively to grab his arm from the other side, while Arnoldo murmured something reproachful in Italian, his right hand reaching for Friedrich's shirt. Faster than either was Fintan. The rather rotund, softly spoken man - known around the concert hall as a fusspot, a gentle but ineffective presence - leapt to his feet, reached across the table and grabbed Friedrich by his coat lapels. Altogether, the scene resembled a strange, theatrical tableau.

"Let go of her, immediately." Fintan spoke with a quiet authority.

Elsa's tormentor blinked and hesitated but still held onto her.

"I said, let her go."

"Or what?" the other man sneered.

Fintan sighed, drew back his right hand and using the heel of his palm dealt the man one sharp blow to the solar plexus. Friedrich staggered, seemed to trip over his own feet and fell to one side, as Elsa pulled away in the opposite direction. Caught off guard, her assailant released his grip, wobbled towards Arnoldo, bent over slightly and stumbled again. This time, Teresa was forced to sidestep smartly to avoid disaster. The man flailed his arms for a moment, but it was no use - he fell backwards into a table, sending beef, salad and cutlery flying. A rogue splodge of mashed potato landed on a woman's head and several diners found themselves wearing lettuce leaves and pureed beetroot. A general outcry went up, and the husband of the unfortunate mash victim tried to grab Friedrich as he lay on the ground, on top of the smashed table. Fearing a full-scale brawl, half the service staff rushed to intervene, and for a few moments absolute chaos reigned.

Elsa finally saw Teresa and let out a sob. Gone was the cool, composed German conductor and in her place was Emer Kelly, a lonely kid from the inner city who had come up the hard way. Teresa gathered her in her arms and comforted her, as if she was one of her own kids. Over the young woman's shoulder, Teresa could see Lisa. Her friend raised an eyebrow but asked no questions. Indeed, the violinist's attention was soon claimed by Arnoldo, full of anxious questions.

"Are you all right, dear Lisa?" He draped his arm around the back of her chair and looked soulfully into her eyes. "You are trembling, *caro*, I can see it. Lean your head on my shoulder, and I will protect you…"

Lisa gave him a long look, that Teresa found difficult to decipher.

"Never mind me." The violinist turned to Fintan and said admiringly, "That was amazing, Fintan. Well done."

"Oh." Fintan's face went slightly pink. "It was nothing. I've done some Kenpo. For self defense. It was a reflex reaction. Elsa, are you okay?"

Elsa's sobs had subsided and with a visible effort she pulled herself together. "Thanks, Fintan. Yes. I'm okay."

She looked around rather anxiously, prompting Lisa to stand and peer over people's heads to see what was happening.

"They have him under control," Lisa reported, "He's still lying down."

Teresa turned to look. As she watched, the crowd around the prone figure of Friedrich seemed to recede of its own accord, in some unspoken common reaction. Only two of the waiters remained, kneeling either side in the debris of the table and its contents.

A woman pushed her way through, saying, "I'm a doctor, let me see."

Mai arrived at Teresa's side. "Are you okay, we saw what happened but we couldn't get to you."

"Hush," Teresa said quietly, her eyes never leaving the scene playing out beside her. Mai fell silent but Teresa could feel the girl's comforting presence. At last the doctor stood up and shook her head.

"You'll have to call the Gardaí, I'm afraid."

Elsa clutched Teresa's arm so tightly, the older woman almost cried out. The doctor spoke quietly but her words carried in the now silent restaurant.

"He's dead."

Chapter 6

Detective Malachy Flynn watched as his junior partner, a young garda detective sergeant by the name of Harry Dempsey, examined the body. The forensics team stood by, eager to assume control of the scene and the State Pathologist, Dr. Lorraine O'Toole, sighed pointedly.

Malachy just smiled at her. He was a patient man and a careful one. If asked he would have told them, *"No point rushing these things."*

Dempsey straightened up and nodded at his boss. "Definitely a puncture wound, lower abdomen."

The pathologist rolled her eyes. "If you don't mind, Detective, could you perhaps wait until *I* determine cause of death?"

"Be fair, now." Malachy grinned. "He never said that was what killed him. He just said there was a puncture wound. We'll not step on your toes, Lorraine, I promise."

He indicated to Dempsey to move away from the body. "Come on, lad. Let's get out of the good doctor's hair."

O'Toole shook her head but wasted no time in moving her team into place. The area around the body had been cleared of people as soon as Friedrich was pronounced dead, with the diners and staff now huddled on one side of the room. The main lights had been turned on, revealing the gaudiness and gilt of the decor to be surface glamour only. The balcony and its trendy crowd were largely silent now, save for the uniformed Gardaí moving through them, taking statements, retrieving footage from mobile phones.

Malachy had little time for social media but he appreciated the fact that crimes in public places were often caught on camera now. Anything that made his life a little easier.

"We'll chat about what you observed later," he told Dempsey. "For now, let's get the lie of the land. We need statements from anyone up there, especially near the balcony. They might have seen more from their vantage point that anyone down here. Send a uniform up there, don't let anyone leave."

He cast an eye over one smaller group, seated at a table slightly apart from the rest of the restaurant guests. These were the people immediately involved in the incident, or as he liked to call them, "the suspects." In his slightly cynical opinion, the people on the scene were often the ones to look at most closely. He was a little surprised to recognise Lisa Kennedy, whose uncle had regrettably fallen foul of the law some years previously. She was a violinist, he recalled, and was doing a line with that young fella in Mrs. O'Brien's music shop. He felt sure he recognised the blonde woman from somewhere, but nothing sprang to mind yet. The older man he instantly recognised as Fintan McLaughlin, from the same case that had introduced him to Lisa and his favourite music shop keeper, Teresa O'Brien.

As if summoned by his thoughts, the redoubtable old woman turned in her seat and smiled at him.

"Good evening, Detective Flynn," Teresa said. "I was hoping it would be you."

"Were you, indeed?" Malachy tried to sound severe but couldn't help smiling. He had twice found himself dealing with the redoubtable old lady, and his admiration for her spirit was only matched by his appreciation for her brain.

"She thinks like a gangster," he had once told young Harry Dempsey and he had meant it as a compliment.

Dempsey did not share his sentiments. An audible groan left the younger Detective Garda's lips at the sight of the music shop owner. Malachy ignored him.

Lisa looked relieved to see him, he noted, and the blonde woman looked indifferent. In fairness, she looked as if she was in shock. Fintan nodded distractedly, and the other man, whom Malachy privately castigated as a bit of a poser with his floppy dark hair and dramatic air, stared at Teresa O'Brien but said nothing.

"I'm Detective Inspector Malachy Flynn," the detective introduced himself, "and this is Detective Sergeant Harry Dempsey. Now, I'm sure you're all as anxious as I am to clear this matter up. As you can see, we are taking statements from everyone who was present for the incident, but we will need to talk to each of you in depth. Perhaps we can start with you, Mrs. O'Brien."

He was nearly sure Dempsey ground his teeth at this suggestion and suppressed a chuckle. The younger man had the makings of a good detective but he was still at that stage where ego overruled self-interest at times. Malachy had learned early on to recognise and utilize the talent around him. Dempsey, he hoped, would come to it given time.

Teresa stood up and followed the Gardaí to a table out of earshot of the others. As they sat down, Malachy was surprised to see young Mai Khan push through the crowd, neatly sidestep a uniformed garda and approach the table. The teenager's face was set in grim lines and her fists were clenched.

"You're not going to interrogate her without a witness!" Mai's voice was slightly shaky but she met Malachy's eyes defiantly.

"Mai, it's fine," Teresa protested. Mai shook her head.

"It's not, Mrs. O'Brien. They can't possibly suspect you, it's ridiculous. You should be ashamed, Detective Flynn. I'm not letting you question her alone."

Malachy made a valiant but not altogether successful attempt to keep a straight face.

"Ms. Khan," he said, gently. "I'm not interrogating her. I have the utmost respect for Mrs. O'Brien. Sure, hasn't she practically solved two cases for me? I just want her insight, and her advice. Okay? You're a good wee lass to worry about her, but there's no need. Now, is that your mother I see over there? And your dad. Go on now, back to them and let me do my job. I'll send Teresa over to you as soon as she's done here. Oh, and could you ask one of the staff to bring her a cup of tea? I'd say she could use one."

Mai hesitated, but a smiling nod from Teresa seemed to reassure her.

"Okay. But -" she glowered at Dempsey in particular, "I'll be watching."

Malachy sat down, grimacing as the rickety chair swayed. "She's fierce fond of you, that young one."

"She is," Teresa said smugly, "if a trifle overprotective. So, Detective, we meet again."

"We really have to stop meeting like this. It's becoming a habit."

"It's not by choice, I can assure you. I came here for a nice birthday dinner - it's Mai's seventeenth, you see."

"You were here with the Khans, then?"

"Here's how it was." Teresa gave a succinct account of the situation, starting with Mai's birthday arrangements to Lisa's new role as soloist and the invitation to dinner to discuss the concert season. Malachy listened with interest while Dempsey - after a sharp elbow in the ribs from his boss - took notes.

"So, you see, the dead man - Friedrich - wasn't in their party at all. He rocked up, roaring drunk, and just generally roaring."

"What do you know about him?"

"Nothing really. Never saw him before, but from what he said at the table, he knew Elsa. He was most aggressive towards her - well, I told you, he downright assaulted her. And from what the others have been saying - after he was killed, while we were sitting waiting for you - I think he's been hanging around the concert hall, making a nuisance of himself." Teresa hesitated, but added, "I think you need to talk to Lisa about that. And you need to talk to Elsa."

Malachy's ears pricked up. There had been a peculiar emphasis on the word "need," which in his experience meant there was something the other was reluctant to tell him but thought he should know.

"Appreciate it," he told Teresa. "I'll be taking statements from everyone, in turn."

He glanced at Dempsey who seemed oblivious to the undercurrent and sighed.

Teresa added, "There's a lot going on, in my opinion. I can't give you anything more than a gut feeling, but if Arnoldo Messini didn't know the victim, I'll be stunned."

"What makes you say that?"

"When Friedrich turned up, it's hard to be sure, but on the whole, I'm inclined to think he recognised the man.

Incidentally he was useless when Elsa was attacked, which is odd, because Lisa tells me Elsa and Arnoldo are great friends. It was Fintan who dealt with him. Now, that's another strange thing. Fintan McLaughlin is not known as a man of action, yet he took on a much bigger, stronger, drunk with hardly a thought."

Malachy nodded. "It's the little things, isn't it? Right, anything else you think I should bear in mind?"

Teresa frowned. "I'm not sure. But if I were you, I'd start with Lisa and then Elsa, leave the men sit there."
Malachy grinned. "Let them stew, eh? I wouldn't imagine that pair have much in common."
"No." Teresa stood, grimacing slightly. "I'm stiff from sitting on these awful chairs."

Malachy nodded. "You get off home. Dempsey, let uniform know that Mrs. O'Brien and the Khan party can head off. I'll call to see you tomorrow, if you're at home?"

"Call for lunch," Teresa said. "I've been baking."
Dempsey escorted the old lady to her friends, while Malachy had a few minutes quiet reflection. He felt sure there was far more that she wanted to discuss with him, but for whatever reason, couldn't or wouldn't right now. If he asked the right questions tonight, then perhaps tomorrow she could help fill in some of the blanks…

"Honestly, " Dempsey reappeared, huffing in annoyance. "I don't know why you put up with her, I don't. Interfering old baggage."
"You're just sore because she proved you wrong last time," Malachy said reasonably. "You need to let that go."
Dempsey gave him a sour eye. "Whatever. Who's next?"

"Lisa Kennedy," Malachy said. He wasn't sure why Teresa

had made such a point of it but he was going to take her advice. "When she's done, Elsa Von Streng next. We'll leave the men until last."

Lisa sat down heavily, her eyes red rimmed and her face pale.

"It wasn't his fault!" She glowered at Malachy, reminding him forcibly of young Mai.

"Whose fault?" he asked mildly.

"Fintan's. He only pushed that man -well, sort of a push - but he only did it to stop him hurting Elsa. The other man, I mean. Friedrich. He had Elsa by the shoulders and was shaking her like a rag doll. Fintan had to step in. He didn't mean to hurt him that badly."

Dempsey opened his mouth but shut it again when Malachy looked sharply in his direction.

"I'm sure he didn't, and of course we'll take all the circum-stances into account," the older detective said smoothly. "You can help your friend greatly, by telling us everything that happened as best you can remember it."

There was a pause, then Malachy continued, "Start with this. Have you ever seen the deceased before tonight?"
To his surprise, Lisa's cheeks flushed and she shifted in her seat. "Before tonight?"

"Yes, Lisa. Before this evening, have you met, seen or spoken to the unfortunate Herr Friedrich…what was on his ID, Dempsey? Oh yes, Herr Friedrich Mann."
Lisa swallowed. "Um. I don't know him, no."

Malachy raised one eyebrow and waited.
"I don't," Lisa protested. "I-I may have seen him before though."

Malachy waited a little longer.

"Oh look, I can't be sure about this. Not one hundred percent. I don't want to give you the wrong impression - or have you arrest the wrong person. Again." Lisa cast a sour eye at Dempsey, whose previous blunders were obviously not forgiven by anyone in Mrs. O'Brien's circle.

"We won't, I promise you. No haring off in the wrong direction." Malachy held up his hands, in mock surrender. "Just you tell us what you know and let us worry about how it all fits together."

Lisa gave in. "Okay. Well, about a week ago - I'd have the exact date in my work diary - after rehearsals I overheard voices arguing in one of the rehearsal rooms. That's backstage at the concert hall, near the dressing rooms."

"I remember," Malachy had been in the inner sanctum of the Hibernia orchestra when Lisa's predecessor had met a rather grisly end.

"I recognised one of the voices - but the other one was a stranger. It was a very distinctive voice though, German accent, harsh and gravelly. Then, earlier today I was a little late back from lunch. There was a man hanging around the backstage door - it was him, Friedrich. He said he was there to visit a friend and when I said I couldn't just let him in, he tried to push in. Security had to come and help me - you can check with them. And there is probably CCTV footage. And - when he spoke, I recognised his voice. He's the one I heard arguing, before. I'm sure of it."

Malachy waited until Dempsey had finished laboriously noting all this down.

"That's most interesting, thank you."

"I don't see how it helps though," Lisa insisted. "I mean, it has nothing to do with…with what happened here. That was an accident. Fintan didn't mean to hurt him."

"Was the other voice in that argument, the one you did

recognise - was that Fintan McLaughlin?"

Lisa started. "Oh, no," she blurted out. "No, it wasn't him. I doubt Fintan ever set eyes on that man before tonight."

"Then, who was it? Come on, Lisa. Did you think we'd just gloss over that bit? Who was Friedrich arguing with?"

Lisa looked at him miserably but answered truthfully. "I thought it was Elsa. But - I did ask her about it and she denies it. So maybe I was mistaken."

Malachy gave her a quizzical look but didn't comment. Instead, he sent her off with Dempsey to be processed and sent home.

When he returned, Dempsey asked, "What do you make of all that?"

"Nothing - yet. Keep an open mind, lad. Bring Elsa over now and we'll see what she has to say." He glanced over at Dr. O'Toole, who was busy directing her forensics team, and pursed his lips. The pathology results would take at least a day, even with a rush, but he was fairly sure he could tell the cause of death. Even without Lisa's description of Fintan's intervention and "push" - a push which other eyewitnesses had described as a cross between a Bruce Lee karate chop and a John Wicks movie stunt.

He looked up to see the cool blue eyes of the famous conductor studying him.

"Ah. Ms. Von Streng. Take a seat."

Elsa sat gracefully and waved aside an offer of tea or coffee.

"I couldn't. The staff have been surprisingly kind, we've been handed tea and even food every ten minutes."

"Yeah. It's funny, they may act snotty and highbrow but it's all show." Malachy smiled at the young woman. "Put on to make Chez Maurice the hippest place to be."

Elsa nodded. "Well, Inspector, you have questions for me?"

"I do. Ms. Von Streng, did you know Friedrich Mann?"

A tiny hesitation, but she answered calmly. "Yes. I knew him."

"I see. And would you please explain to us, what was the nature of your relationship with him?"

Elsa drew breath.

"He was my husband. Now my ex-husband."

Dempsey nearly dropped his pen. "Husband?"

Elsa turned towards him, stared at him for a long moment, then repeated coldly, "Ex-husband."

Malachy ignored Dempsey's interruption.

"Go on. This is an interesting turn of events, you'll appreciate. So, I'm going to assume that you were the one heard arguing with him last week?"

"Lisa told you that?" Elsa's mouth twisted. "I suppose it was inevitable."

"She told me but only reluctantly, I may add. And she tried to tell us that she was mistaken about recognizing your voice."

Elsa smiled. "Ah. I see."

"She's loyal, that young woman."

"I'm beginning to appreciate that. And Teresa is too - she hasn't told you about me, has she?"

Malachy leaned forward. He was a man who appreciated music, and the spoken word. He wouldn't claim to have Lisa's delicate ear but the unmistakable, if faint, German accent had faded away and in its place was something familiar, something surprising.

Something that suggested the narrow streets and cobblestones of Dublin's Liberties rather than the broad avenues of Munich.

"I think I'd better start at the beginning," Elsa said. "I'm sure you'll find out anyway, so it'll save time all round. My name really *is* Elsa Von Streng - now. But I was born Emer Kelly, in the inner city of Dublin. Not half a mile from here. The flats, you know - the ones they pulled down ten years ago. Yes, Detective, *those* flats. I moved to Germany, changed my name - legally- and left the poverty and the snobbery behind. Emer Kelly couldn't get a job conducting a school orchestra, not with a Dublin accent and an address in the worst part of the city. Not to mention two uncles in prison and a brother on remand. But Elsa Von Streng could become the first female conductor to win the Baton D'Or, the first to conduct the Moscow Symphonic, then the Munich and now, the first woman to lead the Hibernia in its hundred-year history."

She regarded the two Gardaí proudly. "I don't regret becoming Elsa, not for one minute. But I do regret some of the people I left behind me, in order to succeed. I miss Cathal O'Brien. He and Teresa were the only people to ever believe in me, to see past the rough kid. When I heard he'd died, I felt awful for just disappearing. I wanted to come home and see her. I've barely spoken to my family in years. I wanted to make it right."

"Understandable. But, where does our poor dead Friedrich come into it all?"

"Detective Flynn, I married Friedrich ten years ago. He was the lead violinist in the orchestra in Munich. He was - charming. Funny, lively, life and soul of the party. Popular, too, and I was not. I've never been good with people. When he showed an interest in me, I was deeply flattered. I fell madly in love, and accepted his proposal - six months after we first met. We got married almost immediately. "

She looked at Malachy, and for the first time he saw sadness.

"It went to pieces immediately, too. The moment he had a ring on my finger, it started. I could do nothing right. He was insanely jealous, not just of other men but of any professional achievement. Every mention in a news article, every good review, every successful performance, seemed to eat at him like acid. And then there was the drinking. He couldn't hold a job, he was utterly unreliable. He lived off my earnings, while resenting me for it."

Malachy felt for her. "That's a sad and very common story, I'm afraid."

"Yes. Well, I put up with it for far too long. Then - as I said, I heard about Cathal dying. I began to think about Ireland, and my family. I missed them. My brother, the one who was in remand, turned his life around. Marriage, kids, a decent job. He sent me emails, and pictures, and I largely ignored them until then but suddenly, I wanted to go see them. Friedrich said no - actually, he went absolutely ballistic." The Dublin accent returned in force for a moment. "He said he'd leather me if I set foot here."

"He wanted you under his thumb," Malachy said. "If you reconnected with family…"

"Exactly. Well, there were some other things too. Taken altogether it was a wake up call. I'd had enough. I divorced him. That was about two years ago. I waited until an opportunity to come home arose, and now here I am."

"Was he ever charged with it?" Malachy asked.

"Charged with what?" Dempsey looked up from his notebook. Both Elsa and Malachy gave him withering looks.

"What do you think, you eejit? With Domestic Violence." Dempsey frowned, obviously replaying Elsa's story in his head until the penny dropped and he managed to read between the lines. "Oh. Sorry."

Elsa rolled her eyes. "No. But he fell foul of the law in other ways. He's done time in prison, over the years. I hoped moving here would shake him off finally but it seems he followed me. He managed to slip into the Concert Hall. He threatened me, and I told him I'd call the cops here on him too. He left."

Malachy doubted very much that the argument was quite as simple, but filed it away for a later time. "He came back though."

"He tried, but I'd already asked security to be more vigilant. I'm sorry he frightened Lisa."

"And tonight? What did he hope to gain by confronting you here. What exactly was he threatening you with?"

Elsa shrugged. "He knew I was insecure about my roots. I made the mistake of confiding in him many years ago, when we were first together. He thought I would do anything to stop him from telling people I was only Emer Kelly, not the great Elsa Von Streng."

"And would you?" Dempsey interjected. "Weren't you desperate to keep your secret?"

"Are you daft?" Elsa sounded exasperated. "I didn't want it to be common knowledge, no. But I'd already reconnected with some old friends. Teresa, for a start. I planned on reaching out to my family and explaining. It wasn't as if the Hibernia could fire me for it. Anyway, what does it matter? Maybe, in his head, it was why he caused a public scene. But no one could have foreseen the accident."

"Ah, yes. Well now, I'm not sure we can call a blow to the chest an accident..." Malachy mused.

Elsa tensed. "Fintan McLaughlin stepped in to stop my ex-husband physically attacking me. I assure you, his *push* was entirely justified. Entirely. I won't have that poor man blamed. Friedrich was drunk, and he swayed off balance. He almost knocked Teresa O'Brien off her feet, twice. He would have fallen even without Fintan touching him. Besides, we all had our hands on him - I was pushing him off me. Lisa was trying to pull him away. Even Arnoldo grabbed at him. So if you blame Fintan, you may as well blame all of us - the man was a savage."

Malachy nodded. "Interesting. Well, we'll bear all that in mind. Now, young Dempsey here is going to take you over to finalize your statement. You'll be free to go then. Have you anyone you can call? You've had a shock, it would be good for you to have company tonight."

Elsa Von Streng was every inch the cold, impervious, conductor as she replied. "No. I shall be fine, thank you. I assume you'll be in touch tomorrow."

She stood, smoothed down her skirt and added, "Please tell Fintan I shall wait for him, over there."

Malachy watched her walk away, mulling it all over as he did. Her decision to wait for the musical director struck him as a declaration of loyalty. Whatever the truth of the events in Chez Maurice that night, Elsa seemed determined to protect the man who had stepped up to her husband. It was an interesting development.

Fintan McLaughlin looked an unlikely hero as he sat down heavily, his face white and a faint sheen of sweat glistening on his brow. He was a pleasant-faced man in his early forties, slightly chubby and of just average height, with thinning brown hair and gold rimmed glasses. His hand trembled slightly as he stuck it out towards Malachy, introducing himself quietly as "Fintan McLaughlin. I'm afraid this is all my fault."

"Is it now?" Malachy pointed at the chair. "Sit yourself down there and tell me what happened. In your own words. There's no rush."

A reproachful cough from Dempsey prompted him to add, "Unless of course, you'd like to wait until you've benefit of a solicitor..."

Fintan shook his head.

"I'd prefer to get it over with. I'm sure you'll need a formal statement later to charge me..." his voice trailed off and he looked sick.

"Let's worry about that when we come to it," Malachy said.

"Okay. Well, I'm sure you know the gist of it. We - that's Elsa, Lisa, Arnoldo and myself - we were having dinner when that man pushed his way over to our table -"

"Why?" Malachy interrupted. "The dinner, I mean. What was the occasion?"

"We're all colleagues at the Concert Hall. Well, I work for the Hall, the others work for the Hibernian Symphony, but it's the same difference. We work closely together. Except for Arnoldo, he's a visiting guest soloist. A tenor."

"Any good?"

"Yes. I mean, a bit flashy, and he's not much good above E5, if you ask me. Bags of character though, and he can sell a part." Fintan sounded far more confident now he was on a familiar subject. "We're lucky to snag him, he's in great demand. He appeals to a wider audience, you see..."

"Good, good. So, it was a working dinner, to discuss the upcoming concert. Was it partly a welcome dinner for this Arnoldo?"

Fintan blinked at him. "Um. Half and half. We had a lot to discuss - some of Elsa's ideas are a bit out there, to be honest.

But it was also a welcome dinner, if you like to look at it like that."

Malachy smiled. "Good, good. Now, you're all sitting around having a nice time - it was a nice evening, I take it? - and then up crashes poor Friedrich Mann, drunk as a skunk."

Fintan nodded slowly. "He was roaring and shouting, detective. He screamed in Elsa's face, which was bad enough. It was all very confused - something about being an old friend, more than friends, and then he said, *"What if they knew the truth?"* or words to that effect. Then he grabbed her by the shoulders. Look, Detective, it was quite obvious he was used to roughing her up. I'm not just saying this to excuse what I did but ask anyone. He hurt her."

"You hit him." Malachy prompted. "Tell me now, was it a push, a shove, or a karate chop?"

"It was Kenpo."

"Kenpo? And how do you come to know a martial art like that?"

Fintan's face hardened slightly. "I'm not a big man, Detective. I'm not sporty. I'm into books, and music. I grew up in an area where boys liked sport and fighting. I survived school, only to find that it doesn't matter if you're rich or poor, there are violent people everywhere. I was in university when some lads on the rugby team decided it would be fun to rough up the music nerd. Broke my hand. I went from a career playing viola to teaching. Then composing and now, musical director. I haven't done badly, don't get me wrong. But after that incident I took up Kenpo for self-defense. No one will ever bully me again and I won't see someone hurt either."

"I'm sorry," Malachy said. "Did you press charges against your attackers?"

"Yes." Fintan met his eyes with a hard stare. "They got off. Their daddies were well connected. Never even made it into a courtroom."

"I see. Galling. I can understand why you felt compelled to intervene tonight."

" I had no intention of hurting him so badly, but I did hit him. Palm of my hand to the solar plexus. He lost his balance and fell over. I am fully prepared to take the consequences of my actions."

The musical director had squared his shoulders and straightened his spine as he spoke. With his slightly martyred air and tense expression, he put Malachy in mind of a faithful hound unjustly accused of eating the Sunday roast. An observation he wisely kept to himself.

Aloud, he said, "I see. I appreciate your frankness and it's as well to be honest with us. We're far more reasonable than people realise, you know. You should of course seek legal advice. But for now, we'll take your statement and let you get some rest. I'll need you to come into the station at some point, but we'll be in touch."

"You're not arresting me?" Fintan blurted out.

"Not at the moment." Malachy gave the other man an encouraging pat on the shoulder. "Look, I'm not saying you should relax, but if what you describe is accurate, you have a good case for defense of another. I meant to ask, did you recognise the man?"

Fintan answered. "I never heard of Friedrich Mann in my life."

Malachy sent Dempsey away with him while he pondered the very precise nature of that last answer.

He was soon interrupted, however, by the arrival of the last of the dinner companions, Arnoldo Messini. The young man threw himself into the nearest chair, flicked his head of dark hair and stretched out his arms imploringly towards the Garda.

"Detective! Inspector, yes? What can I tell you? What can I do? Such a tragedy, such a night." He leaned forward, adding, "It was a horror, truly. My nerves. My voice. I fear for both."

Malachy regarded him coolly. "Mr. Messini, yes? You were supposed to wait until my colleague brought you over."

"Wait? Bah! What have I done all evening, except wait?"

"Nevertheless, you should have waited a little more."

Arnoldo rolled his eyes and gesticulated with his hands for emphasis. "I could not wait. Did you not hear what I said about my nerves? And my *voice*? Ah, but you are a policeman. You don't understand. My voice is my instrument. It is easily upset. Late nights, shock, trauma, endless talking while we wait. My nerves, too. You are finished with the little man, and his story. Why not come over and get on with this?"

Malachy sighed. "Well, you're here now."

"You should have started with me."

"We started with the most important witnesses," Malachy said, "and worked our way down."

Arnoldo's eyes narrowed. "Elsa and Lisa are more important than I? Fintan is more important - well, I suppose, he is the assassin, yes? but the women - why are they more important?"

"We have not yet determined cause of death," Malachy replied blandly. "Elsa and Lisa were more directly involved in the conflict than you, according to eye witnesses."

Arnoldo's cheeks flushed. "Ah. This is because I did not rush in, fists flying, yes? Like that fool, Fintan? *I* was trying to defuse the situation. We wouldn't be in this mess if he had let me deal with the man."

"So, describe to me, what exactly did you do to help?"

"Well, I did not have a chance to do much - as I say, Fintan rushed in too quickly. I was trying to calm the situation…"

Dempsey puffed up to the table, giving Arnoldo a hostile look. "Couldn't wait, eh?

"Arnoldo here is just telling me, he didn't have a chance to calm the situation down." Malachy raised an eyebrow and Dempsey snorted. "According to witnesses, Mr. Messini here didn't do much at all, just sat there."

Malachy turned to Arnoldo. "Did you, now?"

Arnoldo shrugged. "I put my hand out, so," He extended his right hand, "I tried to stop him, but I was also trying to calm him."

"I'd be angry if someone grabbed a female friend and started shaking her." Dempsey pointed out.

"Well, yes, I was concerned for Elsa."

"Concerned. You didn't stand up though. " Dempsey held up his notebook. "Some very clear descriptions in here. All in agreement."

"There was no room to stand." Arnoldo's tone was sulky. "Anyway, so what? I did not strike the man. I did not cause this."

Malachy ignored this. "Tell me, Arnoldo. How long have you known Elsa?"

"About ten years, maybe a little more."

"Ah. You would have been well acquainted with the deceased, Friedrich Mann."

"I? No. I do not know him."

"You don't know your good friend's husband?"

Arnoldo smiled suddenly, a warm smile full of great charm. The sudden change in attitude made Malachy sit up.

"Ah. You know then, that he is Elsa's ex? I am sorry. She is a very dear friend, you understand. It was not possible for me to betray such information about her. I did not wish to make matters worse."

"So you lied?" Dempsey had a knack of putting things in their simplest, least diplomatic form.

"Lied…oh no! I would never lie to the police." Arnoldo said comfortably. "But it's not my place to tell you this, if Elsa didn't want you to know. But I am glad she told you. Friedrich was a bad husband, and a bad person. She was right to leave him."

"Were you surprised to see him here?"

"Here? In Ireland? *Madre de dio*, of course."

Malachy could feel the waves of irritation rising off Dempsey like heat.

"So, you'd no idea he was here?" Dempsey asked sharply. "Your good friend Elsa didn't let on he was harassing her?"

Arnoldo hesitated. "Was he? Poor Elsa. I had no idea."

Dempsey looked as if he was about to pursue this line of inquiry, but Malachy forestalled him.
"Ah well, no doubt she was embarrassed. I think that's enough for tonight, Mr. Messini. We'll talk further tomorrow."

Dempsey looked sullen at the interruption but Arnoldo looked uneasy.

"That is it?"

"For tonight."

The tenor stood, but hovered uncertainly, staring at the detective.

"Unless there's something you need to get off your chest?" Malachy added blandly.

"No!" Arnoldo replied hastily. He extended a hand to shake goodbye and Malachy noted with interest that he was left-handed, known in Irish as a *"citeog."*

"Good evening," the Italian said politely. Dempsey escorted him to the uniformed garda waiting on the side, then stalked back to Malachy looking like a man with his nose thoroughly out of joint.

"I suppose you bought that, then? Him saying he didn't know Mann was here?"

"Did I?" Malachy smiled broadly. "Dempsey, I wouldn't trust that slippery fish if he told me water was wet."

"Then why let him off so easy?"

"Because right now, we don't know what happened here. Did that man die from a blow? was that puncture wound the cause? Until Dr. O'Toole tells us, we are operating in the dark. You press a character like that too closely, they'll clam up. And worse, he might be on the next flight out of here and back to *bella Italia.* No, we wait."

"And if it was a stabbing, and not a tragic accident?"

"Then, my lad, we have a murder inquiry. And four suspects, all of whom had their hands on the victim."

Chapter 7

Sunday, the morning after the terrible events at Chez Maurice, was a lovely August morning, so sunny and pleasant that the events of the night before felt unreal. Teresa had set the table on her deck, overlooking her back garden, with a pot of tea, plates of homemade buns and cakes and sandwiches. She prided herself on being a good hostess, which is why she waited until Detective Flynn was amply fed before launching into the topic at hand.

"I expect you saw the wound to the man's abdomen?" she asked, pouring a hot drop of tea into his cup.

Malachy laughed. "I did. I was wondering if you had realised that he was stabbed, or if you thought it was the blow or the fall that did for him."

"Well, it could still be any of those," Teresa pointed out. "But on the balance of probability, it seemed unlikely that such a short fall could have killed him. He was extremely drunk, you know. He was more likely to have bounced back up, than anything. Of course, a blow to the back of the head - these freak accidents do happen. I remember a cousin of Cathal's, fell backwards and hit his head off the pavement. He almost died."

"Hitting someone in the chest can cause all kinds too,"

Malachy replied.

"Yes. But a great big stab wound does tend to present itself as a prime suspect."

"It does, I agree. Of course, there was a lot of cutlery on that table - we haven't ruled out a freak accident in that regard either."

Teresa said nothing but her face was a picture of skepticism. She appreciated the Garda keeping an open mind but it was highly unlikely that even a steak knife could have found it's way into the man's front and then dislodged itself, to disappear from the scene.

"I know," Malachy said, "It doesn't really hold water. But we're hampered until O'Toole gets back to us. And it being a Sunday, I'm not holding my breath."

"Well, then. Let us proceed. The unfortunate man - Friedrich - approaches the table. He's lurching, obviously drunk, aggressive. He grabs Elsa - who naturally puts her hands on him to push him away - and then from what I observed, and from what the others said, Lisa grabbed at him to try to stop him, Arnoldo reached out towards him from the other side and then Fergal struck him a blow from the front."

"Succinct," Malachy nodded approvingly. "I do admire your ability to condense things to the essential facts."

"Years behind a counter," Teresa replied. "You learn to deal with the long-winded and the indecisive. Also, my Cathal was a divil for the details. No patience, unless it was a story about an instrument and half the time he wasn't listening, only thinking about whatever violin or cello he needed to repair. I soon learned to get my point across quickly."

"Well, I appreciate it. So - any one of the four could have stabbed him? In full view of the others at the table. And then there's the big question, why?"

Teresa sipped her tea and munched thoughtfully on a custard cream.

"Hmm. There's one reason you'd take that kind of risk - if you felt in immediate danger."

"Perhaps Friedrich was about to blurt something out. For example, that the great Elsa Von Streng was born plain Emer Kelly." Malachy couldn't resist a little smile but if he hoped to disconcert Teresa O'Brien, he would have to try again.

"Ah. I'm glad she came clean about that," Teresa said, pouring herself a fresh cup of tea.

Malachy conceded defeat. "You knew her back then, I hear."

"Yes, indeed. Cathal and I were very fond of Emer, as she was then. Very fond. She came to see me when she returned."

Malachy shook his head. "Well, that puts me in my place. Is there anything you don't know?"

"Many things," Teresa grinned. "I don't know the full story between Elsa and her late husband, for one thing. He was abusive, that much is clear but I think he was more than just a bad husband. Just a feeling, you understand. And her decision to return to Ireland, her reluctance to let her family know what's been going on...I think I need to talk to her about it all."

"You might talk to that young one, Lisa, while you're at it," Malachy suggested. "I'll be asking her what exactly she overheard between Elsa and Friedrich. And of course we need to look into Fintan's interactions with him."

"Were there any?" Teresa sounded doubtful.

"He suggests not, but I'll have to be sure. We've found where Friedrich was staying. The Lowry Hotel, on Baggot Street. Single room, booked for three weeks. He arrived about ten days ago. Dempsey says he was known in the hotel for drinking late into the night. Didn't stint himself on fine dining, either but did all of it alone."

"No visitors?"

"No. Disappeared off out most days but didn't get friendly enough with any of the staff to tell them where he was going."

Teresa sighed. "That's a pity. The Lowry is a nice hotel. Pricey."

"Yes. So, we're back to the four at the table. One of them must be responsible, and more than one probably knows more than they're letting on."

"I wish Lisa hadn't been there, it's not fair on her. That young woman is not able for this kind of thing."

Malachy blinked. "Well, now. She was well able to tell me off, so she was. She tried to hide the fact that Elsa - *Emer* - knew the deceased."

Teresa waved her hand airily. "Ach, that's nothing. Instinctive loyalty. These orchestras, they're like families. Dysfunctional and strange families but kin nonetheless. She could detest Elsa and still protect her."

"I notice you call her Elsa - but you must have known her originally as Emer."

"Of course. But Elsa is what she wants to be called. It's her legal name, by the way - she told me she changed it in Germany. But even if it wasn't, I respect anyone's right to be called by whatever name they prefer."

"Oh, I agree," Malachy said. "No argument from me. Well, I think you know as much as I do right now. I don't have to tell you, I'm sure, but I'd be grateful for any insights you pick up. These are your people - musicians, orchestras, that benighted concert hall - if you hear anything ..."

Teresa promised him. "You know I would even if Lisa wasn't

mixed up in this mess. And Elsa. I'm fierce fond of that young woman too. Also - you remember the Super Ukers?"

Malachy laughed. "How could I forget them?"

The Super Ukers were Dublin's premier Ukulele group, and four of their members had operated as Teresa's unofficial army of sleuths the last time they had crossed paths.

"They are playing in the Concert Hall, in a few weeks. In aid of The President's Charity Fund, no less."

Malachy's ears pricked up. "Are they now? And will they be doing any rehearsing in that hallowed hall?"

"Lots." Teresa recalled the conversation she had had with Clara. "Starting very soon."

"Well, now. Isn't that interesting? Between Lisa and the four nosiest ukulele players in Ireland, I'm expecting great things."

"Detective, if there's any gossip to be found - we'll find it."

* * *

Lisa slept late that morning, having finally fallen into an uneasy doze in the early hours. An insistent buzzing from her phone was what roused her - her camera doorbell sending alerts. Her little flat over a corner shop was handy for the bus route into town, and her landlady had installed the security doorbell when she realised Lisa would be living there alone. Lisa opened the app, peering with bleary eyes at the screen.

Michael Clancy was on her doorstep, arms laden with what looked like a shelf-full of groceries.

She let him in, still heavy and sluggish from her disturbed night. He kissed her on the cheek and without any small talk, set about making a breakfast of scrambled eggs, rashers of bacon, fried mushrooms and a pan of fat sizzling sausages. A cup of strong coffee appeared in front of her, and he laid the Sunday newspaper on the countertop.

"Sit. Relax." He instructed her. Lisa felt a wave of affection, as she watched him potter good-naturedly around her kitchen. He might not be the most exciting of men, but he was definitely the kindest.

"Thanks," She gulped a mouthful of hot coffee and instantly felt brighter. "You didn't have to -"

Michael looked at her sharply. "What? After what happened last night - you thought I'd stay in bed having a lie-in?"

Lisa managed a smile. "Well, I suppose - actually yeah, now I think of it, this is the least you could do!"

"Exactly. Now, hush and drink your coffee. And have a read of the paper if you want."

She eyed the Sunday Press doubtfully. "I don't know. Is there much in there about the...about him?" She cast an eye across the headlines and winced. "It's the main story. Lots of speculation, lots of drama. And look, people saying they saw the victim, and one girl claims she spoke to him, just before he got stabbed. Honestly, people are ghouls sometimes."

"Oh. I'm sorry, love. I didn't think. Maybe best leave the paper for now, eh?"

She took out her phone, instead, and looked at the slew of messages crowding her screen. Ollessa had texted several times, in between about twenty phone calls. Other orchestra members had texted too - varying from genuine concern to naked curiosity. She fired off a quick text to Ollessa and ignored the rest. She paused as she saw Elsa Von Streng's name pop up.

"Elsa's texting me," she looked at Michael, who shrugged.

"Open it. She's probably checking to see if you're okay. Or

maybe she's upset and wants to reach out."

Lisa opened the message and read it aloud.

"I hope you are okay. Please make sure everyone knows rehearsals as normal tomorrow. Arnoldo and you must preview the duet."

"Wow." Michael shook his head. "That's cold."

"It's just her manner," Lisa said. "She was genuinely shook yesterday."

"Still."

Another message came hot on the heels of the first. *"Police will need full statements. I have explained some things to them. I would like to explain them to you too. Can we meet before rehearsals?"*

Lisa responded immediately. *"Of course. I can come early, nine o'clock? we can go for coffee."*

"What do you think that's about?" Michael placed a full plate in front of her, and despite being sure a few minutes earlier that she wouldn't be able to touch it, Lisa's stomach growled in hunger.

"I'm not sure. This is lovely, thanks."

"Eat up. Maybe she knew the man?"

"Ah. I need to fill you in on some bits…" She recounted the story again, from having overheard the row to the man claiming to know Elsa.

"I waited until Detective Flynn was finished with her, and we left together, but she didn't say a word. That younger detective, Dempsey, he sent a uniformed garda out with us. She stayed with us til we both got taxis, so there was no chance to talk."

"Ah. That'll be it then. She wants to explain who he was to her."

"I guess."

"And - how did that Arnoldo fella deal with it all?" There was an edge to her boyfriend's voice as he asked.

Lisa felt her cheeks redden, which was ridiculous. Arnoldo was just a colleague, a fellow artiste. It wasn't her fault if he was handsome, charming, funny and famous. He was also, in her opinion, slightly over dramatic and ridiculous.

"He was upset, obviously, we all were."

"I can't believe it was Fintan who punched the man - I didn't think he had it in him. And this Arnoldo - he just sat there?" Lisa frowned. "It all happened so quickly."

"Right." Michael sounded skeptical and Lisa felt an irrational desire to defend Arnoldo.

"Arnoldo is a sensitive person, Michael. And maybe he was right not to interfere. Possibly if Fintan hadn't struck him, Friedrich would be alive. He must have injured himself in some way, falling like that."

"Poor Fintan. What a thing to live with."

"Anyway, it wasn't Arnoldo's fault that Fintan jumped up like that. Maybe if he'd let Arnoldo deal with it…"

Michael's eyebrow shot up. "Oh. Right. I wonder if Elsa would agree. From your description, she's lucky not to have been seriously hurt."

Lisa opened her mouth to argue but managed to stop herself. "Maybe."

It was ridiculous, arguing with Michael over Arnoldo. If she was honest, she had been annoyed at the tenor for not intervening and admiring of Fintan for stepping up and now she was contradicting all that - it must be lack of sleep!

"Never mind me," she apologised. "I'm like a bear this morning."

Michael looked instantly contrite. "Ah, here. It's my fault. I shouldn't be badgering you. You were there, not me." He gave her an awkward hug. "Let's just have breakfast and try to relax, okay?"

Lisa nodded, and she would try, but her head was already spinning. What was it that Elsa needed to explain? And how on earth could she turn up to rehearsals on Monday and play that duet as if a man hadn't died in front of her, less than 48 hours before?

* * *

Sunday or not, Teresa wasted no time in rallying the troops. When they had last investigated together, a WhatsApp group had been formed, nicknamed 'The O'Brien's Irregulars,' in an homage to Sherlock Holmes. It had dwindled eventually into an occasional exchange of news or memes, but now it was time to revive it for its original purpose.

"*Lisa ran into some trouble last night,*" Teresa typed, "*I think we should meet up, if ye are interested in helping.*"

She knew her audience - the four Super Ukers members wouldn't need any further details to persuade them. They didn't disappoint her. Within minutes Clara had answered for herself and her husband, Peadair, who validated it with a thumbs up. Catherine Sweeney - a tall, willowy ethereal young woman who happened to be a solicitor with a razor-sharp mind behind her dreamy facade - replied with a suggestion. They could all meet up tomorrow in Fancies café for breakfast at eight a.m. Clara countered with lunch, in the same place, at one p.m. and a reminder that she was retired and Peadair was not yet back lecturing. The last member of the band was Eamonn Lyons, and he simply put "*Count me in. See ye 1 pm.*"

A few minutes later, somewhat to Teresa's dismay, another

message popped up - this time from Mai. She had forgotten that the teenager was part of the WhatsApp group.

"That suits me, I've a half day."

Teresa wondered if she could persuade Mai not to get involved, then laughed at herself. No power on earth could persuade Mai from a course of action, if she was determined enough. And she had been present at the scene, after all. It was hardly fair to exclude her now. If she was really honest, Teresa would also have to admit that they needed Mai's youthful insight - she had a knack of looking at things from a new point of view.

"Sure, one more won't make matter," Teresa thought, quoting an old saying of her late husband's. Cathal's extended family hailed from Wicklow and he had picked up the phrase in his youth, applying it to everything from having one extra biscuit to doing one more favour for someone.

"I'm free too!" Setanta Kapoor's name popped up and Teresa sighed. Like Mai, the young college student had been embroiled in their first adventure - if you could call their brush with a ruthless and slightly deranged killer an "adventure." Setanta's mother and grandmother owned Kapoor's Emporium, Stephen Street West's chic boutique and Ashmara Kapoor was one of Teresa's closest friends. She could only hope Ashmara wouldn't mind her roping him in again.

"Okay, Fancies at one. Before then, I have some jobs for you -"

Teresa typed quickly, her mind busy sorting and planning. Between them, the O'Brien's Irregulars had a wealth of knowledge, contacts and resources and she wanted them ready to employ them all. Tasks assigned, she settled back to enjoy the rest of her Sunday - or at least, to silent contemplation of the threads that had brought Elsa Von Streng, Lisa, Arnoldo and Fintan to cross paths with Friedrich Mann in an absurdly posh Dublin restaurant, on a random Saturday night.

Nothing, she thought, was ever truly random.

***

"It was totally random," Mai said. "Honestly, Mam, you can't blame Chez Maurice's for what happened."

Her mother sniffed. "Can't I? It's a ridiculous place, in my opinion and just the sort of place something like that was bound to happen."

Her husband glanced up from the Sunday newspaper. "That's a little unfair."

"Is it?"

"Yes." He folded the paper firmly and set it down beside his plate carefully avoiding the remains of a hearty Sunday brunch. "Chez Maurice is …yes, it's pretty silly. But it was fun. I had a good time. The kids enjoyed it. I'll concede, the food was a little strange but it was quite tasty. What happened after was," he waved one hand in the air, as if conjuring up the correct phrase, "unfortunate. But it was hardly the fault of the staff, or the restaurant."

"Hmm. In my opinion, when you cram people in like cattle, deprive them of food or the basic tools with which to eat it, and generally treat them with disdain - it was almost inevitable that tempers would boil over."

Mai couldn't help but roll her eyes at her mother, but she did it discreetly because she wasn't stupid.

"Mam! That's so unfair."

"What's unfair is that they ruined your birthday!" Her mother's eyes were suspiciously bright and her voice wobbled a little. "I know how much it meant to you, going to that - that *madhouse!*"

Instantly contrite, Mai leaned over to hug her mother, almost upsetting the teapot in the process.

"Ah, no, Mam! Obviously, I'm terribly sorry about that poor man, but before that, I had such a great night. And really, all I wanted was to be able to say we went."

Her father held out the folded paper towards them, with a rueful smile.

"I think everyone knows, pet."

Mai let go of her mother, who looked pleased, if slightly bewildered by the unaccustomed show of affection.

"Let me see." Mai shook the paper open, scanning the front page quickly. "Oh. My. Goodness."

"What is it?"

"Mam, we're on the front page. A photo." Mai wasn't sure if she was excited or mortified. "It's all of us, leaving Chez Maurice, with Mrs. O'Brien, they must have taken it just as we stepped out. Look, you can see that Garda Detective, the young one, Dempsey, right beside Aunty."

"What's the caption?"

"*'Present at tonight's tragic scene were well-known local business figures Teresa O'Brien and The Khan family.'*" Mai looked up, her eyes shining. "Well-known, how's that for you! And in brackets after 'Khan Family' they've put '*Local Restaurateurs.*' "

A treacherous little voice whispered in Mai's brain *'Doesn't that sound better than fast food shop owners?'* She bit her lip, looking anxiously at her parents. Her father shook his head and remarked, "Ah, well, it'll soon be forgotten. These journalists have to fill space somehow. Once they have an update from the Gardaí, they won't waste time caring who else was there."

"But what if people think we were involved, somehow?" Her mother seemed inclined to look at things in the worst possible light. Mai smiled brightly and reassured her.

"Mam, no one will think that. Tomorrow, they'll be focused on whoever was at that table. Which is hard lines for poor Lisa, isn't it?"

"Oh. That poor young woman. Teresa said she was only there because it was a work event - with that new conductor. Surely they can't suspect Lisa?"

"Nah, she hardly knew the man." Mai decided not to mention the WhatsApp group messages. No point in worrying her mother further. "Actually, I promised to meet Mrs. O'Brien for lunch tomorrow, after school. Make sure she's doing okay. I'll ask about Lisa then."

"That's a good girl." Mrs. Khan nodded approvingly. "Tell her we're all thinking of her. And tell her from me, Michael Clancy should take better care of her. If they were engaged, which they should be by now, I doubt very much she would be at dinner in a mad restaurant by herself. With that Italian."

Mr. Khan raised an eyebrow. "The Italian, my love? I wondered if you'd noticed him." He winked at Mai before adding, "Should I be jealous?"

"I have a pulse, Amir." His wife replied calmly, one hand patting her dark hair. "No straight female could overlook that young man, let me tell you. But he's not suitable for a young woman like Lisa. If she had a mother to look out for her, she would never let her waste her time with someone like that. Too good-looking. Too slick. Michael is a fool."

Mai said nothing, but privately she was inclined to agree. Arnoldo Messini was a gorgeous specimen, no doubt about it. He looked like he'd be a great deal of fun, but Lisa wasn't a teenager. She was, in Mai's opinion, not exactly old but at an age when she should be thinking about settling down. Michael too. What they were playing at, she'd never understand.

Mr. Khan grinned. "Well, maybe the darling Michael will wake up a bit, eh? With a good looking, famous singer sniffing around…" He chuckled, thought for a moment, then added sternly, "But you stay well away from him, Mai!"

Chapter 8

When Teresa arrived, Fancies café was busy with the lunchtime rush. Making her way downstairs, she was just in time to see Mai run towards the only free table surrounded by comfortable, brown leather couches. Mai threw her schoolbag on one sofa and herself into the other, draping her coat over the one solo armchair. Keeping seats in a Dublin café at peak times was an art form, and the teenager was a master of it. Glaring at a pair of tourists approaching hopefully with their coffees, she looked relieved to see Teresa's trim figure appear on the stairs.

"Over here, Mrs. O'Brien," Mai waved enthusiastically.
"I can see you, Mai." Teresa rebuked mildly. "And everyone can hear you."
"Good. There's a group of students at the till upstairs, I was sure they'd be down trying to nick our seats. Spread yourself out, until the others come."

Teresa sat down in the armchair. "I've ordered lunch, have you?"
"Yeah. Well, I told Setanta what I wanted and he'll get it once he's in. We thought it was best I came and grabbed a table." Mai looked at the older woman, her expression serious. "I am glad you're looking into this. Not just because I enjoy helping

you. Because it's a terrible thing to have happened. That man - one minute up and about, making a nuisance of himself and the next, gone."

Teresa gave a sympathetic nod. "I know. He wasn't a good man, Mai, by all accounts. In fact, in some ways, he was a thoroughly bad one." A memory of Elsa, glossing over the horrors of her marriage to the man, her face white and strained, made her clench her fists. "But it was still wrong, what happened to him."

"What did he do?" Mai's eyes were alight with curiosity.

"I'll tell everyone the story, once they're all here. How are your parents?"

"Mam is fuming, she seems to think it's all Chez Maurice's fault. Like, it's all of a piece with the place being overcrowded, having a tiny menu and making us get our own cutlery. Dad is grand, he takes everything in his stride. And they're both worried for Lisa."

"I don't think she's a serious suspect," Teresa said, "although, of course, it's not a nice situation for her. She's a material witness, at the least."

"They're not so worried about that, as they are worried about her hanging around with Arnoldo Messini, without our Michael."

"It was a work dinner," Teresa protested.

"He was all over her," Mai countered. "Anyone with eyes could see it."

"She can't help what he does. As long as she doesn't encourage him, it's not her fault if he wants to make a twit of himself."

"Agreed." Mai peeped at her from under her long eyelashes, a picture of mischievous innocence. "As long as she *doesn't* encourage him."

Teresa was spared from answering by the arrival of Clara and Peadair Walsh, both looking eager. Peadar was a man of few words, at least when in the presence of his chatty wife. He took his place on the sofa opposite Mai and nodded at both. Clara sat beside him, beaming at the others.

"I am *so* glad you called, Teresa. To be honest, we were thinking of calling you when we saw the headlines yesterday, but didn't want to disturb you. Well, if I'm honest, I would have but Peadar wouldn't let me. I said, she'll be *glad* to hear from her friends but you know my husband. No moving him when he's made up his mind. So when you texted, I said "Peadar, we should have rung her, I told you so." But sure, here we all are now so it doesn't matter, does it?" Clara looked around and added smugly, "I knew you'd want us to help."

"You're very good to drop everything and come help. Both of you." Teresa gave Peadar a sympathetic smile.

"Oh, we'd do anything for you. And young Lisa. How is she?"

"Shocked," Teresa said. "I rang her last night, and she was doing okay. Michael was with her, which is good. But she's back to rehearsals first thing today, which I think is a bit soon."

"Oh. I would have thought they'd hold off for a day, wouldn't you?" Clara shook her head disapprovingly.

"The show must go on," Mai said. "I bet that Elsa wouldn't miss rehearsals if she'd been stabbed herself."

"She's a cold fish, by all accounts."

"She's not what you'd expect," Teresa caught sight of Eamonn and Catherine, making their way towards their table, both carrying trays of food. "Ah, here we are. Let's wait until everyone is settled, before I get into the whole story."

Mai insisted that they wait for Setanta Kapoor. The college student was helping out in his mother's shop for a few hours, and had to extricate himself, then queue for his and Mai's lunch. They passed the time in pleasantries and chit-chat until he arrived, looking slightly frazzled.

"Sorry, sorry. I know we said 1 o'clock, but Mam had me unpacking a crate of clothes, then she couldn't decide where to put them, then this woman came in and asked to see every single jacket in the vintage section. I was lucky to get out at all. Mai, here's your tuna melt. Budge up and let me sit down. Now, what have I missed?"

"Nothing," Mai assured him. "I wouldn't let them start until you got here. Mrs. O'Brien is about to tell us all about that German conductor. Elsa Von Streng."

Setanta looked up expectantly. "Gwon, then. What's the story?"

Teresa drew a deep breath and launched into the story, as far as she knew it. How Elsa was really Emer Kelly, from the inner city of Dublin and how the young woman had reinvented herself, moved to Germany, achieved fame and then made the unfortunate mistake of marrying Friedrich Mann. How she had returned to Dublin, after the breakup of her marriage, determined to rebuild her relationship with her family and old friends. How Friedrich had followed her, and how Lisa had become embroiled in their business.

She was impressed that even Clara listened quietly. Catherine scribbled down notes at intervals, a habit of hers that had proved very useful in the past, but no one interrupted the story.

"So, that brings us to Saturday night. Mai and I were there with her family, for her birthday celebrations. Lisa was there with Elsa, the Hibernian's musical director Fintan and a tenor from Italy - Arnoldo Messini."

"We've met Fintan," Clara volunteered. "He's the liaison for the Super Ukers concert."

"Did you meet Elsa?"

"Not yet, no. He did say we'd have a rehearsal with her and the orchestra, before the event - but to be honest, I got the impression she wasn't impressed with the idea. Your man, Fintan, said she was very busy, and not to expect much input from her."

"Which is a polite way of saying, *'She's only doing the concert because she's contractually obliged,'*" Eamonn remarked.

Catherine paused in her note-taking. "Ah, yes. Fintan was nice, though."

"I see." Lowering her voice discreetly, Teresa explained. "Well, here's the problem. They are waiting for the pathologist to confirm, but it seems highly likely that Friedrich was murdered. Stabbed, at the table, by one of the four people seated there."

A burst of shocked gasps and exclamations greeted this revelation. Teresa hushed them.

"I had a visit yesterday, from Detective Flynn. He's fairly sure of his ground on this. It's hard to see how he could have been accidentally wounded. Now, there is the added complication that Fintan hit Friedrich, a blow to the solar plexus, with his hand."

"Well, I suppose if he was stabbed, a punch wouldn't make any difference..." Clara winced as Peadar elbowed her in the ribs. "What? I'm only saying."

"Actually, Clara is right. Pending the pathology report, we need to assume it was the stab wound, not the punch."

"So that lets Fintan off the hook, then." Eamonn chewed his

fruit scone thoughtfully. "Better to be the one who punched him than stabbed him."

"Unless he used that rather dramatic martial arts move as cover to actually stab him," Setanta pointed out.

"It was madness at that table," Teresa sighed. "If only I hadn't been stuck behind Friedrich, I might have seen exactly what happened. Everyone agrees on the basics but you know how it is - no two people remember the same tune exactly."

"And of course, if one of them *did* stab him they're hardly likely to volunteer the information," Catherine said.

"Yes. It would be worth talking to the staff. When the commotion broke out, one or two of them must have looked over at the very least," said Eamonn.

Mai snorted. "You've never been to Chez Maurice. The staff barely look up from their phones. They spend more time taking selfies than helping guests."

"It's a very unusual set up," Teresa agreed. "But Eamonn has a good point. I'll ask Malachy. I'm sure the Gardaí will have taken statements from everyone."

"Hmm." Mai sounded doubtful. "I bet they all say they saw nothing, heard nothing, and probably deny even being there. Chef Maurice is famous for being paranoid. He makes the staff sign non-disclosure agreements - you know, when famous people have to stop their maids telling everyone how messy they are and what's in their rubbish bins?"

Catherine, respectable solicitor, tried and failed to hide her laughter. "Mai, you have a way of putting things - I'd love to see you argue in a court of law."

"Maybe someday. I haven't decided what I want to be yet," Mai responded with all the confidence of seventeen years. " I might do Law yet. But that's the right term, isn't it? NDA? So, yeah, they will lose their jobs if they say anything he doesn't like."

"Surely not, when it's a murder investigation?" Clara sounded shocked.

"He once fired a sous chef for posting a picture of a new dish on Insta-pic. Said a competitor could copy the meal."

"What was the dish?" Clara asked.

"Beef stew. Like, there's only so many ways you can make beef stew, right?"

"Mad stuff." Clara shook her head of brightly coloured, magenta curls. "Mad. I'd quite like to go now, hearing about it."

Peadar looked alarmed, so Teresa hastened to move the conversation on before Clara booked the whole group in for an impromptu dinner.

"Maybe they'll be less discreet talking to one of us," she suggested. "Setanta, you'd be of an age with them. You could ask after part time work and see what you can get out of them."

"You can count on me." Setanta was pleased as punch to get an assignment, judging from his grin.

"Now, obviously we have Lisa in the Concert Hall, but she can hardly snoop around too much. Not while she's as much a suspect as anyone at the table." Which is a horrible thought, Teresa realised. Her young friend was innocent but would be tarred with the same brush until the murderer was caught. "Could the Super Ukers wrangle their way in, using the anniversary concert as an excuse?"

Clara perked up immensely.

"Absolutely. I'm on the committee. I can say we need extra rehearsals - oh, and the four of us are doing a solo set, did I tell you that? We've taken famous Irish tunes and rearranged for Ukulele! Catherine and Peadar on Tenor, Eamonn on Concert and I'll be on my trusty Soprano…but that's not the point, sorry. The point is, I can say we're horribly nervous and need a couple of extra rehearsals."

"Perfect. Mai, you and I are going to find out everything we can about Friedrich Mann." Teresa hoped to keep Mai safely occupied. She had a guilty memory of their last adventure, and having to tell the Khans that their child was in hospital with a head wound. That, she told herself firmly, would never happen again. "And you can help me with some other stuff, as long as you don't let it interfere with your studies."

Mai nodded obediently but her eyes were dancing and her lips twitched. "Grand. Well, the *O'Brien Irregulars* are on the case. Tell Lisa she has nothing to worry about."

* * *

Lisa would have been glad to know someone was thinking of her as she suffered through the Monday morning rehearsal. To say the atmosphere was strained would be an understatement. Lisa was conscious that Ollessa was watching her anxiously and others in the orchestra sent her sympathetic glances. More again were eyeing her with barely disguised curiosity and several whispered conversations stopped abruptly when they realised that she was looking in their direction.

Claire openly gawped at her when she walked in, whispering to her fellow cellists, "There she is! Bit heartless, turning up like nothing happened."

The excellent acoustics of the Concert Hall ensured that her comment whipped around the auditorium, as clearly as if she had shouted it. Lisa ignored her, glad to see Claire's face redden with embarrassment when the others hissed, "Shut up, will you?"

If her reception was awkward, it was nothing compared to that Elsa received. Most people fell silent, suddenly deeply absorbed in their sheet music, or frantically tuning their instruments. The Timpani section had a minor panic attack at the sight of her, with Diego Montefuego accidentally crashing into the cymbals while Aidan McKenna dropped his mallet and hid behind the kettle drum. A stern look from Ollessa kept the string section under control but the woodwind broke into a shocked murmur that was worse than the din created by the timpanists.

Elsa walked to the podium, head held high, and stared them down, plunging directly into a section-by-section examination of the Beethoven.

Lisa tried to concentrate on her playing, but her mind was spiraling furiously. She and Elsa had met for breakfast as arranged, Lisa assuming the conductor wanted to talk about the terrible events at Chez Maurice. She had been prepared for whatever reaction Elsa might be experiencing, expecting either tears or stoic resolve. What she hadn't imagined was that the conductor would sit down, rub a weary hand over her pale face and remark, in an unmistakable Dublin accent, "Janey mac, it's a mess."

For a moment Lisa wondered if the woman was making some kind of wildly inappropriate attempt at humour, mocking the accents all around her. She cast a nervous glance at the barista, whose own Dublin accent was pronounced.
"Um, Elsa," she began to protest, but the other woman cut across her.

"Emer. Emer Kelly. Oliver Bond Flats, late of. That's my original name. This is my real accent - although I can do posh Dublin too." Elsa's voice segued into a collection of strangled vowels and affected drawl. "Loike, it's a gift I have."

Lisa stared at her, trying to make sense of what she was hearing.

"Emer?" she asked finally.

"Yup. I was born Emer Kelly. I changed my name, my entire identity, when I moved to Germany. Look, you have to understand - ten, fifteen years ago, it still mattered to people where you came from. What your address was, where you went to school. I was in a stuffy, upper crust university and nothing I did was good enough for them. But everyone I grew up with - friends, family, neighbours - they thought I was getting above myself. It was okay to be a musician, just not a classical one. If I had stuck to trad, or pop, no bother. But orchestras? Concert halls? Nah."

Lisa had a sudden memory of her uncle, the previous conductor of the Hibernian, currently doing life for murder, sneering at a player for the way he pronounced "Wagner." "Actually," she conceded, "I can imagine. It must have been hard."

"It was. You know Teresa O'Brien, right? It was her husband who got me to try conducting. I owe them everything, really. I would never have had the confidence to try on my own." She gave a bitter little laugh. "I repaid them by changing my name, hiding who I was and completely ghosting them, as the young people say."

"Oh." Lisa tried not to look disapproving. "Does Teresa know? Did she recognise you?"

Elsa picked at her scrambled eggs. "Yeah. I visited her as soon as I got back to Dublin. Hearing about Cathal passing. Ah, that really shook me. I suppose, I always thought there would be time, you know? I could come back, explain everything, make it up to him."

"But you left it too late?" Lisa reached for Elsa's hand and held it. "You couldn't have known. I'm sure Teresa didn't hold it against you."

"No, she was great. But it made me think, I need to reconnect with my family. They haven't a clue what I've been doing, really. We just drifted, you know. I mean, I write but they never asked to come visit and I stopped coming home and here we are. I'm Elsa Von Streng, now. Emer Kelly is just a memory."

"But you can meet up with them," Lisa insisted. "Honestly, you're lucky. I have only one relative to speak of and he's in Mountjoy Jail. Ah, it's okay. Everyone knows, but we all pretend it didn't happen. I would love to have a brother, or parents, or even a cousin under the age of thirty!"

Elsa managed a grin. "Yeah, you're right. Teresa said the same, basically. Although, I think I'd wait until this mess is cleared up, it's not how I imagined my glorious homecoming."

The ice broken, it seemed Elsa was only too glad to talk. She told Lisa about Friedrich, not just the way he had plagued her over the previous weeks but how they met, their life together, how she had finally escaped. It was clearly painful for her, but at the end, Lisa felt sure that Elsa was in a better frame of mind. And now, she thought angrily, the mean-minded gossips among her colleagues were trying to pull her back into isolation.

Even now, they were taking every opportunity to whisper and mutter, in the middle of rehearsals.

Before Elsa could tap her baton on the podium in her customary wake-up-and-listen mode, Lisa sprang to her feet. Her voice rang out, causing even the timpani to freeze and be quiet.

"We have only a few weeks to first night," Lisa said, looking sternly at Claire and her cronies in turn. "There are several passages that need work - Cellists, you especially should be paying attention to the score and not to idle chit chat. We all know of the weekend's unfortunate events, but if Elsa can dig deep and show up for us, despite her personal loss - well, the least we can do is the same. Is that clear?"

Claire looked mutinous, but the murmur of approval around the orchestra silenced her. "Hear hear," and "Well said," came from the majority of the musicians, even Charles McKay joining in from behind his Double Bass. Lisa gave one short nod, then turned to Elsa.

"We're ready, Madam Conductor."

Elsa drew a deep breath, struck the podium once with her baton and raised her arms.
"From section B, please. Tempo, Tempo, Tempo - let's keep in time, shall we?"

* * *

While the orchestra wrestled with their time keeping, Detective Malachy Flynn sat in Fintan McLaughlin's office and broke the news to the musical director. He had not in fact killed Friedrich Mann with a blow.

Malachy watched with interest as a wave of emotion crossed Fintan's face. First came sheer, naked relief. Then a frown, then confusion, then shock and horror.

If the man was acting, Malachy thought, he should be a professional. He'd win an Oscar. Still, it was surprising how convincing people could be when there was a lot at stake. He had sat across a table from too many suspects whose pleas of innocence sounded genuine but turned out to be big fat lies.

"I'm so - I mean, I'm still so sorry for that poor man, but I am so, so relieved that it wasn't me." Fintan rose abruptly, rounded the desk and grasped the detective's hand, shaking it earnestly. "I really appreciate you coming to tell me. Oh, thank heavens!"

"There's still the small matter of a stabbing," Malachy replied mildly.

Fintan nodded. "Of course, of course. What do you suppose happened? Wait - a stabbing? But surely, that's impossible. Or did the poor man fall on a knife?"

The initial pathology report supplied first thing that morning by Dr. Lorraine O'Toole was fresh in the Garda Detective's mind.

"No. Not unless you can explain how he was stabbed in the front, by a knife he fell on with his back? A weapon that subsequently disappeared."

Fintan flushed, sitting back down on his own side of the desk. "Ah. Stupid of me, I see. Who could have stabbed him? I mean, he was fine when he arrived at our table. Okay, not exactly "fine," the man was stinking drunk, but there was no blood, he wasn't doubled up in pain..."

Malachy waited patiently, watching as the musical director's face changed expression.

"Oh." Fintan said.

"Yes. I'm afraid so. It does look as if one of you four at the table, did the job."

Fintan blinked, his eyes round and wide behind his wire-rimmed glasses. "That's impossible."

"Why?"

"What do mean, why? You can't possibly suggest that one of four people stabbed the man, in full view of the others, at a table surrounded by guests. A table everyone was staring at, Detective, because Friedrich Mann was causing such a scene. It's ludicrous."

"Is it?" Malachy's mild tone of inquiry seemed to inflame Fintan even more.

"It is."

"But from your own eyewitness accounts, it was chaotic. And every one of ye had your hand on the man at some point."

"What? Well, yes, but not with a knife in hand."

"A small knife," Malachy supplied. "A small, thin blade. Easy enough to conceal."

Dr. O'Toole had been as cautious as ever in her report, but the selection of knives bagged at the scene had helped narrow the field. They hadn't found the exact knife yet but the size and shape of the wound matched other thin, slicing blades used in the restaurant. Chez Maurice's gimmick of having the guests choose their own cutlery meant anyone could have taken one from the pile on the communal table.

"But then what? Where's this knife? I know I and my belongings were thoroughly examined by your team. If any of us had it, wouldn't you have found it?"

"We're still looking for that." Malachy conceded the point with an amiable smile. "But for now, let's concentrate on the sequence of events. Talk me through it again, from the time Mr. Mann approached your party..."

Fintan repeated the same version he had supplied the night of the death, a version that dovetailed neatly with his fellow witnesses' accounts. Malachy encouraged him through it, from start to finish, then asked seemingly random questions. He noted that Fintan, while obviously a bit shaken, answered fully and with every appearance of wanting to help.

Was the man instinctively law-abiding or just very clever?

"Well, thank you for your time. I'll be talking to everyone present, you understand - it's vital we get an accurate picture of what occurred. But you've been most helpful."

Fintan looked openly relieved.

"Look, I'm just glad it wasn't my fault. I - I have barely slept, I felt so guilty. I'll do anything I can to help."

"Appreciate it. I'll be around for a while yet. I want to chat to Elsa Von Streng, I believe she's in rehearsal at the moment?"

Fintan consulted his watch. "The morning session is over but there's a special rehearsal right now. A community group is playing a charity concert here at the end of September, they've just started a run-through. You'll catch them on the main stage."

"Thanks. And if anything should occur to you, any detail, let me know. You have my number."

As Malachy wound his way from the Musical Director's office into the bowels of the Concert Hall, towards the sound of an orchestra in full flight, he tried to make up his mind about Fintan. A fussy little man, by some accounts. A righteous defender of the vulnerable, if you took Saturday night at face value. A man genuinely horrified at the thought that he had harmed someone or a clever man, acting a part.

He couldn't quite decide.

Chapter 9

Setanta looked around Chez Maurice in astonishment. The blinds were raised on the large street-facing windows, allowing the bright sunshine to pour in and the interior of the restaurant was stripped of any glamour under its scrutiny. He wondered at Mai wanting her birthday in such a crowded, rather dingy space - although, he admitted, few of the pubs and nightclubs he and his mates frequented looked good in broad daylight either! Still, knowing that he was standing in Dublin's hottest, most expensive restaurant and seeing streaks on the mirrored wall, tables arranged higgledy-piggledy wherever they could fit and the floor - well, he tried to ignore the way his shoes stuck to it slightly as he walked.

Before he could approach anyone to ask for the manager, a willowy young woman strode towards him, her face stern.

"Are you from the agency?" She looked him up and down openly. "Oh, dear."

Setanta made a quick decision. "Yeah. The agency. But like, they told me nothing. Just sent me here."

He had worked enough ad hoc gigs in college to know, this was the eternal complaint of temporary staff, sent to replace the usual staff at events.

"Typical! Look, we lost two waiters this morning - I assume

you heard what happened here on Saturday? Good. Well, half this lot are spooked," she waved a contemptuous hand at a huddle of young people gathered around the back of the space, "and the other half are using it as an excuse to do nothing. I need to know, right now, are you a man or a jellyfish?"

Setanta nodded earnestly. "Man. I mean, it was awful, right? And sad, yeah? But like, it's nothing to do with the work."

"Exactly." A glimmer of what could have been approval crossed her face. "Go on, then. See that woman with the clipboard, the one who looks like a scared rabbit? That's Nora. Give her your name and details and she'll tell you what to do. We need this place cleaned up, that'll be your first shift. Then come back tonight and do the evening rush. We probably won't need you after that, but Maurice is paying double today. It'll be worth your while. Plus, you'll get a share of tips."

"Grand so," Setanta said cheerfully. He smiled at the girl, a smile that young ladies and old women both found charming. "I'm Setanta, by the way. Setanta Kapoor."

She looked at him for a long moment and he wondered it he'd overstepped. But at last, she smiled in return. "Chrissie. Chrissie Long."

"Thanks, Chrissie. Chat later," Setanta gave her a cheeky wink and was pleased to note she half-smiled back. He made his way to the lady with the clipboard. Nora, unlike most of the other staff standing around, was neither particularly young, nor was she trendily dressed or nicely made-up. Her rather mousy hair hung in limp waves, ineffectually tied back with a scrunchie and her face looked scrubbed and rather pink. But she smiled kindly at Setanta as he approached.

"Are you from the temp agency?" she asked hopefully.

"I'm here to do a couple of shifts," Setanta replied, keeping as close to the truth as he could. "I've to give you my name and details, Chrissie said."

"Oh, yes. Good. Did she explain it's only really for today? Set up now and then a shift this evening."

"Yeah, no bother. That suits me. I'm only looking for a bit of work around lectures, you know how it is."

"Oh, I do," Nora smiled at him. "I worked in bars when I was in Uni."

"I do bar work, lots of retail, bit of waiting too." Setanta handed her an ID card with his tax details, and his university ID card. "There you go, that's me."

"And bank details?" Nora lowered her voice. "You'll get the basic rate, and then Maurice is giving a bonus for the short notice. Your tips will be cash-in-hand, okay?"

Setanta nodded and Nora handed him over to Liam, who pushed him off onto Wiktor, who eventually sent him to Precious, who at last gave him instructions and helped him get to work. Precious was a drop dead gorgeous, six-foot tall, part-time model. To Setanta's relief, she was also far more friendly than her co-workers. As they stripped linen from tables and reset chairs, she chatted about her family in Kenya and her adventures travelling. Setanta confided his dream of back-packing for six months after his degree, and she supplied him with a stream of suggestions - the best hotels, the worst cities, the cheapest airlines.

The ice thoroughly broken, Setanta took a chance.

"Hey, were you here on Saturday. When it happened? Chrissie said everyone is dead spooked about it."

Precious glanced around. "Hush. Yeah, I was here. But Nora warned us all this morning, if we're caught talking about it - well, I don't want to get fired."

"Oh, no, of course not. Sorry. I didn't realise - like, it was almost the first thing Chrissie said to me."

"Yeah, well, it's different for her." Precious smiled at his confused look. "She's Maurice's daughter. He's not going to fire her. Well, probably not. He's capable of anything. "

"I've heard he's fierce eccentric."

"Eccentric? He's - what's that you Irish say? He's as mad as a bag of cats."

Setanta chuckled. "Janey Mac. But, sure, it was pure blind chance it happened here, no? A bunch of strangers having a fight is just bad luck."

Precious paused. "Well, not exactly strangers. I mean, the poor man who died was and most of the guests at that table. But…"

"Go on," Setanta encouraged her.

"I've seen the blond one before. The famous conductor, the papers called her. With the German name?"

"Oh yeah. Elsa?"

"That one. She's been in here. Last week."

"Oh. Well, it's a popular restaurant."

"No, I don't mean that. I mean, in the kitchen. Talking to Maurice. She's a mate of his."

Setanta hid his surprise, the conversation moving on. There was no opportunity after that to pump her for more information, and Setanta was afraid to appear too interested. He worked the shift diligently, went out of his way to be friendly and before it was time to leave was on good terms with a number of staff. All he could do now was come back that evening and see if he could find out anything more.

* * *

After his interview with Fintan, Malachy went in search of Elsa Von Streng. He was expecting to find the orchestra in full string but he was unprepared for the sight of the Ukulele players from the Super Ukers, grinning at him from centre stage. Clara gave him a very indiscreet wink. He bit down on the urge to ask what they were doing, and tried to look like a man who had never crossed paths with the four irrepressible amateur sleuths.

He approached Elsa, who nodded but didn't miss a beat with her baton. He waited patiently while she instructed the ukulele players to please keep time, told the oboists that they were a disgrace to their profession and asked the timpani if they needed time off to reconsider their career choices. She praised the viola section but cast aspersions on the lead cellist's ability to play a B flat. Eventually she turned to Malachy, who felt sure she was about to give him a critique of his detective skills, but instead she raised an eyebrow and asked, "Detective, I presume you are looking for me? Or is it Lisa?"

"It's yourself, this time." Malachy smiled at her, careful not to show even a trace of irritation at being kept waiting or at her rather rude tone of voice. He nodded at the assembled musicians and added, "That sounded lovely. Especially the Oboes."

A titter of nervous laughter rippled through the room and Elsa pursed her lips.

"Now, if we could just have a word, Ms. Von Streng. This will take a few minutes, so let's step out here. Is there a room we could use?"

He noted that Elsa followed him calmly, while chatter broke out behind them as they exited the stage area. He hoped the Super Ukers were listening to the gossip, whatever else they were up to. Elsa led the way into a small room, not much bigger than a cupboard, lined with shelves containing piles of sheet music. It also boasted a couple of rickety chairs and Malachy placed them a foot apart, facing each other, and sat into the one nearest the door. Elsa hesitated, but took the other one, her face a mask.

"Well, now." The detective produced a small, black, battered notebook, a habit from his early days as a garda. He retrieved a biro from his jacket pocket and sat poised to take notes. "I'm sure you're anxious to hear what's been happening with the investigation."

"Naturally." Elsa's mouth tightened.

"First things, first. The cause of death. It wasn't the blow from Fintan."

Elsa's face relaxed. "But that's great news. Poor Fintan! Have you told him?"

Malachy eyed her sternly. "I have."

Elsa looked at him, as if surprised by his tone. "It is good news, yes? He didn't - he wasn't responsible. A tragic accident - well, the way Friedrich lived, drinking constantly, it was probably inevitable. His heart, I assume?"

Malachy shook his head. "A stab wound to the abdomen."

If he had hoped to shake the woman's cool facade, it worked. Elsa's face froze, then crumpled. She looked younger, smaller and suddenly frail.

"No. What do you mean, a stab wound?"

The detective's voice was gentler as he explained. "I'm afraid someone stabbed your ex-husband, possibly while on the ground in the confusion but, according to the pathology report, more likely while he was still standing."

"While he was still - you mean, at our table?" Elsa looked at him in horror. "You're saying, one of us, the four at the table, stabbed him?"

"It's looking that way, yes."

"No." She shook her head. "No. I've known Arnoldo for years, he's not violent. Lisa - that's absurd. She didn't know him. And you saw poor Fintan, he was devastated when he thought he had hurt Friedrich by accident. No. You're wrong."

The flatness of her denial was convincing, Malachy had to admit. And it was far from clear where the man had been stabbed, standing or lying. That had been a stretch of the truth on his part. But what possible reason could a bunch of waiters or guests have to randomly stab a drunken stranger? Annoyance that their posh dinner was on the floor was not a strong enough motive, even considering Chez Maurice's ridiculous prices.

"I'm sorry. But it's the most likely explanation, so as you can imagine we must proceed accordingly."

"Am I - am I a *suspect*?" She said the word as if it was contaminated.

"You and the others, yes. Again, I'm sorry but that's the reality."

Elsa blinked rapidly. "Okay. Tell me what you need to know. You have to find the culprit, Detective. Otherwise we'll all live under a cloud."

He nodded sadly. "You will, it's true. But it's all very well telling us to do our job, Ms. Von Streng. If people don't tell us everything they know, if they keep secrets and hide things from us, the truth may never be known."

"But what else can I tell you?" Elsa's cool facade broke, her voice pleading. "I told you all about my background. I told you about Emer Kelly. You know Friedrich was my husband

and that he was a pig to me. What exactly do you think I'm hiding?"

The detective smiled. "Let's start with your relationship with Arnoldo Messini."

"Arnoldo?" Elsa rolled her eyes. "He's an old friend. You can't possibly think - we have no relationship other than friendship. None."

"Very well," Malachy made a show of taking notes. "Fintan, then."

Elsa opened her mouth, shut it again and then sighed deeply. "Fintan. You think he and I are having an affair, is that it?"

Malachy waited silently.

Elsa waited silently.

Malachy raised any eyebrow pointedly.

Elsa rolled her eyes again.

"Right. So we're clear. Fintan and I have never been anything more than colleagues."

Something in the way she said it made Malachy's sixth sense tingle. "Never? How long have you known Fintan, Elsa?"

Elsa bit her lip then conceded, "Look, he has no idea. He didn't recognise me, not even for a second. But the truth is, we were in college together. It wasn't a happy time for me, Detective. I didn't do as well as I should have, for a number of reasons, and it wasn't until my final year that I found my calling. The other students were snobs, rich kids who had beautiful instruments and lived in student flats on campus. I was a scruffy kid from the flats and if it wasn't for Cathal O'Brien, my violin would have been an orange box strung with catgut. I had to play trad sessions in pubs for the tourists, just to afford music books. Fintan was one of the golden ones - oh, the lecturers loved him. He was obviously set for a great career. He interned here, did you know that? Before he even had his degree, he was "in" with the orchestra leaders."

She paused and looked at Malachy. "I hated the rest of them. They sneered at me, they made sly digs at every opportunity. Fintan was the exception. I was mad jealous of him, I admit it, but he was kind to me. He even stood up for me and that took guts, because he was a quiet young fella."

"He never recognised you?" Malachy was doubtful. "Emer Kelly is long gone," Elsa replied, a little wistfully. "I shouldn't think my own brother would recognise me now." "The brother that was on remand?" Malachy recalled her statement at Chez Maurice's.

"Ah, he reformed. That was childish stuff. He went back to school, got a good leaving cert and went into finance." She sounded proud. "He's done very well for himself, lovely house and a family, thriving business. He's come far." "So have you," Malachy pointed out. "I'd say he would be glad to know that."

He knew the moment he spoke that it was a misstep. Elsa's face shuttered and the cold, distant look was back in her eyes. He changed tack.

"But Teresa O'Brien recognised you, didn't she?" "Of course. But she's *Teresa O'Brien*. Mind like a steel trap, and the memory of an elephant. You could use her at airports if the facial recognition technology ever broke down."

"True. Well, I assume you haven't told Fintan yet that you used to be Emer Kelly?" "I have not." From her tone of voice it was clear she had no intention of remedying that situation any time soon.

"Who choose the restaurant, by the way?" Emer shrugged. "I did. I read about it in the Evening

Independent."

"And how would Friedrich have known you were there?"

"I have no idea, Detective."

"Have you not? Would Signor Messini have told him, do you think?"

"Arnoldo? I can't imagine so."

"Weren't they friends?"

Elsa paused. "Arnoldo and Friedrich were friendly, yes. They were "mates" rather than close friends. When I moved to Germany, Arnoldo had just moved there too from Italy. We hung around together. He knew my ex-husband through mutual friends, and I suppose for a while, we all knocked around together in a larger group. When Friedrich and I started dating, Arnoldo was delighted - he sometimes claims that he introduced us, but that's not really the case."

Malachy nodded. "So then, when the marriage broke up, Arnoldo was more on your side?"

"That's fair to say," Elsa agreed. "I mean, I'm sure he was still friendly with Friedrich but by then, most people were fed up with his antics. Friedrich got fired from every job, fought with every conductor and performer, borrowed money off everyone...I never asked, but I am fairly sure he borrowed money from Arnoldo and never paid it back."

She added, rather bitterly, "People didn't seem too concerned about his behaviour towards me, but they soon dumped him when he owed them money. At least Arnoldo cared about how he treated me."

Malachy felt a stab of sympathy. It sounded as if Friedrich Mann had been a nightmare of a husband but there was no denying it. Of everyone at that table, Elsa was the one with the strongest motive to stab her husband.

"I'm going to ask you a question, Elsa," the detective said, his face carefully neutral but his voice gentle. "And you may think about it before you answer me. Is it possible, bearing in mind that your husband had been violent towards you previously, and that you had every right to be frightened of him and that he accosted you suddenly and aggressively in front of friends and colleagues…is it at all possible that in the heat of the moment, in fright, you reacted? You had a knife in your hand and without perhaps meaning to, you lashed out?"
He watched her carefully but she met his gaze calmly and unflinchingly.

"No. I was frozen. I was scared. I wish I had punched him. He deserved it. I didn't even do that. I certainly did not stab him."

Malachy closed his notebook and smiled. "I'm glad to hear it."

* * *

While Elsa protested her innocence to Detective Flynn, and Fintan sat in his office stewing over the news that Friedrich had been murdered, the Super Ukers took full advantage of the gossip ripping through the orchestra. As soon as the conductor left the stage, excited chatter broke out, led as usual by the cellist, Claire. Lisa was about to rebuke them until Clara winked at her. The four ukulele players attached themselves to various groups and shamelessly eavesdropped.

Eamonn found himself stretching his legs by the timpani section, where at least one member insisted that it was common knowledge the deceased was a Russian, poisoned by either Elsa or Arnoldo in a fit of jealous rage. In Elsa's case, a crime of passion and in the tenor's case, professional jealousy. Eamonn then tried his luck with the flautists - at least they knew the dead man had been German. One older lady informed her listeners that Elsa and Friedrich had been married, were the subject of several unsavoury rumours and she also knew someone who knew someone who had sat next to the unfortunate Friedrich in a minor orchestra.

"So, what I was told was…" she lowered her voice and heads moved closer together to hear. "He was well on his way down at that point. I'm not saying he was an angel, but my source says she bad-mouthed him across Europe. Poor man couldn't get a gig playing in a pub without her trying to get him fired. Bitter, she was!"

Catherine found herself talking to the viola section, where a pleasant woman introduced herself as Ollessa and gave a tiny nod in Lisa's direction.

"We're all a bit shook up by recent events," Ollessa excused her colleagues. "I'm sure you heard."
"Of course. We were nearly afraid to ask for an extra rehearsal, with all this going on. It was kind of Ms. Von Streng to agree."

Odessa's eyes twinkled. "I'd say Fintan insisted, to be honest. He takes our community concerts very seriously."

"Well, we're grateful anyway." Catherine smiled at the other players and added, "How are ye all holding up?"

Everyone professed themselves "shook to the core" by the news, although they did admit that no one actually knew the dead man. Most had only a vague idea of what had happened, based on speculative media articles, and if anything seemed to think he had a heart attack. The main reason for their interest lay in the fact - now common knowledge to many - that Elsa was once married to the poor man.

Clara didn't fare much better, despite flitting around the string section offering sympathy and a willing ear. In among the confusion were general nuggets of accurate information but nothing new. Disappointed, she returned to her seat to find her husband Peadar smiling smugly. In his inimitable way, he had managed to glean something when everyone else had failed.

She leaned in, dying to hear what he had to say, but Peadar just shook his head. When Catherine and Eamonn made whispered inquiries, they met the same answer.

They would all just have to wait until later.

* * *

Teresa had hoped that Mai would be too occupied with school, and with the sudden notoriety the weekend's tragedy had bestowed on her, to insist on being heavily involved in the investigation. She was soon disabused of this notion. The teenager appeared in the early afternoon, still in school uniform, clutching her laptop and two coffees, ready for action.

"I've been googling all day," Mai confessed, "We had two free classes and it was a godsend. I found out loads - absolutely loads - about Friedrich Mann. And that singer fella, the one sniffing around Lisa."

Teresa arched an eyebrow and looked skeptical. "I think he's just naturally flirty."

Mai looked scornful. "Nah. He's one hundred percent invested, thinks he has rizz."

Teresa blinked. "Could you say that again, in old person speak?"

"He's trying too hard, Mrs. O'Brien, and he thinks he's God's gift to women."

"Well, isn't that what I said?"

"No, you don't understand. He's low-key creeping - I mean, he's always a bit flirty. But where Lisa is concerned, he goes into overdrive. He is trying to get between her and Michael. Mark my words."

Teresa sighed. It had crossed her mind that the Italian tenor was more than usually attentive to Lisa, if she was honest.

"Ah well. It's not whether Arnoldo flirts with Lisa, is it? It's only a problem if she reciprocates."

Mai didn't reply, becoming suspiciously interested in her laptop. Teresa waited. A long moment of awkward silence followed.

"Look," Mai gave in finally. "I'm not saying Lisa would encourage him, but - you have to admit, Michael is awful laid back. He doesn't make an effort. Lisa is beautiful, talented, and absolutely sound. Nicest girl you'd ever meet. If Arnoldo Messini sees that, and makes her feel special - can you blame her if it shows up how Michael acts?"

Teresa's first instinct was to defend Michael. Her second thought was that Mai made a very good point, and hadn't she tried to get Michael to step up a bit herself?
"I see your point," she confided. "But we'll just have to let them work it out for themselves."

Mai shrugged. "I'm not sticking my nose in. But when she elopes with the tenor and they're a world-famous power couple, remember I said it first. Now, look - I've made a timeline tracing any stories about Mann online. And it's interesting!"

Teresa peered at the screen. Mai's presentation was clear and easy to follow - she had put her free classes to good use, although maybe Mrs. Khan wouldn't agree. There was a surprising amount of information online about not only the victim, but other players in their drama. Elsa and Arnoldo were the subject of articles ranging from rave reviews to fluff pieces, including "at home with the famous conductor" and "a day in the life of the fabulous Messini." Poor Friedrich wasn't as lucky, she noted. Some early articles had titles like "Rising star" but it soon veered into gossip pieces - "Well-known Musician makes scene at Restaurant" and "Rumours swirl at Bach Recital."

A quick glance at the stories themselves gave Teresa the gist of the problem - an increasingly erratic, truculent and often drunk Friedrich turning up at concerts, gigs, events and causing trouble. Elsa had already outlined her ex-husband's decline, but it was terribly sad to see it in such public terms. The world of classical music is terribly small, Teresa reminded herself. It must have been agony for Elsa, never knowing what Friedrich would do next.

"And then, he got arrested." Mai pointed at a newspaper article she had linked to, and added, "It's in German, but it basically says he was sentenced to eighteen months. Which isn't surprising considering the way he was carrying on but what caught my eye was this paragraph here. It says it was for drug related offenses."

"What?" Teresa stared at the screen. "That's unexpected. Elsa never mentioned anything to do with drugs. Does it say whether it was for possession or supplying or what?"

"Nothing. I looked and looked and can't find anything further. Maybe Detective Flynn could find out?"
Teresa nodded. "I think he should."
"Does it matter?" Mai sounded doubtful.
"I don't know. It might. Anything else of interest?"

"Maybe. See what you think of these…" Mai clicked on a few links in her document and several tabs opened. She started with one that was obviously an Italian newspaper. "It doesn't translate well into English but basically it says, "Handsome face, Golden Voice." It's a vanity piece, you know the type. But look, there's a photo of Arnoldo and "friends," and see, there's Elsa and Friedrich."

"Well, we know they were all friends at one point."

"Yeah, but," Mai pointed to the paragraph of text beside the photo, "It says, "Arnoldo Messini with his childhood friend, violinist Friedrich Mann." Childhood friend is a bit more than mates from work, Mrs. O'Brien."

Teresa nodded. "It is. That's interesting. Anything else."

"Yes, a few things. Here's a piece on Arnoldo from the gossip pages of a magazine. Him and some supermodel, falling out of a nightclub in Milan. It doesn't say anything out straight, but it hints at him being a bit of a wide boy."

Teresa hid a grin at the teenager's use of an old Dublin phrase. "A ladies' man?"

"More than that. Roughly, "*Messini has already fallen foul of the management at La Scala, with rumours of late starts and - um, let's see - failures to show up to rehearsals.*" There are quite a few articles like this, he seems to have a reputation for being difficult to work with and partying a bit too hard. I thought singers had to watch their voices?"

"They do," Teresa agreed. "It seems Arnoldo and Friedrich had more in common than we thought."

"Once I saw these, I went looking for pieces about Elsa. She didn't not go down the same road as her husband and Arnoldo. Not a hint of any gossip or partying, just articles about how professional and dedicated she is. How on earth did she end up hanging around with that pair?" Mai shook her head. "I just can't put them together."

"Ah. Well, love is a strange thing, Mai. People don't think logically, they follow their hearts. From what Elsa told me, she hoped she could save Friedrich, help him get back on track. By the time she realised who he really was, it was too late."

"That's so sad."

"Well, she got away in the end. It's better late than never, Mai."

"I suppose. Oh, look! Here's another bit of info you might find interesting. I found an online forum for musicians, and there's a sub-forum for orchestral players. Took a bit of digging but I found an exchange from a few years ago between a couple of players, moaning about Elsa and how tough she is. Lots of chatter about her persecuting her Ex and making sure he couldn't get a job. She really does seem to have hated him."

Teresa sipped her coffee. "You've done a good job, Mai, but to be frank it's hard to see if any of this will help."

"I know, but the more we know…" Mai grinned. "You never know what might be important."

Her optimism was infectious.

"You're right," Teresa said. "Who knows what will come in useful. Let's keep digging. Hopefully the others will turn up something too."

* * *

Mai had just left to do her homework and wait for her mother in the Noodle Palace when the Super Ukers burst through the door of the music shop, causing the glass showcases to rattle and the instruments to sway gently. A soft hum of strings resonated, echoed by the bodhráns stored in rows on shelves above the counter. Teresa could see from their faces that they had some news but no one spoke which, considering Clara was there, was a miracle.

"Any news?"

Three of the four uke players turned towards Peadair, who smiled smugly.

"I might have," he said. "A wee bit."

Teresa waited. Clara poked her husband in the ribs and hissed, "Peadair!"

"Ow. Okay, okay, would you give over? Let me tell it in my own time." He gave the ghost of a wink in Teresa's direction. It wasn't often Peadair got to be the one with the gossip, she reminded herself. Let him enjoy the moment.

"Take your time."

"Thanks, Teresa. Well now. While this lot were wasting time listening to the auld biddies gossiping in the orchestra, I went and had a word with the ushers and stagehands. You know, if you want to know anything about an organization you should always start with the ones who do all the real work. They're the ones who hear everything."

Teresa tried not to look impatient, just nodding in agreement and hoping Peadair would get a move on.

"So, I spoke with Tommy, he's in charge of the lighting. Lovely chap, very knowledgeable about the history of the Concert Hall. Did you know the building used to be a hospital, back in the 19th century?"
Another elbow in the rib from Clara got Peadair back on topic.

"Anyway, he told me that Elsa and Friedrich had more than

one row last week. The man kept slipping into the Hall and trying to see her. Then Tommy called over a young lady by the name of Leslie." Peadair beamed at Teresa. "Leslie is a cleaner, and she's in and out of every room in the place. Friday evening, she walked into Fintan's office to find him and Friedrich Mann, sitting there sipping glasses of whiskey, as friendly as can be."

Teresa blinked. "Fintan? With Friedrich Mann?"

"Isn't it bizarre?" Clara obviously couldn't contain herself any longer. "I thought they were strangers!"

"So do I. Peadair, well done. That was excellent work. It certainly casts Fintan in a new light."

She thought back to how the musical director had reacted to Friedrich's appearance in Chez Maurice. How he was so quick to attack. They had all assumed it was a chivalrous attempt to rescue Elsa from her violent ex-husband but what if they were wrong?

What if Fintan had reasons of his own for wanting to silence Friedrich?

Chapter 10

Teresa lost no time in relaying everything they had discovered so far to Malachy Flynn. It was a long phone call and the detective professed himself grateful, although he agreed it was hard to see where most of it might be relevant. The fact that Fintan and Friedrich were not only acquainted but seemingly on friendly terms was the most interesting piece of the puzzle. He assured her he would be paying a visit to the musical director in short order.

Teresa was left with a sense of dissatisfaction. She could think of half a dozen reasons why anyone at the table that night might want Friedrich dead, with the exception of Lisa of course. The violinist was now the only one who genuinely didn't know the man, and whose encounters with him were wholly innocent. But why on earth kill him there and then?

She discussed it with Michael over a cup of tea, both of them seated in her tiny office space at the back of the shop.

"You see, either someone saw a chance and took it - and took a terrible risk in doing so - or they had no choice. Friedrich was about to say or do something that would expose them, ruin them? A scandal, maybe?"

"Here," Michael swallowed the last of his cake. "Has anyone looked into Friedrich's finances? How did he get here, after being in and out of prison and pretty much unemployable? And how did he afford that hotel? it isn't cheap, you know."

"And Malachy said the man made himself conspicuous, drinking heavily and eating in the restaurant." Teresa's pulse quickened. "Where did he get the money?"
"Ring Flynn back," Michael suggested, "Ask him was it cash or credit card? Have they checked the man's bank account?"

"I am sure the Gardaí have thoroughly investigated…" Teresa protested but she made the call. Malachy answered almost immediately, sounding as if he was shouting over the noise of a concert.
"Hang on! I need to - Dempsey, for the love of all that's holy, would you turn down that infernal racket? Honestly, it's as bad as driving with a teenager. Sorry, Mrs. O'Brien, my partner likes to deafen us both with his awful taste in music. Keep your eyes on the road, lad, and slow down."

Teresa waited until the detective paused for breath. "Malachy, I just wanted to ask a quick question. We were wondering, if Friedrich Mann was down on his luck, just out of prison - how did he make his way to Ireland? And then stay in a decent hotel, drinking late into the night?"

"I hear you. Dempsey, pass me that file. We've just got access to his bank account. Two interesting things cropped up. Despite his long-term employment problems, his account was very healthy until a few months ago. Regular payments in from the one account - we're trying to get access to details about that. Those payments stopped, and he ran through the balance. Thousands every month. At the moment, it's pretty empty. He paid for his airline ticket with his debit card, you can see where he paid in three hundred euros just before he bought it. The ticket cost just over fifty euros, and he spent a fair bit at the airport on drink. He had one hundred and fifty euro left in his account after hitting Dublin, and that's whittled away in dribs and drabs -for god's sake, Dempsey, you nearly had that bicycle! - sorry, where was I? Yeah, he used that up in small purchases over the week and half he was here."

"But he's been spending freely here. Was he paying cash in the hotel?"

"Wads of it. And we found a good stash of it in his room." Malachy answered.

"How much is a "good stash?" Teresa asked.

"Five thousand, give or take. I would estimate, given his rate of spending, he must have started with at least eight thousand."

"Had he anything on him when he died?"

"Only a hundred. I wonder how someone like him, in his state, got into Chez Maurice? The bar is for the young and lovely, and the restaurant is reservation only."

Teresa and Michael exchanged a look.

"Well, I should probably tell you. Setanta Kapoor, you know the young lad whose mammy owns Kapoor's Clothes Emporium? Maybe that's something he could answer. He's doing a few shifts at the restaurant, starting tonight. Pure good luck, eh?"

There was a long moment of silence, then Malachy sighed. "Of course he is. Well, tell him to be careful and keep the head down. And if he does find anything out, let me know."

A muttered commentary from Dempsey interrupted the older detective. Malachy sighed again, answering his colleague with a sharp tone.

"You can't stop a young fella taking a part-time job, Dempsey. It's a free country. Teresa, thanks for the call. We'll talk soon."

Michael stifled a laugh. "I'm almost sorry for Dempsey. He's a miserable git but it sounds like Detective Flynn is hard on him."

"Ah no. If I'm not mistaken, Dempsey has the makings of a good detective but he's got blind spots. His ego won't let him take help, and he has a brusque manner. Malachy will whip him into shape."

"Tough love," Michael grinned.

Teresa eyed him thoughtfully. "Sometimes we all need a bit of tough love. In the spirit of which, let me ask you a question."

"Fire away."

"What in the name of god are you playing at with Lisa?"

Michael spluttered, almost choking on his mouthful of tea. "What?"

"She's a beautiful, kind, talented woman. You seem to like her. Most men would be nailing that down, taking no chances."

Michael stared at her, a look of genuine bewilderment on his face.

"Michael," Teresa said. "You take Lisa for granted. Old married couples make more romantic effort than you do. Dinner in Lannigan's Pub, for goodness sake! Lisa lands the biggest break of her career and you take her to an old man's pub, to have a stodgy pub dinner?"

Michael flushed. "Lisa likes Lannigan's," he began defensively but Teresa cut him off.

"You're a very laid-back person, Michael, and that's fine. No one is asking you to change or to pretend to be something you're not. But if Lisa is important to you, you should be making more of an effort. You assume she likes Lannigan's - well, she probably does for a bite of Sunday dinner or a quick pint after work. But for a date or an important occasion, would you not have booked somewhere better?"

"Somewhere like Chez Maurice, I suppose?" Michael's tone was sulky and Teresa knew she had hurt his feelings. It made her miserable, but she ploughed on.

"I'm not criticizing for the sake of it. I love you and I love Lisa and you're a great couple. I just don't want to see you lose her for want of a bit of care. That young woman needs to feel special, especially now."

Michael's expression was impossible to read. It reminded her of when her own lad was a teenager. But Michael wasn't a kid, she reflected, and he needed to hear this before it was too late.

"Michael, I'm sorry if you feel I overstepped. But I couldn't watch you blunder on without saying something."

Michael nodded, said curtly, "I need to get back to work," and strode from the room, stomping up the stairs to his workrooms like a disgruntled elephant. He worked until 5 p.m. on the dot, then took his leave with a rather subdued air, leaving Teresa feeling as if she had kicked a faithful puppy.

"Oh dear," she told herself, "I'm an interfering auld baggage. I probably should have kept my mouth shut."

But at least Michael couldn't say he hadn't been warned.

* * *

Setanta Kapoor made sure he was half an hour early for his shift at Chez Maurice, neatly dressed in black trousers, shoes and shirt, his dark wavy hair properly styled instead of flopping across one eye. Chrissie Long, the willowy hostess, gave him a sharp once-over, then smiled.

"You look smart. Maurice will be pleased. Half the staff turn up looking like they were dragged through a hedge backwards.

I was going to put you in back-of-house, but I reckon you'll be grand out front. You know how this works, right? Your job is to get the guests to their tables, point out the tableware station, make sure they don't scald themselves or knock the food off the table. Give each party ninety minutes, then get them out of here. They can go upstairs to the bar, if they don't want to go home but get that table clear. We have three seatings a night, we can't afford to have people lingering over their coffees. Understood?"

Setanta bit back the impulse to protest. It sounded like a horrendous dining experience, and it went against the grain to treat people like that, but for the sake of the mission, he nodded obediently.

"Go on, then. Nora will set you up."

Nora was as frazzled as she had been that morning. She recognised him and greeted him with relief.

"Thank heavens. You're early, which is a miracle around here. Where does Chrissie want you?"

"Out front."

"Good. You know what to do?"

"She ran through it with me," Setanta said. "But to be honest, she's very rushed. Did she really mean that I've to just point out where the tableware is, and let people help themselves?"

Nora sighed. "I know. It's mad, isn't it? But Maurice wanted the place to be different, make people talk about it, and Chrissie came up with this. It's worked, you know. Place is packed every night."

"She said. Ah well, wouldn't be my idea of a nice meal out but each to their own."

Nora smiled. "Mine either, if I'm honest. Chrissie is a bit of a genius at the marketing, though. Who knew people would be willing to pay through the nose to be treated like an inconvenience."

Setanta found himself liking the older woman. "Yeah, but the novelty will wear off. What then?"

She shrugged. "I suppose we'll try something else when that happens. At least we're doing well now."

"Thanks to Chrissie. I'd say she's employee of the month, eh?"

"The year. Not that her dad gives her much praise for it."

"It's no joke working for family," Setanta said with feeling.

"I suppose not. Oh, for goodness sake! Don't put those there, Kate, they'll get knocked over. Sorry, Setanta, I need to crack on. Just do your best, and thanks for pitching in."

Nora bustled off, dragging a sulky young waitress in her wake, while Setanta busied himself counting the tables in his section and looking at the menu. It offered a ridiculously narrow choice for such a posh restaurant, in his opinion. It also made life very easy for the kitchen staff. Maurice wasn't exactly wearing himself to the bone cooking.

He tried chatting to some of the staff before the rush started but didn't get anywhere. There was no sign of Precious yet and he was soon swept up in the first influx of diners, eager to experience the unique set up at Chez Maurice. Some were bewildered, obviously unaware that they were expected to act as their own servers, while others seemed to relish being part of the madness. Setanta felt a rush of affection for his fellow Dubliners, willing to try anything, a quip at the ready for any occasion. He soon settled into a rhythm, sympathizing with the reluctant and making jokes with the more adventurous.

More than one group asked him breathlessly if he'd been present for the "terrible accident." He was glad he was able to say no and felt a stab of sympathy for the staff who had faced these endless inquiries since Saturday. No wonder they were reluctant to talk about it.

The hardest part of his job proved to be getting people to relinquish their tables at the allotted time. Dubliners liked to get the full value of a meal out, which meant enjoying a few drinks or coffee after their dessert. Chrissie operated a ruthless, no-lingering policy. When Setanta failed to shift a group in the first wave of diners she strode over to the table, banged down the leather covered folder containing the bill and said pointedly, "Out. Unless you want to be barred. Chef Maurice won't have you back if you outstay your welcome." Setanta was stunned at how effective this was. It seemed the fear of being excluded from the capital's hottest restaurant outweighed everything.

He got better at moving groups as the evening progressed, but it hardened his resolve to never fall for this type of "marketing" himself. If he went out to dine, it would be in a nice place that respected their customers. Poor Mrs. Khan, he thought. Mai was a wee divil to have dragged her mother to this bedlam.

At last, one of the other servers appeared at his shoulder, hissing in his ear, "Take your break. Half an hour, mind. I'll be timing you."

Setanta found a quiet spot in the back, out of the way of the kitchen but near enough that he could observe the comings and goings. There was no sign of the great Chef Maurice, only a couple of sous chefs ordering the rest of the kitchen staff around. Still, he kept his eyes open, enjoying the bustling scene. Orders were shouted out from the pass, by a stern looking woman to whom everyone deferred with a solemn "Yes, Chef!" followed by a flurry of activity. Waiting staff grabbed plates and swept in and out of the kitchen looking cool and collected despite the heat. Whatever chaos reigned outside in the dining area, the back of house was run with precision and efficiency. His respect for the flamboyant and elusive Chef Maurice increased.

And at last, just as Setanta was about to give up and return to his post, the great man himself strode into the kitchen. He was tall, heavily built, sporting a very bright white chef's uniform, his reddish hair visible under his chef's hat. Setanta blinked. The man had an undeniable presence but there was something almost theatrical about his appearance. The young man watched as the chef exchanged a quiet word with his deputy, who nodded before turning to her underlings and shouting, "Good work, everyone!" Setanta could almost feel the energy recharge, the juniors smiling at each other. Maurice knew how to motivate his staff, he thought, although he didn't seem to spend a lot of time in the kitchen actually cooking.

He watched as Chef Maurice made his way to the office at the far end of the kitchen. A moment later, Chrissie bustled through the kitchen in his wake, looking harassed, her face pale under the layer of carefully applied makeup. It was really past time for Setanta to get back to work, but he couldn't resist. He followed the girl, trying to look busy, grabbing a tray as he went and fussing over it, half expecting to be stopped by an irate cook or one of his fellow waiters. But no one spared him a moment's thought, and he found himself outside the office door, in the shadows, close enough to hear the conversation inside without being seen himself.

This caused him a momentary stab of guilt. His parents, the elders in the temple and his teachers in school had all shared very strict views on honourable and honest behaviour and he had never before in his life sneaked around and eavesdropped. However, Mrs. O'Brien was relying on him and after all, being undercover meant you had to do a few things that might look underhand in other circumstances. He put aside his scruples and applied himself to listening carefully.

"Dad!" Chrissie sounded exasperated, "You can't turn up halfway through service and interfere. Julia has everything under control. Leave her alone."

Setanta was expecting the famously rich, plush tones of Chef Maurice, the face and voice of Modern Cuisine on Irish television. But instead, the man who replied had the unmistakable accent of Dublin's inner city, rich in its own way but a far cry from the cultured, middle class accent the chef usually affected.

"Ah, Gwon outta dat. It's my restaurant, Chrissie, and don't you forget it. The staff like to see me, makes them feel appreciated. Stops them gossiping about me being absent, for that matter."

A sigh from his daughter. "Dad. You're supposed to be *resting*, that's the problem. You know what the doctor said, no work for at least another month."

"I'm not workin' though, am I? I'm sitting on me - I'm sitting at home all day with my feet up, twiddling my thumbs. It's doing me head in."

"I don't care. You had a heart attack, Dad. A *heart attack*."

"I had very minor heart event."

"You were in hospital for two weeks! Have you any idea how hard that was to keep quiet? Imagine the shareholders finding out?"

Setanta bit his lip. Whatever he had expected to hear, it wasn't this. This was personal and not at all his business, and he needed to withdraw before he was caught listening in.

"If only you'd told that stupid woman to bog off," Chrissie added bitterly, "instead of letting her have a table at the last moment. Someone at her table stabbed that poor man, and now we're a murder scene on top of everything else."

"You leave Elsa out of it," Maurice replied sharply. "She's a good friend, an old friend. It's not her fault that waste of space she was married to showed up. Not that it's damaged business, has it? We're full to capacity every evening since."

Chrissie sniffed. "Maybe. But I still don't like her sniffing around, Dad. What if she tells people?"

Maurice snorted. "Tells people that I'm not some posh lad from Howth, is that what you mean? Tells people I started off as Morris Murphy, from the flats?" There was a sharpness to his tone, Setanta thought. And an element of hurt.

"Ah, Dad." Chrissie sounded weary. "We've been over this, a dozen times. Like, no one wants a celebrity chef from the inner city."

"And it wouldn't look good in front of your posh pals, either? Oh, don't bother denying it. You've always been afraid of people finding out Dear Daddy wasn't born rich. And more fool me, I've been happy to go along with it. But you know what? I don't much care anymore."

"I just don't want us dragged in any more than we already are," Chrissie said, "I've had to stop the staff gossiping as it is. Bad enough that he was upstairs drinking for an hour. Have you seen the Insta-pic reels? Anyone who caught a glimpse of him has their footage up…"

Feeling he'd heard enough, Setanta inched away carefully holding his breath until he was clear of the office and back out on the floor. He got a sour look from his replacement, but it couldn't be helped.

The rest of his shift flew by, but he kept an eye out for Chrissie, who soon returned to the reception desk, dripping her customary disdain for the general customer but smiling at the favoured few. She was clever, he thought and still very pretty, but he was a little disappointed with her snobbery. Maybe if he'd been brought up in a posh house, going to a snobby school, he'd be the same. But then, Mai was in one of the poshest schools in Dublin, and she wasn't ashamed of her parents, and her background. And she wasn't fake.

He turned over what he'd heard as he worked, including the confirmation that Elsa and Maurice were old friends and that Elsa had begged a table at the last moment.

He wondered what Teresa O'Brien would make of it all.

Chapter 11

Tuesday morning saw the detectives back in the Concert Hall, and once again facing the unfortunate Fintan behind his polished mahogany desk, in his neat little office. He peered at the Gardaí through his gold-rimmed glasses, his face a picture of anxiety.

"I thought we had cleared all this up," he said plaintively, his shoulders hunched over his desk. "I don't know what more I can possibly tell you."

Malachy sat down opposite Fintan, while Dempsey remained standing, his six-foot muscular frame looming rather impressively over the seated musical director.

"Well, now," Malachy said amiably. "You could start by explaining your relationship with Friedrich Mann."

Fintan flushed, a mottled red creeping across his cheeks. "Relationship? I told you, I didn't know the man."

"Oh, yes. Let me check my notes…indeed, that's what you said." Malachy smiled. "Which makes me wonder - doesn't it make you wonder, Detective Dempsey? - why did you lie?"

"I didn't!" Fintan protested, his eyes round behind his spectacles. "I don't understand…"

"You didn't know the man, but you had him in here for a wee chat, drinking whiskey and shooting the breeze?" Dempsey's tone was incredulous.

Fintan's face whitened, his eyes blinking rapidly.

"Come on, now," Malachy chided him. "It's pointless to lie. You were seen, in this very room, having a private conference with our victim, plying a known alcoholic with whiskey. You lied, Mr. McLaughlin."

The detective's stern tone seemed to be the final straw for the man.

"It wasn't like that!"

"How was it then? How are we expected to interpret this - this blatant lie?"

Fintan drew breath, exhaling slowly, his hands palm down on the table. It struck Malachy that it was a calming technique, the kind of thing you learn in therapy. He caught Dempsey's eye and shook his head. Better to let their man calm down, and maybe then they'd get some sense out of him.

A moment's silence seemed to settle Fintan's nerves. He looked at Malachy and nodded his head as if he'd made up his mind about something.

"Detective, I owe you an apology. I - I lied. I have no excuse, only I was afraid. I was so relieved when you said I hadn't killed the man. Then you said he'd been stabbed and I was terrified you'd think I was a suspect again. It was a moment of cowardice and I am ashamed."

Malachy gave the man an approving nod. "Good. Now, explain yourself. What was the nature of your relationship with Friedrich Mann?"

Fintan winced. "There was no "relationship,"" he insisted. "Oh dear. It's such a mess. You have to understand, I didn't actually know Friedrich, he wasn't a friend. He wasn't even an acquaintance. And I just wanted to help. He was harassing her, you know that. Wouldn't leave her alone. I saw her face, she tries to be so hard and tough but she was terrified of the man."

Malachy frowned, his brain working overtime to decipher this incoherent confession.

"By "her," do you mean, Elsa Von Streng?"

"Of course," Fintan answered impatiently. "You must know by now, he put her through hell."

"I do."

"Well then, what would you expect me to do?"

Even Dempsey looked thoroughly confused. Malachy and his junior exchanged a look. To the older detective's surprise, Dempsey took the lead but this time his voice was gentle.

"Fintan, why did it bother you so much? Who is Elsa to you? Wait! Don't lie to us again, man. You tried to intervene with her ex-husband. It was you who defended her, physically, when he attacked her at the restaurant. That's more than colleagues. So, I'm asking you again - who is Elsa to you?"

The unexpected kindness in the young detective's voice seemed to break Fintan in a way no amount of browbeating could have achieved. He sagged in his chair, every trace of defiance vanished.

"I love her," he said quietly. "I always have."

Malachy felt a piece of the puzzle clink into place as he stared at the man in front of him.

"You remembered her," he said, his pulse quickening. "You knew she was Emer Kelly, all along."

"Of course I did," Fintan replied. "How could anyone forget her? She's - she's so beautiful, and so talented. Oh, don't look at me like that. I'm not stupid. I know she'd never look at me. I'm a short, balding, round middle-aged man, Detective, who never made it past musical director of an orchestra. She's a wonderful, famous, gorgeous woman with the world at her feet. I don't want or expect anything from her. But I'm allowed love her from afar."

There was a quiet dignity in the way he spoke, that impressed Malachy. Even Dempsey looked touched.

"You said, you always loved her. I assume this started from your college days?"

"She was the only one I could stand," Fintan echoed the very words Elsa had said about himself. "The rest were awful stuck-up. The only reason they tolerated me was because I did well in the exams and the lecturers liked me. I was tipped for a good position from second year onward so they wanted to be on good terms. But they made fun of me behind my back. I knew it. Elsa was actually nice to me. She is the most genuine person you'd ever meet."

Dempsey raised a skeptical eyebrow. "Genuine? The woman has been living under an assumed name for decades."

"She changed her name," Fintan replied. "Who cares? A name is nothing. It's who you are underneath that matters and that never changed. I've followed her career for years, you know. Elsa has sponsored dozens of young musicians, from marginalized backgrounds, from poor areas, some of them refugees. She's arranged tuition, got them into orchestras, promoted their careers. Maybe her name changed but she never forgot who she really is. That's far more important." Malachy was inclined to agree. Part of him wished the steely conductor could be present to hear it. It might do her good to know someone thought so highly of her.

"It must have been a shock when she came home, especially when she came to the Hibernian."

"I was delighted. Oh, I knew she wouldn't remember me and I wouldn't embarrass her by mentioning our past. I just - it was nice to have her around."

"Then Friedrich turned up," Dempsey prompted. "How did you feel about that?"

Fintan shifted in his seat and looked directly at Dempsey. "Until he started bothering her, nothing at all."

"And when he upset her?"

"I was raging," Fintan conceded. "But I know from my own family, these things are complicated. My mother, she put up with a lot. Should have left my Dad, no doubt about it, but she couldn't bring herself to do it. I understood. I hoped she would report him to the guards when he started hanging around the concert hall, but - for whatever reason, she just couldn't."

Dempsey's response came eagerly. "So you decided to take matters into your own hands. eh?"

"What? No!" Fintan protested, looking at Malachy now. "Oh, for god's sake it wasn't like that at all."

"Explain it me," Malachy said.

"I thought - I thought, maybe the man just wanted to be heard. If he got to air his grievances to someone, maybe it would calm him down. I used to sit and listen to my dad while he ranted and it often worked. When I caught Friedrich wandering the corridors backstage, I invited him into the office. He was - I know you shouldn't give an alcoholic drink but when they're in the throes of addiction they can't function or concentrate without it, you see. I poured a small amount into a glass. It relaxed him, enough to have a conversation."

"That makes sense." It did, in a strange way. Malachy had dealt with enough addicts in his time to see the practical wisdom in Fintan's actions.

"He was a very angry man," Fintan continued. "Kept saying he'd been cheated, he was there to collect what was owed to him. I suppose, after leeching off Elsa for years, he thought he was entitled to money from her. I just listened. Then he started on about loyalty, and how people underestimated him. Everyone was against him, Elsa had made it impossible for him to get a job, his friends had deserted him. Then - well, he cried. Drunks are often sentimental, you know. He said wouldn't be doing it, if Elsa had helped him."

The Gardaí remained silent, loathe to interrupt. Telling them his story seemed to be a relief for Fintan.

"I thought, now's my chance. I offered him money, five hundred euros, if he'd go away and leave her alone. I told him, the orchestra season was starting and it was vital that our conductor wasn't distracted and that we would be prepared to help him out as a gesture of goodwill. To be honest, I was prepared to go higher - I could afford about a thousand euro - but he wasn't interested. He laughed in fact. Said that was an insult, that he was owed tens of thousands and that he wasn't leaving without it. That he was promised money, for some kind of job, I think. Or maybe like, a loan. He became very incoherent. That's when it all went a bit wrong."

"Wrong?"

"Yes. Up until then he'd been amiable enough. Glad to sit and talk, you understand. But now he got extremely angry. Accused me of trying to trick him into talking. He was agitated, pacing up and down, shouting, and then he threw open the door, shook his fist at me - really, it was like something from a stage villain in an opera - and he ran out. I went after him, but security caught him at the end of his corridor and bundled him out. Honestly, Detectives, I swear to you, I never saw him between that moment and the restaurant."

Malachy pursed his lips. "We have only your word for that, Fintan, and you haven't exactly been truthful with us up til now."

"I'm telling you the truth," Fintan pleaded. "You have to believe me. I am so sorry I didn't tell you all this before, but surely it's irrelevant. You know he was here, annoying Elsa."

"We'll be the judge of that. We'll leave it here for now, but you'll come to the station later and amend your statement, understood? Good. Now, if you think of anything else, contact us."

As the Gardaí stood to take their leave, Fintan looked up at them. "You won't tell her, please? She doesn't need to know how I feel about her. We have to work together and it's not fair to her."

Once again, Dempsey surprised the senior detective. "No. No, we won't say a word. Although, you might be surprised. She thinks very kindly of you."

With that, they took their leave. Dempsey shook his head in exasperation as they walked out through the labyrinth of corridors backstage. "I really thought we had our man, for a second."

You've changed your mind?"

"Ah, Flynn, come on. He's not a killer. He's a lovelorn eejit. He'd do a lot for that woman but can you see him stabbing a man in cold blood, in a crowded restaurant?"

"No." Malachy shook his head. "I can't."

* * *

Lisa had been fortunate to get Rehearsal Room 1 on Tuesday

afternoon, usually booked weeks in advance or reserved for visiting soloists. She suspected a word from Elsa Von Streng had freed it up. She was grateful, whatever the cause. There were passages she needed to practice, and the acoustics in her tiny bedroom simply weren't good enough. Plus, she needed to concentrate and truth be told, when she was at home she couldn't help wonder if Michael would call, or if he was too busy to meet up - it was an uncomfortable feeling. No one wanted to be the person running after the other in a relationship.

No, here in the concert hall, only music was important, and her only problems were easily resolved by practice, by technical exercises, by giving in to the score. Admittedly she had texted Michael and told him where she would be, but she resolutely put aside any hope that he might suggest meeting up or even come to collect here. Instead, she applied herself to her violin.

An hour flew by, then another and only aching fingers forced her to take a break. She laid down her precious Perry violin, flexed her shoulders and stretched her arms out, fingers interlinked.

"Bravo," Arnoldo Messini said quietly. Lisa jumped, stifling a scream. She hadn't seen or heard the tenor enter the room and had no idea how long he had been there, leaning nonchalantly against the wall, a mischievous grin on his handsome face.

"Oh my god!" Lisa exclaimed. "How long have you been there?"

"A little while. I apologise, Bellissima. I should have made my presence known, but then - I would have disturbed your so heavenly playing."

Lisa felt her cheeks flush.

"You're being kind. There's still a lot to iron out."

"No, *Bellissima*, please. I cannot abide false modesty. It is unbecoming to a great artist. You should own your talent, be proud of it!" Arnoldo waved his hands expressively. "People will value you more, if they see that you value yourself highly," he added, with an unusually serious air.

Lisa smiled. "It's not very Irish, though, is it. We tend to be a bit scathing of anyone having "notions," you see."

"Notions?" Arnoldo laughed. "You Irish, you are funny. But you are an artist, first. You must learn to speak like one. Say to yourself, *I am the greatest.* I am not joking, don't giggle at me! Say it. You are the greatest violinist ever to have lived. Paganini wishes he had been as good. Yehudi Menuhin is only a shadow compared to you."

Lisa couldn't help it, he was so funny it was infectious. "I have no idea half the time if you're serious or not."

Arnoldo grinned. He really did look like a movie star, Lisa thought, with his dark good looks and that cheeky charm.

"Ah, *Bellissima*. You don't take me seriously, but I am, I promise. Well, I haven't been in the past, this is true. But for a woman like you…" He crossed the room so quickly Lisa hadn't time to react. She stood perfectly still, as he lowered his face towards hers. "For a woman like you," he breathed softly, "I would be as serious…as the grave."

Lisa was frozen for a couple of seconds, then pushed her would-be suitor away firmly.

"I know you think it's funny," she said firmly, "but I don't. I'm in a serious relationship."

Arnoldo smiled.

"And where is your boyfriend? I would never allow you to dine alone. Spending hours by yourself, working yourself to the bone. If you were mine, I would take you to the most important places. You would be feted, spoiled, famous. I can open doors for you, my dear Irish rose. Here, let me kiss those talented fingers…"

The tenor reached for her hand in a fit of ardour and received the full force of a smack across his cheeks.

Lisa's voice shook with rage. "*Open doors* for me? What do you take me for?"

He ignored her protests, laughing at her. "You are beautiful when you're angry, Lisa, but don't be angry with me. I can't help that I admire you!"

"Admire me? You don't admire me, ya big gurrier. You think any woman will fall at your feet, just because you're famous." Lisa struggled to keep the Perry out of harm's way as the amorous tenor reached for her again. "I said, get off me, or I'll box your ears."

She managed to place the precious violin down safely on a stack of sheet music and turned her full attention to the problem at hand. Too late! Arnoldo managed to grab her face and bring his puckered lips close to hers…

Chapter 12

Michael paused at the backstage entrance. His eye strayed to the large and very pretty bunch of flowers he had just bought - at a truly ridiculous price, daylight robbery! - and the discreet but distinctive bag bearing the logo of Dublin's most expensive department store. That carried a tiny, elaborately presented bottle of perfume that judging by his credit card bill, must contain liquid gold and essence of diamonds. He had spent the previous hour being gently fleeced by helpful sales assistants, a desperate experience for a Tuesday lunchtime.

But Teresa O'Brien had urged him to make an effort, and an effort had been made. If he was honest, indignant determination had carried him this far, but now that he was about to cross the threshold into the hallowed home of the Hibernian Orchestra bearing his gifts, he felt…slightly ridiculous.

Really, while he had the highest regard for Mrs. O'Brien, there was no need for all this fuss. He was not some lovelorn teenager, to run after a crush. Lisa wasn't some flighty young one to be impressed by flowers and perfume. What did he look like, standing out here waiting for her? She might find it embarrassing, he thought suddenly. After all, this was her place of work. Maybe she'd feel it was inappropriate. He could go home now and put the perfume away for her Christmas present. Far more suitable, really. And sure, he could give her the flowers that evening. A late congratulations for getting the solo part.

He had almost convinced himself to give it up for a bad job when a familiar voice called his name. Ollessa, Lisa's friend and colleague, hurried up.

"Hi! Are you here to meet Lisa? Ooh, look at those flowers - they're gorgeous." She nodded approvingly. "Good call!" Her gave swept across him, noting the tell-tale logo on the little bag dangling from his hand. Ollessa beamed at him. "Yes, very good call indeed. Hang on, I'll open the door - no point in waiting out here."

She inputted the code and the heavy door unlocked. Pushing it open, she beckoned him to follow and Michael had no choice but to go ahead with his grand plan. Ah well, he thought, the decision had been made for him. Hopefully Lisa would be pleased.

And maybe, he admitted deep inside, very quietly, just to himself, *maybe he hadn't made as much of an effort as he should have recently.* Sure, it wouldn't do any harm to spoil Lisa a bit, would it? After all, she really was a dote and he was very fond of her....

He followed Ollessa obediently through the labyrinth of corridors that led to various rehearsal rooms, storage cupboards and dressing rooms. It wasn't his first time in these hallowed spaces but he was grateful for Ollessa's guidance, especially as the place was eerily empty at this hour.

"I left my wallet behind," Ollessa chatted as she walked briskly ahead. "My bus pass is in it, and my credit cards. Typical on the one afternoon we have off, but I couldn't bring myself to go home without it. It would probably be grand until tomorrow but you know yourself, it worries you when you don't know where something is…"

She came to a halt in front of a red door. A black plague with neat white lettering declared it to be "Rehearsal Room 1. " There you go. I'll head off. Have a great evening. And well done," She winked broadly, a delighted look on her face, "Lisa will be made up, honestly. Good man."
She disappeared down an adjacent corridor, her shoes click-clacking away. Michael took a deep breath, fixed a smile on his face and hoped that Lisa wouldn't burst out laughing at the sight of him.

"Lisa? Love?" He opened the door wide, holding the flowers out like a shield. "Surprise!"

His eyes took in the scene in front of him. His girlfriend of almost two years was in the clutches of the Italian tenor, Arnoldo Messini, whose lips were pursed in the unmistakable precursor to an amorous kiss. Lisa looked horrified - whether at the romantic advances of the singer or at the sight of her boyfriend, Michael had no time to decide. He was conscious of a roaring in his ears, a flush of blood spreading hotly across his cheeks and an unaccustomed emotion pulsing through his veins. The flowers dropped unceremoniously to the floor. The little bag of expensive scent still dangled from his wrist as he strode across the room and pulled Arnoldo away. It still swung merrily as he drew back his arm and swung with precision, boxing the other man firmly on the nose.

Lisa screamed while Arnoldo slipped to the ground, moaning and clutching his face.

"MY DOSE." It was less a roar and more a muffled, nasal wail.

"Michael!" Lisa grabbed his arm as he towered over Arnoldo.

"Stop! It's not - I mean, it isn't what you think."

"Isn't it?" Michael thundered. "I think that - that weasel was about to kiss you. If he hasn't already."

Lisa shook her head, her face crimson. "No. He - he did try to but …"

She trailed off helplessly and shook her head. "I know it looked bad, but I swear to you. I didn't encourage him."

Michael gave her a long, cool, appraising look. Then he turned to Arnoldo and said, his voice remarkably steady considering the state of his emotions, "Get up, you eejit. Up. Get out, now. And if I catch you bothering my girlfriend again, I'll finish what I started."

"You have broked my dose," Arnoldo wailed. "My DOSE! How can I ding with a broked dose?"

"I don't care," Michael replied with absolute sincerity. "Now, get out."

Arnoldo hesitated, looking pleadingly at Lisa. She ignored him pointedly. He finally tottered towards the door, but paused to shake a fist at Michael, or possibly both him and Lisa.

"Thid iddn't over. You attacked me! I'll - I'll go to police.…"

Lisa stepped forward, her face still red. "You do that. Go ahead, I dare you. In fact, I'll ring them myself, right now. You can explain why you thought it was okay to corner me in a rehearsal room and *jump* on me!"

Arnoldo's eyes narrowed and the look he gave her made Michael's fist clench again. "You led me on."

"I did not," Lisa tossed her head and pointed at him. "You pretend to be a cheeky, harmless flirt but you're just a lecherous gobdaw. I don't care if you're best mates with Elsa, no one has the right to behave like that. Now get out and think yourself lucky it was Michael who hit you. I'd have rammed that music stand down your neck."

Arnoldo spat out a string of muttered imprecations in Italian, mercifully unintelligible to everyone else. His parting shot as he slunk out of the room however was given in a very clear, precise English, broken nose notwithstanding.

"You'll regret this." He smiled unpleasantly, his nose still clutched in one hand. "You have no idea who you're messing with, no, not at all. You have made a bad mistake."

Michael ignored him, turning instead and picking up the discarded flowers. He looked at them oddly, as if he'd never seen them before.

"Michael," Lisa approached him tentatively. "You do believe me, don't you? It wasn't my fault. He got the wrong idea, but I never -"

"Here." He thrust the bunch of rather battered blooms in her hand. "These were for you. And this -" he untangled the bag from his wrist. "All for you."

"Michael," Lisa's face was white now. "I swear to you, you have to believe me."

"Oh. I know exactly what happened here." Michael turned on his heel sharply and walked away, leaving the door open behind him. He passed Ollessa on his way out of the building, ignoring her shocked glances. He didn't turn back even when he heard Lisa sobbing, and her friend asking her what was wrong.

He left the concert hall like a man on a mission.

Chapter 13

Setanta sat in the office at the back of O'Brien's music shop, early next morning, and recounted his adventures in Chez Maurice to a very appreciative audience of two. Mai - on yet another "free period" from school - and Mrs. O'Brien.

"It's probably not relevant, though, is it?" he asked Teresa. "I mean, it's interesting that there's a link between Elsa and Maurice but then again, we already knew it. The bit I found most interesting is that Friedrich was upstairs at the bar for an hour, according to Chrissie. She said there's footage of him on social media. How was he there so early, if he was following Elsa?"

"I'm not sure yet," Teresa replied truthfully, "but it all adds up. You did a great job though."

"It was a late night," Setanta said ruefully. "The money's good but I couldn't work there full time and keep up in college. Pity, though. Chrissie offered me more shifts if I wanted."

"I bet she fancies you," Mai winked at Teresa, her eyes alight with mischief. "You said she's very pretty…"

"She is." Setanta frowned. "I did kind of like her, but honestly, the way she spoke to her dad put me off. She's a bit of a snob."

Mai shook her head. "You don't know that. I bet she went to a really posh school, yeah? It's not easy, being the odd one out.

If everyone is snobby - well, it's no fun being the odd one out."

Teresa caught Setanta's eye and he said hastily, "Oh, don't mind me. I do understand. It has to be hard on you - I mean, on anyone. I'm sure Chrissie is nice really."

"Has there been much talk in school about the murder?" Teresa inquired, her tone carefully nonchalant.

Mai shrugged. "Yeah, everyone wanted to know what happened, were we nearby, did we see anything? Until Niamh Finnegan shoved her oar in…" The teenager trailed off mid-sentence, sounding as if she was choking back tears.

Setanta frowned but said nothing. Teresa patted Mai gently on the arm, and asked, "Is she up to her old tricks?"

Mai nodded but avoided making eye contact. "She told everyone I was lying," she said quietly, "that there was no way a pleb like me would be let into Chez Maurice. That they didn't serve noodles there, so what would my parents eat, and how would they read the menu? The usual."

"That's awful," Setanta blurted out. "She sounds like a total cow!"

"I'm used to it. And don't you dare tell anyone, Setanta Kapoor. Mam and Dad pay a fortune for that school, they'd be distraught if they knew. But don't go around blaming that Chrissie girl for being sensitive about it either."

"Mai, if you're truly unhappy there - " Setanta began.

"I'm not. I have some good friends, it's not all bad. And I've only a few years left. Niamh is just difficult."

Teresa pursed her lips but didn't contradict her young friend. This was something that required some thought, and Mai was a resilient youngster. If she could handle it, well and good, although it made Teresa's blood boil. From the expression on Setanta's face, she wasn't the only one.

There was no time to pursue the topic anyway as the door to the tiny music shop swung open and Lisa Kennedy appeared, her dark hair looking unusually lank and her face pale and drawn.

"Is he here?" She placed both hands palm down on the shop counter and peered in at the trio sitting in the office. "Is Michael here?"

Teresa bustled out, conscious of a feeling of alarm. It was highly unlike Lisa to be either unkempt in dress or impetuous in manner.

"Michael? No, he's not in yet. But it's only half past nine, Lisa. He's often not in until around ten."

"Have you heard from him?" Lisa rubbed her hand across tired eyes and added, "Please, Teresa, please. At least tell me if he's okay."

"What on earth wouldn't he be okay?" Teresa rounded the counter quickly, almost knocking over a counter display of brass tin whistles in her haste. "Lisa, what's happened?"

The young woman sobbed and covered her face with both hands. "It's awful, Teresa."

The rest of whatever she had to say was lost in a fresh bout of sobbing, and Teresa gave up trying to interrogate her.

"Setanta, go next door and get Lisa a tea, plenty of sugar in it. Mai, ring Michael's mobile. Use my phone and if he answers, pass it to me. If he doesn't, send him a text and ask him where he is and tell him to get to the shop asap. Lisa, come back here with me. Sit down, sit. Breathe, deep breaths."

Within a few minutes, she had the girl breathing quietly and a hot, strong tea with plenty of sugar clutched in her hands.

Mai got no answer from Michael, but dutifully sent a text as requested, sending one from her own phone for good measure. She also popped onto social media, checking Michael's accounts. He usually favoured the Insta-pic app but here were no updates from him.

"Okay, Lisa. Tell us what happened. What's wrong?" Teresa struggled to keep her tone neutral, calming. Lisa blinked rapidly, breathing quickly as she tried to calm herself.

"I'm sorry. I didn't mean to scare you. Teresa, have you really not heard from Michael at all? Didn't he tell you what happened yesterday afternoon?"

"No. I assumed he was just running a bit late." It wasn't Teresa's way to stand over her colleague and watch his comings and goings. Michael worked long and hard, but he chose his own hours. "Lisa, do you - area you saying something has happened to him?"

Lisa shook her head. "No. Not like that. Oh, it's such a mess. Teresa, Michael walked in on my rehearsal after lunch. I was in a private rehearsal room, and Arnoldo Messini was there. I didn't invite him, he just walked in on me too. But he- well, he made a pass at me. He was horrible." Her breath caught on a sob. "Then Michael walked in, just at the worst possible moment and he got hold of the wrong end of the stick. He punched Arnoldo! And then he threw a bunch of flowers and a bottle of perfume at me and left. He hasn't answered his phone or texts since. I came to the shop, in desperation."

Teresa, Setanta and Mai exchanged a startled glance but the young pair had the sense to keep quiet. Teresa patted Lisa on the shoulder and tried to think.

"Lisa, I have to ask. You and Arnoldo - did you have…were you having…"

"No." Lisa's answer was flat, and decisive. "I most certainly was not having an affair with Arnoldo, the greasy little weasel.

Oh, he's handsome and very flirty and I thought he was charming in a general way but I love Michael. Arnoldo grabbed me and tried to kiss me. That's what Michael saw, only he thinks it was mutual. He was so angry and so upset. I've never seen him like that."

Teresa bit her lip. "I understand him being upset, but he should have at least asked you what happened."

Lisa was a good and decent young woman, she thought, and if she had been tempted by Arnoldo, she would have broken it off with Michael first. It made her blood boil, to think of the Italian harassing the young violinist and then Michael treating her like the guilty party.

She gave vent to her opinion in one succinct utterance. "*Men!*"

* * *

While Lisa was unburdening herself to Teresa O'Brien, Clara wandered through the hallways of the concert hall, armed with her trusty ukulele and an air of innocence. Employing the age-old strategy of looking like she belonged, nodding hello to anyone she passed and exuding an air of complete confidence, she made her way backstage without hindrance. In fact, she stopped to chat with a burly security guard who helpfully pointed out things like Fintan's office, and Elsa's personal dressing room.

It paid, she reflected, to be a cheerful, harmless, middle-aged woman. Although Peadair might have snorted derisively at "harmless." Her purpose in being there wasn't quite clear, even to Clara herself. When Peadair had objected to her plan, she had simply smiled and replied, "You never know what I might see."

Clara was a great believer in *"you never know."*

She had persuaded Peadair to drop her off at the concert hall, where she thought she might just take a look around and chat to anyone she met. She was the first to admit that Peadair had outshone all of them in gathering intel on their first attempt but she felt sure that there was more to learn.

If anyone had accused Clara of being a gossip, she would have been offended. But people liked to talk about things that happened around them, and she liked to listen. Human nature, she told herself.

Her first port of call was the office of the music director. Fintan had remained aloof, apart from a brief introduction when the Super Ukers had arrived to rehearse with the orchestra. Everything Teresa O'Brien had told her about the man had piqued Clara's interest, however, and she was determined to see for herself. Was he the quiet, unassuming man he appeared to be, or - something more?

She rapped on the door of his office and called out, "Hel-loooo!"

A slightly startled "Come in," was all the invitation she needed, swinging open the door and bouncing in, smiling broadly.

Fintan stared at her, his surprise obvious from his expression. "Oh. Hello -um, eh - Ciara, is it?"

"Clara," She corrected, plonking herself into an empty chair opposite Fintan's desk. "Clara, from the Super Ukers. Your friendly neighbourhood Ukulele group. I must say, we've had some great gigs, Fintan. We played for the President's garden party, you know. We've been to festivals all over Ireland and across Europe. But let me tell you, playing in the Concert Hall is - well, it's special. And playing with the Hibernian under Elsa Von Streng - it's a dream come true, Fintan."

"Oh. Um, well, yes - thank you, Clara. I appreciate your kind words." He looked at her rather anxiously. "I must apologise. I can't remember, did we have a meeting scheduled...?"

"Oh, don't worry. You're a very busy man, sure we can't expect you to remember every little thing!" She winked at him. "No harm done."

Fintan looked stricken. "Oh, I do apologise. It's not like me to forget. I must have forgotten to put it in the calendar."

"Understandable. I'd say it's been a nightmare week," Clara replied. "What with the tragedy at Chez Maurice. So shocking. Lisa told me all about it, how awful it was."

Fintan frowned. "Lisa? Lisa Kennedy? I didn't realise you were acquainted."

"Oh, we're old friends. She's very close to young Michael, from O'Brien's Music Shop. And sure, Teresa O'Brien is an honorary member of the Super Ukers. Ah yes, we're all good pals. And of course, Teresa knows your Elsa well. Such a fascinating woman, isn't she? You did well to tempt her over here, Fintan, what a coup for the Hibernian!"

Like many people faced with the full force of Clara's personality, Fintan seemed hypnotized into replying.

"Ah, yes. Well, Elsa's an international star. I'm very glad we were able to persuade her."

"Bit hard for some of the old guard though, eh? I can tell, lots of them would be happy doing the same old repertoire. Not that there's anything wrong with the classics, not at all. Sure, aren't they popular for a reason. But you need to keep it fresh, as the kids say. And Elsa is such a catch, wouldn't you agree?" Her arch tone brought a deep blush to Fintan's cheeks. He dropped his head shyly and murmured something noncommittal in reply but Clara ploughed on, undeterred.

"Such a good-looking woman, too. That horrible man - I know we shouldn't speak ill of the dead, but *really* - he didn't deserve her at all. Now at least, she's free." Clara grinned. "It's an ill wind, eh? Oh, don't look so shocked. I bet she's relieved. Fancy him coming all the way here just to harass her."

Fintan blinked. "Well, of course. I mean, it's still terrible..."

"Oh indeed. Terrible. But also, well, it could be worse. It could have been Elsa, if someone hadn't stopped him. It could have been our Lisa, the poor wee pet. Or yourself!"
"Me?" He exclaimed. "Are you saying, it could have been meant for someone else at the table?"

"Why not?" Clara had no idea if it was even a feasible suggestion but long experience had taught her that the quickest way to get the other person to talk was to make an outrageous statement, one they couldn't help contradict. Fintan was no exception.

"I don't think that could possibly be the case," he said earnestly. "The detectives seemed certain Friedrich was the intended victim."

"Pooh." Clara said airily. "How could they be sure? There were four people at that table, and then Friedrich pops up and someone just happens to have a knife on them, that has never been recovered, incidentally."

"But it was surely opportunistic." Fintan eyed her doubtfully. "I mean, there were knives everywhere."

Clara raised an eyebrow at this rather startling assertion.

"What I mean is," Fintan explained, "We had to get our own cutlery and plates and things. It was ridiculous. Arnoldo and

I volunteered to collect them for the ladies. There was every kind of knife, just laid out on a huge table. Anyone could have taken a steak knife, or something. They might have just taken it not knowing what the table would need, then used it because it was there."

"Oh. That does make sense. Aren't you clever?" Clara's voice dripped admiration and Fintan sat back with a pleased look. "Who was it, do you think? Arnoldo? You? Elsa? It wasn't Lisa, she's the only one with no motive at all. Who do you think did it?"

Fintan's mouth gaped open. "Madam!"

"Oh, gwon now. You can tell me."

"This is highly inappropriate." He stood suddenly, looking unusually stern. "I have no idea what happened, no more than you do."

"Are you sure?" Clara remained seated. "Oh, I don't mean you're lying. Sit yourself down, there's a good lad. No, I just mean - maybe you saw something you can't recall yet. Think, man, think. You must have noticed something. Someone had to pick up the knife and stab him."

Fintan ignored her. "I really must ask you to leave now, Clara. Thank you for calling in. I'm sure the Super Ukers will have a great evening, I look forward to it. But i do have other appointments..." He moved to the door and held it open, pointedly.

Clara gave in graciously. "Well, thanks for your time, Fintan. Lovely chatting to you and again, just wanted to say how much we appreciate this opportunity." She took her leave murmuring pleasantries and trotted off happily towards her next victims.

* * *

Teresa and Elsa were once again facing each other over coffee in Fancies cafe, but this time there was a marked degree of tension in the air. Once Lisa had calmed down, and Setanta had volunteered to walk her back to the concert hall, Teresa had wasted no time in contacting her old friend.

At first, Elsa had protested that she was too busy and was needed at the concert hall.

"We have rehearsals," the conductor had pointed out. "I can't just disappear."

"Yes, you can. Half an hour, Elsa. Not taking no for an answer."

Now, Elsa avoided Teresa's eyes, busying herself with arranging the coffee cups and plates of cake on the tiny table.

Teresa waited patiently. Elsa might be a polished version of the young lass from Dublin that she used to know, but despite her fame, achievements, travel and new name, it was amusing how clearly one could see the teenage Emer Kelly in the adult Elsa Von Streng. Many a time the younger woman had sat in the shop, sullen and sulky, while Cathal had gently lectured her. To her credit, she had always taken the advice on board, no matter how much she resented having to listen to it. Teresa looked at her fondly. It was no different than her own kids, at the same age. They were all grownups now, and yet to her, they were also still just young people trying to make their way. "Elsa," Teresa said gently, when her companion had finally run out of distractions. "You need to be honest with me."
"Are you accusing me of lying?"

"You can drop that tone with me, young lady. No need to get defensive. You haven't been completely straight about a lot of things. Let's start at the beginning, shall we? When you and Friedrich split up, you deliberately made it difficult for him to get another job with an orchestra. Detective Flynn tells me it's common knowledge in orchestral circles. Now, you're not a vindictive person. You walk away from people who treat you badly, and you cut them off. I know he was appalling, and you'd every right to ill-wish him, but it doesn't seem like you. So, there's something else. Something you aren't telling us. No, hear me out."

Teresa paused, deciding to draw together all the little bits of information she had learned from Malachy Flynn, Setanta, the Super Ukers and Mai's internet searches.

"There are other things that don't add up. Your friendship with Arnoldo. He's a nasty man, Elsa. He made a pass at Lisa, late at night, in the rehearsal room. And by *"made a pass,"* I mean, he grabbed her and tried to assault her. He's not who he pretends to be. Yet you seem to be on the best of terms with him. I'm surprised. Oh, and one other thing - why didn't you tell me you knew Fintan from your college days? And Chef Maurice, another old friend. That seems odd, too."

Elsa stared out the window of the cafe, and for a moment Teresa thought she would simply refuse to answer. Then, those icy blue eyes looked directly into her warm brown ones and she knew she had won.

"I'm glad you think I'm not vindictive, at least." Elsa sounded weary. "Most people were only too quick to point the finger at me. "Bitter ex-wife." You can imagine the story. And yes, it was my fault he didn't get offered many positions but then again, the ones he did manage to secure he lost all by himself, drinking and not turning up for performances."

"Why, Elsa? Why was it so important to you that he didn't

work in an orchestra? Surely, as long as he was well away from you, it didn't matter?"

Unless of course, she had been simply so angry, understandably so, that she wanted to destroy him.

"It wasn't that I didn't want him to have a job. It wasn't bitterness. " Elsa gave a brittle little laugh. "Although, I *was* bitter, make no mistake about it. Holy lord, Teresa, he was a divil of a man. I loved him so much and he treated me like a dog. But once we were divorced, I would have been happy to see him settled, working, as long as it was well away from me."

Teresa nodded encouragingly. "I thought as much. So, what happened to change that?"

Elsa sighed. "I found out something, something awful. You have to understand, when we were together, Friedrich relied on me financially. I earned far more than him, which didn't bother me at all but he hated it. He demanded sole control of our bank accounts - forced me to sign over power of attorney to him. It was his way of keeping me on a leash, I suppose, and making himself feel better about earning less. He started throwing money around, living the high life. I thought it was on my money."

"And was it?"

"Partly. But he had found another income source. He used our joint account, he used my name, he used our position as orchestra members. Oh, it makes me sick even now." She rubbed her face with her hand, in a weary gesture. "Long story short, he was letting a drug dealer hide money in our bank account for a fee. They hid their money, he laundered it. They would "buy" something from him or pretend to hire him - or me - for a performance, all kinds of tricks. They paid him well enough for his services. But being Friedrich, he couldn't even be a straight crook. He started dipping into the cash."

Teresa gasped. "He stole from drug dealers?"

"Monumentally stupid, right? And that's how I found out about the entire scheme. They showed up one night, at our apartment, threatening all sorts if their money wasn't repaid. I liquidated what savings I had, sold off anything I could and bailed Friedrich out. But that was the end for me. I told him, if he didn't agree to a divorce, I would go to the police."

"How did he take that?"

"Badly. That's how he ended up being arrested, for hurting me. Frankly it was worth it though - he realised he had to back off, or he would lose everything. I was just happy to finally be free of him." Elsa shivered. "Then I found out the truth. He had graduated from money laundering, to being a mule. You know what a drug mule is? He hid drugs in the orchestra's instrument cases. We travel a lot in a good orchestra, all over Europe and across the world. Customs don't really search high profile people or open every instrument case to check for drugs. But it was still a terrible risk. If a sniffer dog had been brought in, it would have been a disaster. He risked putting us both in prison. He hid drugs in our colleagues' gig bags and flight cases, especially the heavy-duty ones. He was utterly shameless."

"Dear heavens above," Teresa had suspected something had tipped Elsa over the edge where Friedrich was concerned but not this. "Was he working alone?"

"I have no idea," Elsa said. "None. Maybe they were all in on it? Maybe he came up with it all be himself? Although, no, I don't really believe that. He was crooked, and could be very manipulative, very clever when it came to being cruel. But he wasn't bright enough to work out such an elaborate, daring plan. Oh, I don't know. Don't you think I've tormented myself, going over and over this, trying to work it out? I spent months, looking at the people I worked with and socialized with and called friends, wondering if any of them helped my husband smuggle drugs across the world."

"It must have been awful," Teresa said, reaching for her friend's hand. Elsa let her envelope her slim hand, blinking back tears.

"It was. I was so alone. You asked how I could remain friends with someone like Arnoldo? Well, he's the one who told me what Friedrich was doing. He was touring with him, with an orchestra based in Leipzig. I was in France at the time, doing a guest series with *La Conservatoire*. He was distraught. He told me he had caught Friedrich retrieving a package of drugs from one of the Double Bass cases, quite by accident. The owner of the instrument was with Arnoldo when they caught him. Friedrich blamed everyone but himself, of course. Even turned up in Lyons at my hotel, demanding to see me, full of stories about how it hadn't been his fault. The drug dealer's men had made him do it. He had no choice."

"You didn't go to the police?"

"I had no proof. Arnoldo felt sorry for him, they were old friends. He wouldn't agree to turn him in, just made him promise to resign from the orchestra. Arnoldo persuaded the man whose Bass it was not to say anything either. After that, I kept tabs on Friedrich. If he applied for a job with an orchestra that traveled a lot, I put the kibosh on it. A word from the great Elsa Von Streng was enough, no one wanted to cross me. If it was a domestic outfit, I left well enough alone. It gnawed away at me, though. I kept thinking, what if some innocent person had been caught with those drugs? Between that and wondering who in my own orchestra had been part of his scheme, I couldn't stand it."

"The offer from the Hibernian must have seemed like a godsend," Teresa agreed.

"I was so happy to come home. It felt like a sign. And now, it's all ruined."

Teresa shook her head vigorously. "Nonsense. It doesn't feel like it now but I am certain you did the right thing. I feel it in my bones. I'm beginning to see where all this fits together. Besides, you have family here, and friends. Where else would you be?"

"Family that doesn't even know I'm here."

"That's your own fault. Get up off your behind and ring your brother. Tell him everything and if he isn't just happy to have his sister back, I'll eat my hat."

"Teresa, did Arnoldo really do that to Lisa?"

"Yes. And worse, Michael walked in on it. You know Lisa's been seeing my Michael?" Teresa spoke about the young luthier as if he was one of her own kids. "There's been a terrible scene, Michael's gone off the radar, and Lisa's distraught."

Elsa clenched her fist. "I knew he was a flirty so-and-so, but he's gone too far. I knew he quite fancied her, but he fancies everyone. I thought it was just his way. I'll flay him alive."

"You'll have to get to him before me," Teresa said grimly. "Although from what Lisa tells me, Michael landed a right planter on him. Your precious Arnoldo will be facing the audience with a black eye."

"He'll be facing the business end of my baton when I catch up with him. What an unholy mess. I'll have to have a word with Lisa, too. Apologise for unleashing the wee scalpeen on her."

"Time enough for that," Teresa said. "Lisa is a lovely girl, she won't hold it against you. From the way she stood up for you to Detective Flynn, she's very fond of you. She could be a good friend to you, Elsa. And speaking of friends, you haven't explained about Fintan and Maurice yet."

Elsa shrugged. "There's nothing much to explain. Fintan was in my year in college. Oh, I doubt he even remembered me, but I recognised him immediately. He was the only one I could stand. Maurice and I grew up in the flats together. He was a wild man back then, but harmless. And talented. I know he's a famous chef now with his posh food but back when we were kids, his chip butty and bacon sandwiches were legendary. I'd give my eye teeth for one now. I saw him being interviewed on Sunrise Ireland, and thought, there's a man who'll understand why I'm now Elsa Von Streng and not Emer Kelly. And I was right. It's nice having someone who knew me back then and doesn't judge me for having reinvented myself. You and Maurice are the only ones I trust, Teresa."

"I'm glad of that, love. You and Maurice being old friends, though - that explains how you got the last-minute reservation at Chez Maurice. When did that happen?"

"On the Thursday."

"I wonder how Friedrich knew you'd be there," Teresa mused.

"Oh. I assumed he must have just followed me."

"The state he was in?" Teresa wasn't ready yet to share Setanta's idea about the upstairs bar.

Elsa frowned. "I never thought about it. Maybe it was sheer coincidence that he ended up in the same place as me."

"I can't buy that. He seems to have spent his days stalking you, but his evenings were generally passed in the hotel. He'd have dinner, then drink at the bar until late."

"That sounds like Friedrich all right."

"Which brings us back to, how did he know where to find you?"

"Someone must have told him," Elsa said, her voice almost a whisper. "But, who? And - why?"

Chapter 14

Mai walked slowly, her schoolbag weighing heavily on her shoulders and her worries weighing heavily on her heart. She had returned to school after lunch, her mind full of Lisa's tale of woe, half glad to be back in the simpler environment of lessons, and homework, only to be greeted by another round of teasing from Niamh Finnegan. And it all centred around Chez Maurice and the events of Mai's birthday dinner.

At first, Niamh had told anyone who would listen that Mai couldn't have been present that night, there was no way a nobody like her could get a reservation. When other girls pointed to the news reports, that specifically listed Mai's parents as well-known local business people, the other girl changed tack. She poured scorn on the idea that Mai had known anyone at the ill-fated table. She called her a liar, which didn't bother Mai so much, she was used to Niamh's crude attempts to bully her, but she abruptly changed tack and told everyone it was probably Mai's low-life family that was behind the murder.

The sheer audacity left Mai momentarily speechless. Then words had rushed out, hot and angry, and to her horror Niamh had twisted everything she said. Every attempt to point out that there was no basis for such a slanderous comment prompted Niamh to new heights. Mai's family were, according to her tormentor, *"well-known all right. Infamous gangsters, more like,"*- known, she claimed, for drug dealing over the counter of the Noodle Palace.

In Niamh's narrative, Mai's little cousins became tough, evil men intent on bringing criminality to the streets of Dublin. Mai tried to point out that both the boys attended one of the cities' most exclusive schools and were more interested in art, and Warhammer models, than anything remotely nefarious but she was shouted down by the other girl. Niamh appealed to the crowd, their classmates, and demanded to know how she was supposed to feel safe in her own country with people like Mai running loose?

The appearance of Ms. Geraghty, the formidable P.E. teacher, sent the girls scattering, leaving Mai standing alone. "I'm fine," she responded stubbornly to the teacher's kindly inquiries, "It's fine."

But it wasn't. She took her bag, left the school and decided it was better to risk getting caught skipping school than go back into a class full of horrible girls who obviously hated her. Her own friends hadn't said a word! That hurt most of all.

She wandered around, wondering where best to go. Usually, she'd take refuge in the music shop but at this hour her parents might notice her across the road. St Stephen's Green was the obvious choice but several girls had been caught hiding in there, *"mitching off"* as Mrs. O'Brien called it, and the school had threatened dire consequences to the next pupil they caught in the park. Teachers were always in and out of the place, and it was too easy to bump into one of them.

She took a turn away from the Green and up towards the concert hall. There was a nice café opposite the imposing old building, and no one from school was likely to go past. It would give her time to think, and to decide what to do. Although short of asking her parents to let her switch schools, there didn't seem to be many options.

The café was bright and clean, and she was glad to see nearly empty. She swung into a booth against the far wall, furthest from the door, avoiding the rows of tables along the windows. It was quiet, no background music playing yet, and only the sound of the coffee machines and cups rattling against saucers breaking the silence. Even the two other customers sat alone, silently scrolling their phones and not at all interested in anyone else. Mai ordered a coffee, adding on a slice of carrot cake when the waitress waved a menu at her. Then, when she was sure she was unobserved and unlikely to be disturbed, she put her head in one hand and let the tears fall.

A shadow fell across the table and she started.

"It's only me." Lisa Kennedy slid into the booth, facing her across the white topped table. "I'm sorry, I don't want to intrude. I came in to get a coffee, before braving the rehearsals. I'm not looking forward to it, I can tell you. I'm supposed to be playing a duet with the man who may have ruined my relationship, assuming he can even perform with a black eye and a possibly broken nose. I saw you and wanted to make sure you're okay."

Mai looked at her, unable to hide how she felt. Despite her own woes she felt sorry for Lisa, who looked every bit as miserable herself.

"Have you heard from Michael?" the teenager asked, trying to blink away her tears.

Lisa shook her head but managed a smile. "Never mind him. What has you in such a state?"

Mai shook her head. "It's - it's not important. Just stupid school stuff."

"It's not stupid if it has you this upset. Come on, Mai. You listened to me cry my heart out over Michael earlier. Won't you trust me enough to return the favour?"

Mai opened her mouth to say no, but to her surprise the whole sorry tale of bullying and unjust accusations spilled out instead. Months of pent up hurt, a burden carried alone. It was a relief to let it go, especially when Lisa had such a gratifyingly partisan reaction. She used words for Niamh that Mai didn't think the rather prim and proper violinist even knew. Older people really could surprise you sometimes, she thought.

"No one stood up for me," was the final, shameful confession. It made Mai feel hot and sick to admit it.

"They may have been in shock," Lisa said. "And you said that teacher appeared suddenly. You can't be sure what they would have done, if she hadn't turned up. Let's wait and see, there's no point in assuming the worst. Have any of them contacted you?"

Mai fished her phone out of her schoolbag and turned it on. "They make us turn it off in school, even in the lockers," she explained. "It's so annoying. I grab it when I get my school bag but I keep forgetting to power it on."

As she spoke a series of beeps came from the mobile. Lisa raised an inquiring eyebrow.

The names of her friends popped up in quick succession, as notifications flooded the screen. Then there were texts from others in her class, some that she wasn't particularly even friendly with.

"I don't understand," Mai waved the screen under Lisa's nose. "We don't have access to our phones during the day. They must have snuck into the locker area to text."

"Well, what do they say?"

"Oh." The tight knot in Mai's chest loosened somewhat. "Okay. Mel says *"Niamh is a dirty rat, and we all hate her, please don't be upset."* Carol says they're all mad at her and that even Maura Doherty told her off. Maura is her best friend, Lisa. I don't think I've ever even seen her say 'no' to Niamh."

"There!" Lisa crowed. "You're far more popular than Niamh. She's shown her true colours. Anything else?"

"Oh. My. God." Mai almost giggled. "Triona Butterfield says she took Niamh's maths copy, with her homework in it, and threw it in the bins round the back of the school. Apparently, Niamh is out there now rooting through them. Mrs. McNeil saw her from the classroom window and stormed off to see what she's playing at. That's how everyone was able to grab their phones to text me."

"Ah, Mai. See? I'm so sorry you have a Niamh to put up with, but now you know the rest of them are not like her. I hope she gets a desperate rollicking from the teacher."

"They'll realise I skipped out," Mai said, her heart suddenly falling again. "I was so upset I didn't care at the time, but - I can't afford to get into trouble, Lisa, not for the likes of her."

"Leave it to me," Lisa produced her own mobile, took the school's number from Mai's contacts and made the call. "What's the secretary's name? Bridie? It's ringing - Hello? Is that Bridie? Bridie, this is Lisa from Easy Teeth Dental. I'm ringing to inform you Mai Khan had to leave school early. She was most anxious that I let you know as soon as possible. She had a dental appointment here at two p.m. but found out her mother forgot to tell her year head. Exactly. Parents, am I right? Hah. Well, you have her marked out properly now? Excellent. I'll let her know. She's in with Dr. Murphy at the moment. No, no bother at all. Can't have schoolkids wandering around, can we?"

Lisa grinned impishly at Mai and hung up. "I used to make all the phone calls for my friends, when I was your age. I have a really convincing phone voice."

"You're amazing." Mai looked at her in awe. "Did you really mitch off school?"

"Not often, no. I was too afraid of getting caught. I was a bit of a goody two shoes, if I'm honest. But like I said, I made all the calls to get my mates off the hook."

Mai smiled shyly. "You're lovely, Lisa, do you know that? Michael needs his head examined."

Lisa winced. "I'm afraid he doesn't feel that way. Come on, no more crying over spilt milk. Do you want to come with me? You can sit in the hall and listen to rehearsals. I'd say Elsa will take us apart today, it should be very amusing for you."

Mai hopped up. She felt a lot better, but sitting in the hall beat sitting alone in a strange café.

"I'll come. And if Arnoldo Messini shows his face, I'll blacken his other eye if you want!"

* * *

Clara had spent a rather fruitless hour after her encounter with Fintan. She found any number of people to chat to, as she made her way around the hall, but no one had anything of interest to add. She found a quiet spot and rang Teresa, who brought her up to date on events. She rang off, swearing under her breath at the thought of young Lisa being manhandled by the singer. As if she had conjured the Italian up by thinking of him, Arnoldo Messini stepped out of a dressing room as she passed.

Clara considered all her options, including boxing his ears and poking him in his one good eye, but her instructions from Teresa had been clear. Find out whatever she could and not to antagonize Arnoldo if she met him. For the sake of the mission, she told herself, it was time to play dumb.

"Oh! Mr. Messini, you gave me such a fright. I was miles away, so I was. But it's lovely to see you again. How are you settling in to our little community?"

Messini stared at her, obviously wondering if he had met her before but unable to place her. He was dressed in his usual attire of expensive trousers, linen shirt and cashmere wool jumper but his good looks had taken quite a blow, figuratively and literally. His nose was sore looking and very swollen, and one eye was almost shut with a purple bruise already blooming around it. His usual air of suave good humour appeared to have deserted him, and a sour expression marred his looks as effectively as the black eye.

"Settling in? Madame, this is a den of vipers and savages," he retorted bitterly.

"Oh, dear. Oh, you poor man, I'm so sorry to hear that!" Clara's motherly sympathy worked like a balm to the singer's ego. "What have they done to you?"

She listened with rapt attention as Arnoldo spat out his version of events.

"I have spent hours, hours, with that woman. That ingrate. Teaching her, mentoring her, helping her raise herself above mediocrity. She repaid me by - by luring me into a rehearsal room, throwing herself at me and allowing her boyfriend to beat me! Perhaps she wanted to make him jealous, I do not know. Maybe they thought they would blackmail me? Or she wanted to have her fun, yes, and then when he caught her decided to pretend that I was to blame…"

Clara bit down hard on the urge to kick his shins and forced herself to nod. "Who knows? And this person, the boyfriend, he punched you? Did you call the Gardaí?"

Arnoldo started, his eyes narrowing. "Call the…you refer to the police? Pah. What's the use of it? It's my word against theirs."

"Oh, but your poor eye. And nose. That's proof, surely."

"Perhaps." His tone was wary and his eyes shifty. "I am a celebrity, you know. I have to think of my image. My publicist, she would not like this kind of scandal. I have performances to give…" He trailed off vaguely.

"I'm sure you know best," Clara said soothingly. "I do hope it doesn't hurt too badly?" She tried to hide her delight when he moaned in pain and reached into his pocket for a packet of painkillers. "Oh, you need to take them? Come with me and I'll get you a glass of water. There's a kind of staff room back here, that'll have supplies."

As she ushered Arnoldo through the corridors she caught sight of Lisa in the distance, and what looked like Mai Khan. She installed Arnoldo in a chair in the tiny canteen kitchen where the orchestra took a cup of tea between rehearsals and popped her head out the door. She waved frantically at Lisa, and mouthed Arnoldo's name, miming dramatic singing for added effect. Lisa's eyes rounded in dismay and she grabbed Mai's arm, beating a hasty retreat towards the stage itself.

Satisfied that at least the girl knew Arnoldo was here, and had avoided running into him, Clara turned her attention back to the disgruntled singer.

"Do you think you can sing, with your nose like that?" she asked.

"Sing? I don't know. I must try. It's possible that I cannot. If not, they will pay me anyway. It's not my fault, it was that stupid girl."

"What a terrible time for you," Clara leaned against the door frame and eyed him. "Losing a good friend in such tragic circumstances and now this. Almost like you're jinxed."

This earned a sharp glance from the singer but Clara's expression of gentle sympathy seemed to reassure him.

"Friedrich was not a good friend," He sighed dramatically, then produced a colourful silk handkerchief from his trouser pocket. Clara stifled a laugh as he dabbed at his eyes. "No, not really. I found this out too late, you see. Ah, I was a *magnificent* friend to him, always. But he was an ingrate and a traitor."

Curiously, Clara found herself believing him. There was such a genuine sense of outrage in his voice when he said "traitor."

"Nothing worse," she agreed. "Makes it harder in some ways."

"How so?"

"To lose him in such tragic circumstances, when you weren't on good terms. Sad."

"Hmm, I suppose. Yes. You are very simpatico, I see now. No one else seems to realise how hard it is for me. I am an artist, we *feel* things."

"And to think he was here all that time and never tried to make it up with you." Clara shook her head and tutted. "Dreadful."

Arnoldo's handkerchief disappeared back into his pocket and he sat up straight.

"Here, all that time? What do you mean?" His tone was wary.

"Didn't you hear? My friend Teresa had it straight from that detective. Friedrich was here in Dublin for at least ten days before he died."

"No?" He stared at her, his artistic torment seemingly forgotten. "I thought - I got the impression he had only just arrived."

"Oh no, he was stalking poor Elsa Von Streng for a while before he revealed himself." Clara was enjoying herself now. She wasn't sure what the man's reaction meant for the investigation but she was happy to rattle his cage. "Oh yes, Lisa met him trying to get into the hall, but the security guards said he'd been in and out a few times before that. He was even in talking with Fintan McLaughlin at one point."

Arnoldo stood, almost overturning the tiny table in the process.

"I must go, apologies." He smiled, an echo of his usual charm peeking through. "Dear lady, I shall see you again."
Clara watched him hurrying away, in the opposite direction to the stage. Whatever she'd said, it was enough to make Arnoldo decide to miss the rehearsal.

* * *

Malachy Flynn had not been idle, while Teresa and her O'Brien Irregulars had busied themselves. The problem was his investigation was taking him in an uncomfortable direction and he was far from pleased. On the other hands, his junior colleague was delighted with himself.

"I told you, that woman is up to her neck in it!" Dempsey exclaimed, waving an Interpol report at his boss. "Look, drug smuggling, money laundering, and that's just what they're willing to share with us. She killed her husband to shut him up."

Malachy took the sheets from Dempsey, and read them quickly.

"This says nothing but that they suspect a link," he pointed out mildly, "between Friedrich Mann and a well-known Italian drug ring. It says they can't be sure whether Elsa was involved or even knew about it. That's a far cry from an open and shut case."

"Pah!" said Dempsey, his face scornful. "We've been wondering why Mann followed her here, and who was bankrolling him. Either he was travelling on drug business, or Elsa was paying for him. I'd say he was blackmailing her and she had to silence him."

"In a restaurant, in full view of everyone?" Malachy smiled. "She could have met him anywhere. God knows he plagued her enough trying to make her talk to him. Why wait until there were witnesses?"

"Witnesses who saw nothing," Dempsey pointed out. "She's a cool customer, that one. Nerves of steel. Saw her opportunity to silence him before he could blurt anything out to her new boss, Fintan."

Malachy sighed. There was a thread of sense in Dempsey's argument but he was far from convinced. The lad had a good enough brain, and a reasonable grasp of what it took to be a detective but he lacked both the creativity to think outside the obvious, and the objectivity to appraise the situation without prejudice. The long and the short of it was, Dempsey had taken a fierce dislike to Elsa from the first, and now every piece of evidence he looked at was filtered through that emotion.

Which was why Malachy enjoyed the company of Teresa

O'Brien. The old lady reminded him of his mother and aunts, whose judgments he would trust over most of his colleagues, any day of the week. He wandered away from the incident room, told his desk sergeant that he'd be back in an hour and walked briskly from his office on Bride Street to West Stephen Street. He stopped outside the music shop, staring at the famous red and black sign that hung on a wrought iron frame on the side of the building. Before he could push the door open, Teresa herself stepped out, her keys in hand.

"Oh," Malachy checked his watch. It was four o'clock in the afternoon. "Are you shutting early?"

Teresa chuckled. "Am I what? No, I'm running next door to grab a sandwich, and eat at my desk. I'm on my own today, and it's been bedlam. I had a coffee with Elsa earlier today but I haven't sat down since."

Malachy shook his head. "That's no good. You shouldn't go all day without a break. Come on, I'll stand you a lunch and fill you in on today's madness."

Teresa didn't argue, only too glad of an excuse to leave the shop for half an hour. Inwardly, she cursed Michael Clancy and his disappearing act. This was not good enough. At her age, while she hated being reminded that she wasn't a spring chicken anymore, she definitely needed a bit of help around the shop. Even knowing Michael was upstairs was enough, on the average day. She was thoroughly shocked at his behaviour, very annoyed indeed with her protege and at the same time, really quite worried about him.

To her surprise, Malachy guided her past the café, and down the road to the St. Stephen Hotel.

"You need a bite of dinner," he said firmly. "They do a lovely bit of pork here, with mash and veg. It'll save you cooking when you get home."

He made her take a seat at one of the shining mahogany tables, on a plush, velvet covered chair that managed to be firm and soft at the same time. In no time at all, the Garda had ordered food, secured a large pot of tea and was assured by the bar staff that their meal would be delivered to the table in short order.

"Now, then," he rubbed his hands together. "I'll tell you my news if you'll tell me yours."

Teresa listened to the news of the Interpol reports, and the damning evidence turning up regarding Elsa's ex husband. She reciprocated with an account of her conversation that morning with Elsa. Malachy's eyes widened as he listened.

"Well, now. That is information our friends in Interpol will be interested to hear. Smuggling drugs using an orchestra - I've heard it all now. I can retire from the force. What a shock Elsa must have had, finding that out."

"She was distraught. Stopped him from taking international work whenever she could but she still isn't sure who was in it with him. And she's fairly sure Friedrich hadn't the brains to do it alone."

"It could have been him on the inside, alone, with the cartel telling him what to do," Malachy suggested.

"Possibly but unlikely. Getting the packages into cases without the individual owners suspecting and then retrieving them as inconspicuously - it's a lot for one person."

"I agree. I wonder what they'd have done if someone had discovered their precious violin or cello had a pack of that garbage stuck in it!" The detective shook his head.

Teresa winced. "I have seen musicians come to blows because one of them borrowed the other's resin and didn't put the lid back on correctly. If they opened their cases and found they'd unwittingly smuggled drugs - well, that would be be a motive for murder, right there."

"So, we're in agreement. Someone else was involved, probably at the stage of loading and unloading the instruments for a tour," Malachy brightened up. "Now, that's where Interpol should be concentrating. That outfit Elsa was conductor for, when she was with Friedrich, when they traveled together? Someone must have been employed there, doing the logistics, organizing tours."

"I'll get Elsa to ring you, she can talk you through exactly how they would do it and who would have the best access." "Thanks, Teresa. Although, I feel sure there was someone else, someone in charge, with an operation of that scale."

"Ah, yes. A brain, behind the brawn. And not Friedrich, who appears to have been easily led and unscrupulous but hardly a mastermind." Teresa smiled suddenly. "I think we're inching our way towards a solution, Detective Flynn. Slowly, but surely."

Chapter 15

After her chat with Arnoldo, Clara had joined Mai in the auditorium, enjoying the music as the orchestra tackled the programme for their big debut concert. The teen had looked happy to see her, and surprised the older woman by sitting beside her, one arm through hers as they let the melodies carry them away. Clara was a chatty woman by nature - some used the word "garrulous" - but she knew when to shut up. She asked Mai nothing but was happy to note that her shoulders relaxed and her face looked less drawn and pinched as they enjoyed the experience.

"It was like a private concert," Mai gushed at the end, her eyes shining.

Lisa waved to them from the stage, but Elsa called her to one side before she could join them.

"Come on," Clara said. "We should get you to the restaurant, your parents will think you're in detention at this rate. It's almost five o'clock."

"They'll assume I'm with Mrs. O'Brien," Mai assured her. "And I'll tell them that Lisa brought me into the rehearsal, they won't mind. It's cultural, isn't it?"

"Educational," Clara nodded. "Still, I've to fill Teresa in on a lot. Let's make tracks."

Mrs. Khan had no issue with Mai being a bit late but put her to work immediately.

"We're short staffed," she pushed a dishcloth into her daughters hands. "Just give me an hour now and you can go do your homework then."

"Sure. But, Mam, I'm meeting Mrs. O'Brien at seven in fancies, okay? It won't take long, and I don't have much homework tonight."

Clara left them to it, crossing the road to the music shop where an anxious Teresa was alone.

"Michael hasn't turned up." The music shop owner shook her head in exasperation. "I could wring his neck, the silly boy. He's making a bad situation worse. I got a text from him earlier to say he's okay and not to be worrying, and then nothing since."

"He's fine," Clara said firmly. "He's got a bruised ego and is probably thoroughly ashamed of himself. What a palaver…I didn't think he had it in him, to be honest."

"What, thumping Arnoldo? Hmm. Obviously, I don't approve," Teresa replied, in a tone that suggested she did in fact, very much approve of someone giving Arnoldo Messini a good box. "But it's the way he's treating Lisa that has me fuming."

"Like something from the last century, I know. But he has to work through it himself, Teresa. And we have more pressing concerns."

Once Teresa had locked up her shop, giving a final fond glance at the rows of instruments hanging in glass cabinets, the two women retreated to Fancies. Teresa listened raptly to Clara's unusually succinct recital of her day, while they waited in Fancies for the rest of the O'Brien's Irregulars to arrive.

"How very interesting," Teresa leaned back and stared into space, her mind working away. "How very, very interesting."

"Did I do well?" Clara clapped her hands in delight. "Oh, Peadair will be annoyed. He was full sure I was wasting my time hanging around the orchestra."

"You did very well," Teresa assured her. "I'll make sure Peadair knows. And your chat with Fintan too, very enlightening."

"Was it?" Clara sounded doubtful. "He really didn't reveal anything. Except, maybe, that he has a humongous crush on Elsa." She chuckled and added, "He went as red as a fire engine when I said she was a good catch."

"I can only imagine. Yes, Fintan has been an admirer since their college days."

"Poor man."

"Oh, I don't know." Teresa smiled. "Stranger things have happened. But it's your suggestion that someone other than Friedrich could have been the target that set me thinking."

Clara frowned. "I don't follow? I only said that to get a rise out of him."

"I know. Leave it with me, Clara. It's far from clear yet, but - you know how you have all the different sections of a piece of music? How each separate piece sounds like a weird variation on a melody? It never sounds right, until you put it all together, and then suddenly - perfection. Right now, I've got snatches of melody, variations on a theme and even bits that don't seem like they fit in at all."

"But it'll all come together in the end?"

"It will. It's nearly complete. I just need a little bit more information."

At seven on the dot, Catherine and Eamonn arrived, followed by Peadair. Setanta ushered Mai in, and to Teresa's surprise, Lisa was hot on their heels. She was still pale and her eyes were a little puffy, but she turned a brave face to the group. Teresa admired her young friend; it was easy to mistake her gentle manner for weakness or apathy, but when needed, she could show the steel beneath. The violinist sat beside Mai, who whispered something to her. Lisa grinned and squeezed the girl's hand.

Teresa made a mental note to ask what was going on with Mai, as soon as she could get Lisa alone. She let Clara have her moment, telling the story of her foray into the concert hall with a lot more embellishment and drama than her report to Teresa. It was met with gratifying acclaim, even Peadair generously admitting that she had "played a blinder," much to his wife's delight.

Catherine cleared her throat, somewhat self consciously. "I have a bit to report too. Nothing as exciting as Clara's, I'm afraid but I reached out to a friend who works in Munich. She's in the legal department of a multinational there, but she knows a lot of the local legal community. She's been asking around for me. Friedrich's murder made headlines over there, you know, as he was a minor celebrity. Lots of chatter about the divorce from Elsa, his convictions, his reputation. She came across a lawyer who said his firm dealt with Friedrich just after the divorce, and then again, before his last conviction. So twice, in a relatively short period, a few months apart. Here's the interesting bit - his fees were paid by a company called *"Musikalische Touren International GmbH"* - International Musical Tours, ltd."

"Who are they, when they're at home?" demanded Peadair.

"No one knows. I thought perhaps Eamonn could find out?" The solicitor turned to their resident computer expert. "Do you think you can trace them?"

"No bother," Eamonn was delighted. "Give me a day, I'll have their names, addresses and what they eat for breakfast."

"Excellent," Teresa said. "Yes, indeed. I think that will tell us a lot, Eamonn. Get on it as soon as you can."

"I will," he promised, "but I've a wee bit of intel of my own to share. I have been tracing Friedrich's movements as much as possible, going back a bit further than the Gardaí have - no offense to them. He's obviously been out of the way, in prison, for a good chunk over the last few years. But when he was out, he moved around a lot. I don't mean from house to house, or even job to job. I mean, he traveled out of Germany, and across Europe. And when he was home, he lived quite the high life. I mean, this is a man who couldn't hold down a job. He drank, he got into street brawls, in and out of prison - but he rented an apartment for over three thousand euros a month, dined out, threw parties. Hardly the pathetic existence we were led to believe."

"How could he afford it?" Catherine asked what they were all wondering.

"Well, if he was still involved in drugs," Peadair suggested, "maybe he was doing "errands" for his drug bosses, and they were either paying him or bailing him out?"

"Whoever is behind that company, is behind the drugs." Mai sat forward, almost squirming in excitement. "It has to be."

"We can't jump to conclusions," Teresa warned, "But it seems reasonable to say it's connected."

"But -" Catherine hesitated, then ploughed on. "I hate to be a killjoy, but even if we know who the drug dealer was, does that prove who killed him? Why kill him, especially in public, at a table full of people? It doesn't make much sense."

"Don't drug cartels kill people publicly to make a point? To scare their other donkeys?" Clara pointed out.

"Mules, Clara, not donkeys. And yes, they do but they usually claim responsibility. And it's not generally in a posh restaurant with a stolen steak knife."

"Oh. I suppose you're right, Peadair. Well then, why would they kill him?"

Teresa smiled. "Why kill him there, why kill him at all? Why, indeed."

She refused to elaborate. The meeting broke up, Eamonn anxious to get home to both his family and his private computer on which he kept all kinds of very intriguing software. Only Mai and Lisa held back, waiting for the others to disperse, and they didn't press Teresa about her theories. Instead, with encouragement from Lisa, Mai told Teresa about school, about Niamh Finnegan and about the fall-out from the evening at Chez Maurice.

"You need to talk to your parents," Teresa was gentle but firm. "I'm not saying you should switch schools, it sounds as if you have some good friends there despite everything. But you can't let Niamh continue to bully you like this and to tackle it, you need your parents."

"I feel awful, Mrs. O'Brien. You've no idea what it means to them to send me there. They work all hours just to afford it. It's - it's like a slap in the face to them, if they find out I'm not doing well there."

"But you are doing well there," Lisa protested. "Tell her, Teresa. This isn't her fault. It's that little wagon who isn't "doing well." She's the one who should be thoroughly ashamed of herself."

"She's right, Mai. You've built this up so much, you can't

think straight. You having a problem in school isn't some sort of failure. Even getting into trouble wouldn't be the end of the world. You're young, you're allowed to make mistakes. But you did not cause this problem. Niamh did. Some things we can handle on our own and some we need help with - a virulent little germ like Niamh, you need help with. And your parents are the ones to do it."

Mai didn't seem fully convinced but agreed to think about it. Teresa turned her attention to Lisa then, curious to know what, if anything, Elsa had said to her about Arnoldo.

"I hope she took the time to talk to you about it," Teresa said.

"She did," Lisa assured her, "She was really sweet. Said that just because she was close to Arnoldo, it wouldn't stop her from dealing with him as soon as he shows his face. It was a relief, if I'm honest. Part of me wondered if she'd take his side, but she's a real girl's girl, underneath."

"I'm very glad to hear it," Teresa said warmly. "And I wouldn't like to be in Arnoldo's shoes when she does catch up with him, the wee gobdaw. Clara seems to have spooked him, though. I wonder where he is and what he's up to?"

Lisa shrugged. "I couldn't care less, Teresa. He's poison and I hope he goes home to Italy."

"Do you? I can't agree, I'm afraid. I very much hope he sticks around a while longer." Teresa had a steely glint in her eye. "I would like a word with him myself."

"Not on my account," Lisa tossed her head. "If I need to deal with him, I will, for the sake of the Hibernian. Other than that, he's absolutely dead to me."

Lisa took her leave, with a hug from Mai. The teenager allowed Teresa to walk her across to the Noodle Palace. She stood outside for a moment, watching her parents as they worked behind the counter, a smile and a kind word for each customer as they dished out steaming ladles of hot, tasty food.

"Okay," she said finally, turning to Teresa. "I'll talk to them. About Niamh and all that."

Teresa hugged her tightly. "That's my girl. You'll be pleasantly surprised, I know you will."

***

Expecting to come home to an empty flat and another evening waiting by the phone, Lisa was both surprised and overjoyed to find her friend Ollessa sitting in her car, waiting for her to arrive.

"I was worried," Ollessa confessed, producing a casserole dish, wrapped in a plastic bag. "I made extra and thought you might enjoy it."

She brushed off Lisa's thanks, keeping up a steady flow of small talk until they were both inside, seated at the tiny kitchen table, Lisa tucking into a large bowl of beef stew.

"That was the longest day in the history of days," Lisa told Ollessa as she finished eating, "I was in a café twice today and didn't manage to eat either time. I didn't even know I was hungry until I smelled your cooking."

"I won't ask if you've heard from Michael," Ollessa said. "And I have no advice to give -except to say, if he's meant to be the one for you it will all work out. If not, then let him go and make space in your life for the right person. I want you to watch silly TV tonight, read a book, watch Insta-pic reels, whatever it takes to relax. Then go to bed and sleep, properly. Tomorrow will take care of everything else."

From almost anyone else, that advice would have irritated Lisa. Ollessa had a quietly confident authority, a very gentle but unshakable belief that things would play out exactly as they were meant to, and it worked its magic on Lisa. Once her friend had left, she checked her phone one last time for messages, then powered it off. She turned on the TV, choosing a gentle programme where dedicated crafts enthusiasts learned new skills at a masterclass, this week's offering being loom weaving. After that, a classic episode of Dad's Army was shown, followed by an interesting look at life in a remote Hebridean Island community. Her eyes felt heavy, yawn followed yawn, and a good night's sleep beckoned.

As she drifted off, Lisa wondered if perhaps Michael had finally contacted her, but she refused to turn on the phone. It could, as Ollessa had said, wait for tomorrow.

Chapter 16

Teresa started the day in her garden, with a cup of coffee, enjoying the mild sunshine. There were still enough flowers and colour to make the place cheerful, but the unmistakable tinge of Autumnal colours had cast a faint blush across the trees and there was an earthy smell that reminded her of playing fields, and long walks through forests as leaves fell. As ever, Cathal wasn't far from her mind and she talked to him in her head as she mused over the events of the past two weeks. The sudden return of Elsa Von Streng, the death of Friedrich Mann, the way Arnoldo Messini had exploded all her hopes and plans for Michael and Lisa. So much had happened, in such a short time.

"What a mess, Cathal," she thought. "You'd have loved to see Emer - Elsa, I should say - again. She came home too late for that. But she has a chance to mend things with her brother, if she would only stop being so stubborn. And if that young pup Dempsey doesn't haul her off to prison for murdering her ex-husband!"

She hoped Elsa would see the sense in cooperating with the Gardaí, and by extension, Interpol. It was true she had no proof per se, other than Arnoldo's story of finding drugs in the orchestra's cases, but it was up to the authorities to find proof. If they knew what to look for, they had some chance of catching the drug ring in the act.

"And now there's Lisa and young Michael," she told her late husband. "Ah, I could spit I'm so angry with that young gossoon. Poor Lisa."

And poor Michael too, she thought, sure he loves that girl to distraction. It must have been a desperate shock to see her in the arms of another man. "It's him running off that I'm raging about, Cathal. He should be here, dealing with it, like an adult."

It's none of your business, she could almost hear Cathal pointing out. Let the young folk work it out for themselves. He was always inclined to scold her if he thought she was interfering too much. Their own kids had many a broken heart and drama between them over the years.
"I'm not interfering," she said aloud. "I'm just - interested."

She turned her thoughts towards the biggest issue, the untimely end of Friedrich Mann. What an unpleasant human he had been. Willing to do anything for money or to spite Elsa. Money laundering, drug smuggling, stalking - Elsa had been lucky to make it out alive.

And with that thought, she made up her mind. She knew what the solution was, it was proving it that would be the problem.

* * *

Rather than open the music shop, Teresa sat in her little office and made a phone call to Detective Flynn. He sounded startled by her request but rallied well.

"You want me to gather them all together and bring them to Chez Maurice? For a sort of reconstruction?"

"Yes. Is that a problem?" Teresa waited, knowing it would take the cautious detective a while to weigh up the situation.

"How certain are you?" he asked finally.

"Very."

"Grand so. I'll text you as soon as it's arranged. It won't be before this afternoon, mind you."

"This afternoon is perfect." Teresa had some organizing to do on her own end. She ended the call, feeling more energized now that there was a plan in motion. Everything would hinge on what Eamonn had found in his late-night internet trawling. She had already left a message asking him to ring, but couldn't resist sending another, pointing out the time pressure. She had barely pressed send, when the sound of keys in the lock of the shop door brought her to her feet.

Michael Clancy had finally returned.

Teresa bit her lip, willing herself not to explode in recriminations as she waited for him to round the counter and make his way through the swinging doors into the back. The sight of him drove the words out of her head, however. She had expected either a picture of pale faced misery, or a surly angry head on him. What she most certainly had not expected was to see him dressed head to toe in a stylish three-piece suit of soft green tweed shot through with shades of purple and mauve, like the heather on the Dublin mountains in Spring. Trousers, waistcoat and jacket were paired with a crisp linen shirt and polished brown brogues. His hair had been trimmed and there was a suspicious aroma of expensive aftershave lingering around his shiny face.

In all the years she had known Michael, and even worked alongside him day by day, she had never dreamed he could scrub up so well. If anyone had asked, she would have said he was a good-looking enough chap, and meant it. But it was astounding what an ounce of effort had produced.

"What the absolute -" Teresa exclaimed, hands on hips. "We've been half-demented worrying about you, and you wander in here looking like - like a male supermodel. Like some hipster in a commercial. I've a good mind to -"

She got no further because the young man hugged her so tightly, she had to catch her breath.

"I'm so sorry, Teresa, I never meant to worry you. I just had a lot of thinking to do."

"Hmm." Teresa sat down and gave him another appraising look. "And you couldn't text your poor girlfriend while you were doing all this thinking, no? Too busy getting your hair cut and trying on suits?"

She looked at him anxiously, wondering how he would respond. His face reddened, and he winced slightly, but he looked her in the eye as he responded.

"I was an absolute fool, Teresa. From beginning to end."

"Well, I'm glad to hear you say it," Teresa retorted. "Imagine thinking Lisa would cheat on you with that eejit?"

"Not just that." Michael squared his shoulders. "Far more than just that. You warned me and I wouldn't listen to you. You said I was taking her for granted, that I was complacent, and it was true. Then when Arnoldo turned up, and she was so excited to be working with him, I was jealous. I wouldn't admit it, oh no! But yeah, I was green about it. Then I bought her flowers and perfume, and thought I was a great fella. Wasn't she lucky to have me? Walking in on them, it was like my worst nightmare come to life. Oh, I knew, almost as soon as I punched that little weasel, I knew Lisa hadn't encouraged him. She was struggling to get away from him, if anything."

"So why on earth did you storm off? Why did you ignore her? She's heartbroken over you."

"Is she?" Michael looked up, a spark of hope in his eyes. "Is she really?"

"Michael," Teresa said slowly, "What exactly do you think is happening here? Because as far as everyone else can tell, you decided Lisa was to blame, left the poor girl there crying, and then ignored her."

"What? No! Of course it wasn't her fault. I mean, yes I did storm off but I was angry at myself and Arnoldo. Ollessa was there comforting Lisa. I felt like a heel. I thought about how stupid I had been - romantic dinners in Lannigans, for goodness sake! - and I thought she would surely dump me. I was a useless boyfriend."

"You were," Teresa agreed, "and you're a first-class twit, to boot. She thinks you're raging with her and have dumped her. You absolute gobdaw."

"Oh." It was Michael's turn to sit down. He looked lost in thought, then burst out with, "But if she's upset, then that means she still cares? Right? It's not too late?"

"I don't know," Teresa said. "You need to talk to her, face to face and apologise."

Michael leapt to his feet, hugged Teresa again, saying, "Yes. Right now. I'm sorry to run off again, but I have to see her."

"Wait! None of this explains why you're done up like a dog's dinner? If you were so distraught, where did you find time to do a makeover?"

Michael looked at her as if she had two heads.

"I couldn't propose without making an effort, Teresa. Sure, isn't that the whole point? I need to show her I've woken up, I can offer her more than pub dinners and varnish-stained fingers."

He rushed out of the shop, banging the old door behind him leaving Teresa, for once, completely lost for words.

* * *

On any other day, Michael's declaration would have been the main focus of interest. Today it was rapidly overtaken by more pressing matters, and Teresa pushed it to the back of her mind. She had a dangerous killer to unmask. Michael would have to salvage his relationship with Lisa by himself. She sent up a devout prayer to heaven that he wouldn't blurt out a proposal before repairing the damage he had done to his relationship. After that, he was on his own.

Eamonn didn't text, instead presenting himself at the shop with a smug grin and waving several sheets of closely printed paper at her.

"*Musikalische Touren International GmbH,*" He mangled the pronunciation cheerfully. "The company that paid for Friedrich's lifestyle is also the logistic company behind the Munich orchestra's tours. Responsible for transport of instruments, among other things. It's owned by a shell company, that's owned by another shell company. And behind that is a very hard-to-trace company, that has only a handful of directors. One name in particular, one name you'll recognise."

Teresa read the pages rapidly, her face relaxing into a broad smile. "Oh. Well done, Eamonn, very well done indeed. And in the nick of time. We have an appointment with Detective Flynn in Chez Maurice, if you fancy coming along."

"Try and stop me," Eamonn said. "And what about the others? You can't exclude them, Clara would never forgive you."

"All in hand. They'll be there, as will Elsa, Lisa, and Fintan. I've asked Mai to come too, and Mrs Khan is coming with her. No, don't bother me with questions, there's a good lad. I still need to work a few things out. Just walk with me."

Eamonn seemed more than willing to stroll quietly beside the old lady as they made their way through Drury street, into Exchequer Street, and down Wicklow Street, past the boutiques and small eateries that gave Dublin 2 such a unique feel. Like Setanta, when they stopped outside Chez Maurice, the facade struck them as a bit gaudy in broad daylight.

"It stands out, doesn't it?" Eamonn remarked, "I thought it would be…"

"More elegant? Chez Maurice is not your typical restaurant," Teresa laughed. She tried the door, which was open, and they stepped inside.

"Oh." Eamonn sounded disappointed. "From all the hype, I expected something a bit nicer than this."

"I beg your pardon?" Chef Maurice's daughter Chrissie appeared out of nowhere, her face like thunder. Eamonn groaned and tried to backpedal.

"Um, I just meant we - it's not what I expected. It's very nice, honest, just I thought it would be more, um, more sort of -"

Teresa rolled her eyes. "It's weird to see it in daylight. That's all he meant. You're Chrissie, yes? Maurice's daughter?"

An almost comical look of surprise crossed the young woman's face. "Yeah. You're with them, I suppose?"

She jerked her shoulder behind her, towards a small group standing at the back of the dining area, including the Garda detectives, Lisa and Elsa, and Fintan McLaughlin, plus Mai, her mother and the rest of the Super Ukers. A sulky-looking Arnoldo Messini stood rather pointedly separate from the group. Teresa looked for Michael Clancy but the young luthier was absent, as far as she could see.

"Mrs. O'Brien?" Chrissie asked.

"That's me. Is your dad here?"

"Yeah. But he's busy."

"Not too busy for this. Run and get him, there's a good girl. Tell him he's needed out here."

There was an unmistakable note of steel in Teresa's voice and Chrissie obeyed without arguing, although her face retained its usual scowl. Detective Flynn detached himself from the others, his face troubled.

"It took some persuading to get the go-ahead on this," he admitted. "I don't want to add to the pressure but we need a result."

"I'll do my best," Teresa assured him. "Assuming you're all set up?"

"Ready when you are."

"Great. Make sure everyone stays back - there's no telling what might happen. Clara, if you and Peadair could go upstairs, to the bar area, stand at the balcony where we can see you. Elsa, Lisa, Fintan and Arnoldo, please take your seats."

The four last named stared at Teresa.

"Sit, at the same table as that night?" Elsa asked.

"Yes. Please."

None of the four looked overjoyed at the idea, but they obeyed. Lisa gave Elsa a reassuring squeeze as they took their places, exactly as they had on the night of the murder. Teresa had a momentary pang of guilt at making them re-live the event, but in the end, it was better to face a little unpleasantness now.

"Good, we're almost ready. Ah, Chef Maurice, thank you for joining us."

"I don't know why you need me here," Maurice's cultured drawl was back and he sounded cross. "It is an imposition. I am a busy man…"

"Oh, give it up," Elsa snapped at him. "Morris, everyone here knows we grew up together."

Maurice shrugged but reverted to his real Dublin accent. "Sorry, love. Force of habit. Well, I'm here, missus, but why?"

"Because the story of that night starts with you, in a way. Elsa's decision to bring her guests here was fairly last minute. Usually it takes months, if not longer, to get a reservation. Mai's parents booked their table six months ago, when Mai first started talking about how popular it was."

Mrs. Khan nodded. "And even then we were lucky, there was a cancellation and we got the right evening."

"We're dead popular," Maurice agreed, looking very pleased with himself. "But Elsa's an old pal. I told my Chrissie, stick another table in and make it work."

"How does the bar area work? Can anyone walk in off the street and go upstairs?"

"No way," Chrissie interjected. "I have security on the stairs. Either you have a reservation for dinner and want a drink at the bar first, or you're on the list."

"Need I even ask, was Friedrich Mann on the list?"

"Good god, no. That man? Sorry, I know he's dead and all, but he was a drunk. And about twenty years too old."

Teresa nodded, satisfied. "Well, then. How did he get in?"

Silence greeted her question. Setanta coughed, looking embarrassed. All eyes turned towards the young student.

"Um. My guess is, through the back door and past the kitchen.

There are people in and out all the time, and if you recall, he was dressed in a black shirt and trousers. He would have looked like wait staff."

"Well done," Teresa clapped her hands, and Setanta grinned happily. "But once he was in, what did he do then?"

"Um, I don't know."

"He went upstairs to the bar. Remember? The girl in the newspaper article, who said she was talking to him at the bar shortly before he got stabbed? We all assumed she was just another poster pushing herself into the limelight but then Mai showed me Insta-pic reels of the night. Setanta also mentioned social media. People recorded the row ,obviously but I went looking for reels that were posted just beforehand. There in the background, at the bar, was a young girl and a man of Friedrich's build. You could only see the back of his head, and it didn't register with me, until I began to work out his movements that night."

Teresa pointed up at the bar area, where Clara and Peadair hung over the balcony rail, looking down at the scene below. "It was by far the best place to wait. See, not only did Friedrich know that Elsa would be here, he knew *when* to expect her. He arrived earlier than her. You can see from the timestamp on the videos taken, and I am sure by now Detective Flynn has tracked down the young lady and confirmed all this?"

"We have." Malachy nodded. "She says Friedrich was upstairs for at least half an hour before she began talking to him. She first noticed him standing where Clara and Peadair are, looking down at the dining area. He avoided the bar itself, which is why the staff didn't remember him. At least, that's the version we'll go with, Chef. Not that your staff were told not to tell us if they had seen him, eh?"

Chrissie looked at the ground, and her father shrugged.

Malachy continued, "The need for a drink must have won out though, because he pushed through the crowd, picked up a pint this young one had ordered for her boyfriend and tried to walk away with it The girl told him off and you can imagine his response. There were a few heated words exchanged, then he went back to his post at the railing. We have witness statements as well as camera footage."

"We all assumed he followed Elsa here, but he was up there half an hour before Elsa arrived, at least." Teresa said pointedly. "And even then, he didn't confront her immediately."

"No, we were on our main course before he came over," Elsa said. "Was he - was he watching us all that time?"

"It seems likely." Teresa replied. "Maurice, are the CCTV cameras in here?"

"Of course. I gave the footage to the Gardaí, immediately." Maurice said defensively.

"Do any of them cover the balcony up there?"

"Oh. Well, no, not directly. More the bar itself, and of course the dining area, and the cash register."

"And when you checked it, Detective Flynn, did you see the victim approach the table?"

"We saw a lot of things," Malachy replied grimly. "We saw Ms. Von Streng's party arrive, we saw who fetched the plates and cutlery from that table back there. We saw the food arrive, and we saw Friedrich Mann approach."

Teresa turned and fixed a beady eye on the party of four, seated around the ill-fated table.

"So many little things, little individual notes. Each one seemed so inconsequential. But put together, in the right order - ah, that's a different tune. It started long before that night.

Elsa, it began for you when you fell in love with that dreadful man. He was a terrible blight on your life, wasn't he? Liar, cheat, violent drunk, money launderer and criminal and finally, just when you thought you were free of him, he turns out to be a drug smuggler. He used you, and the career you love - that you sacrificed everything for - and you couldn't get rid of him."

She looked at Lisa and smiled. "At least, you had nothing much to do with him. It was unlucky that you overheard him bullying Elsa, but that was the extent of your involvement. Be grateful, my dear."

"I am," Lisa muttered, fervently.

"Fintan was unlucky too, weren't you? After years of silent, distant adoration, you finally had Elsa back in Ireland, and better still, in your orchestra. Everyone thought you were fretting over her changes to the repertoire, but it was far more personal than that. You were nervous about seeing her again. I don't think you had any hopes of a relationship with her - you just wanted to be near her, maybe rekindle your friendship - but there's no question that you love her. And then that man turns up, the one who almost ruined her, who made her life hell. Here, in your concert hall, in your city." Teresa frowned down at the musical director, who was now red-faced and sweating. "You were furious, weren't you?"

To his credit, despite his obvious embarrassment, Fintan looked her in the eye and answered calmly.

"Yes. I hated him. Elsa was worth ten of him, and he didn't appreciate her. Instead of being proud of her talent, he tried to destroy her. I've heard a lot over the years, the music world is very small. I knew - I *know* - you'd never look at me, Elsa, not like that. But it didn't stop me wanting the best for you."

"You were very quick to tackle him," Teresa prodded, "when he put his hands on Elsa that night."

"I was half expecting him to do something like it, " Fintan replied. "Ever since he showed up at the Hall. It would be just like him, try to show her up in public. The minute I set eyes on him that night, I was ready."

"Fintan." Elsa sounded shocked. "I had no idea. I didn't realise you had recognised me, let alone…"

"It's all right, Elsa. I can't help how I feel, but it's not your problem. I - I care about you deeply. I always have. It doesn't matter that it's not reciprocated. I would do anything for you."

"Even kill her ex-husband?" Teresa asked.

Fintan started, his face going through a rapid change from red to white and back again.

"What? No!" He looked around wildly. "I didn't! You have to believe me."

"Oh, it's okay." Teresa waved her hand at him. "I don't really think that. I couldn't resist. No, no. It wasn't you. Of course not. Only one person had murder on their mind that night, and it wasn't poor Fintan here. By the way, Fintan, stop telling Elsa she couldn't have feelings for you. She might start believing you. No woman remembers a man as fondly as she remembers you, because he was a good mate. You two need to talk after all this."

She turned to the last person at the table, and said, "It was Arnoldo of course. But killing Friedrich was an accident."

Chapter 17

Half of those listening gasped and repeated, "Arnoldo killed him!" and the other half gasped and said, "An accident? how?"

Detective Dempsey expressed his feelings in a loud groan and even Malachy was moved to ask, "Are you quite sure?"

Teresa ignored them, her eyes never leaving Arnoldo's face.

"You didn't intend to kill Friedrich. The moment I realised that, everything began to make a lot more sense. Maybe you'd have had to get rid of him anyway later on, but that night, you had quite another outcome in mind." She sighed. "You and Friedrich were the best of pals, once. When he was caught money-laundering, you came to Elsa's aid. Helped her pick up the pieces, helped her get away from him. Why was that, Arnoldo? Not because you were helping a lady in need. We all saw your true colours recently - you're no gentleman! No. Because Elsa was still in a position to be of use to you. Have you worked it out yet, Elsa?"

"No," Elsa admitted, "I mean, what could I do for Arnoldo? He didn't gain anything much from choosing me over Friedrich."

"Of course he did. He gained access to your orchestra." Teresa waited then sighed as no one seemed to be following. "Ah come on, lads. Arnoldo is the drug smuggler. The brains behind it. He recruited Friedrich to launder drug money and then he used him to do the dirty work. Put the drugs in the cases, retrieve them before the owners claimed their instrument. That's why initially, even after Friedrich was caught with the money in his account, he played up their old friendship and not wanting to abandon his old pal. But when that Double Bass player in Munich stumbled across the drugs in his case, Arnoldo had to work fast. He broke the news to Elsa, he destroyed the evidence, he persuaded the Bass player to remain silent. In public he cut off Friedrich, took Elsa's side and waited for the dust to settle."

"But it didn't settle," Elsa said slowly. "I wouldn't let it. I hounded Friedrich, to keep him from getting another job travelling with an orchestra."

"Yes. You didn't want to risk him doing it to another innocent player, even if you couldn't prove anything. So Friedrich ceased to be of use to Arnoldo, and grew increasingly erratic. Arnoldo needed to get rid of him, but then there was still the problem of Elsa. If anything happened to her ex-husband, but the drug smuggling continued and ever came to light, she would of course come forward with everything she knew. And if Friedrich was dead, it would stand to reason someone else was behind the scheme and it would bring the spotlight far too close to Signor Messini. You worked in the shadows for so long, so successfully, you weren't going to risk that."

Malachy moved closer to the table and Dempsey mirrored his actions. Everyone else sat or stood in rapt attention on the drama playing out in front of them.

"Lisa, take Elsa over to the bar," Malachy said quietly. Arnoldo looked at him sharply and made a movement as if to stand up. The detective placed one hand firmly on his shoulder and pinned him in place. "Ladies, away now with ye."

Fintan McLaughlin stood too, but stayed at the table, looking determined. Malachy didn't ask him to move, perhaps remembering his martial arts skills.

Teresa sat down in Elsa's empty seat, looking as composed as if it was an afternoon tea party. She continued, "There you were, Arnoldo, with two problems. You came up with a very clever, very nasty, plan. You paid Friedrich handsomely to come to Ireland. You put him up in a nice hotel, kept him sweet with plenty of spending money, and told him to harass Elsa. I bet he didn't need much persuading. He'd have done it for free. As far as he knew, he was supposed to cause a scandal in public, embarrass his ex-wife."

Teresa looked at Elsa. "But being who he was, he just couldn't stick to the plan. He showed himself too early. It must have been a bad shock, when you heard from Clara that he'd been roaming all over the place, talking to God knows whom. He was drunk too and rambling and indiscreet. It was quite a risk using him, you know. But I suppose, if everything had gone according to plan, it would have all added to a very convincing picture. You staged it beautifully, I'll give you that. He was to roar and shout at Elsa and reveal something he thought would embarrass her. A little secret really, in the scheme of things. We all know it now but it would have been easy to convince that bully that she'd be mortified."

"This is nonsense. nonsense. I had no reason to kill Friedrich, and why would I humiliate Elsa? I am no drug dealer…" Arnoldo began to shout, but a not so gentle squeeze from Malachy silenced him.

"Quiet now, there's a good chap. You'll get your chance. Go

on there, Mrs. O'Brien."

"it's pointless to deny it, Arnoldo. We know that you funded Friedrich's trip through that company you set up - Eamonn here has all the details. You own it. And the same company had special flight cases made for instruments and donated them to Elsa's last orchestra. I'll bet when the Munich police examine them, they'll have special compartments built in. You thought you had covered your tracks but there's a paper trail."

"There's always a trail, if you where to look," Eamonn whispered loudly, elbowing Catherine in the ribs. "Between us, we got him."

"Yes, thank you Eamonn. And Catherine. But if I can continue? Arnoldo here can deny it all he wants but he was the mastermind. Which brings us back to that night, here in Chez Maurice. Friedrich knows to wait until the middle of the meal to ensure the place is packed, full of witnesses. Maximum dramatic effect. He's supposed to confront her but his violent temperament gets the better of him. You were hoping for that, weren't you Arnoldo? It was almost a certainty that he would lay hands on her, which is when you planned to stab Elsa."

A shocked silence fell over the group. Teresa waited serenely.

Finally, Fintan spoke. "Mrs. O'Brien, are you serious?"

"Oh yes. Elsa was always the intended victim. Everyone would see her ex-husband grab her, and shake her, then she would fall down, stabbed. No one would question that it was him. Arnoldo palmed the sharpest knife he could find at that ridiculous tableware station - you really have to ditch that, Maurice, it's very annoying and not at all safe. At the perfect moment, Arnoldo put his hand on Friedrich, as if to restrain him, but it was his right hand. You're left-handed, aren't you? It would have been natural to put out your dominant hand, but you couldn't because you had the knife hidden in your left hand. You went to strike…but Fintan intervened. He broke Friedrich's hold on Elsa at that very moment, pushing Elsa to one side, turning Friedrich slightly and instead of Elsa, you stabbed your accomplice."

It was Detective Dempsey who reacted first.

"Are you kidding us? He was trying to kill Elsa Von Streng and frame Friedrich?"

"Yes. Oh, he would no doubt have helped Friedrich get away from here, in the aftermath. I'm sure he had a plan worked out. He would have been the only person to know where Friedrich was hiding, and it would have been easy to get rid of him then. Maybe he already had some of his lowlife friends on standby to "hide" him, then make him disappear. Permanently."

Arnoldo slumped in his seat, head down, looking defeated.

"You are a *strega*. A Witch. Well then, you are so clever. Except - you cannot prove a thing. No one saw me stab anyone. I am not going to admit to it, am I? I am a respectable citizen of the EU and you cannot detain me without proof." He raised his head, his expression arrogant, and a smile playing about his lips. "It is all nonsense. So what if I own a company that arranges tours? And donates equipment? This is not a crime! I am sorry if someone interfered with those cases - very expensive, top-quality cases. But it has nothing to do with me. Friedrich's death - pah, nothing to do with me either." He smiled complacently and added, "Best of luck proving any of it."

Teresa tilted her head and smiled. "Ah. Proof. You really didn't listen did you? There's CCTV camera footage showing you taking the exact type of knife that was used in the murder. There's footage from the balcony up there of the row, it's in the hands of the Garda forensic team now. Lots and lots of footage, all those influencers filming the excitement below. Clara, Peadair, what can you see up there?"

"Everything," Clara called down.

"No matter how quick you were, they'll find it - the moment you plunged with the knife. And then there's the fact you bought Friedrich's ticket, paid for his hotel, loaded him with cash while he was here. Now we know you own those shadow companies, the Gardaí will find the transfers between you and the victim."

"We will," Malachy agreed. "We're fierce thorough. And Interpol are on the case too."

For the first time, Arnoldo looked shaken. He tried to regain some of his bravado, muttering in Italian and shrugging his shoulders. Teresa continued as if he hadn't interrupted.

"Detective Flynn also tracked down the Bass player who found the drugs in his case. He told us how you threatened and bullied him. He also confirmed that he found *you*, with Friedrich, rummaging through his case. Give it up, Arnoldo. It's only a matter of time. You can do yourself one last favour and cooperate. But whether you do or don't, it's over for you."

Arnoldo reacted so quickly, he caught both garda detectives off guard. Gone was the foppish exterior, and in its place, a dangerous animal quality, as he tensed his muscles and threw off the older man's hold on his shoulder. He sprang to his feet, overturning the table and launched himself at Teresa, before Dempsey could react. Teresa didn't flinch. As Arnoldo reached for her, Fintan McLaughlin threw himself at the tenor with a bellow. Teresa could see the shock on the Italian's face, as he realised that the rather round, mild mannered musical director had seized him in a headlock and was raining blows on his head. There was a pause while everyone enjoyed the spectacle, then the Gardaí took over and held Arnoldo down.

"Curse you, you interfering old…" Arnoldo spat. "You'll regret this. I'll make sure of it."

"Arnoldo," Elsa's voice cut through the chaos, icy and controlled. "I thought you were my friend." She walked up to him, as he struggled between the two detectives. "I believed you, trusted you. I can't believe you could do any of this. It's not true. You're not capable of it."

Arnoldo sneered. "You are a fool, and you always were. My god, I listened to you whining on and on about Friedrich, how he treated you, blah blah - if you had a backbone you'd have left him. Instead, you cried over him like a lost puppy. It made me sick. I wish I had stabbed you, instead of him. At least he was some use to me!"

Elsa stepped back, smiling her coldest smile. "Thank you for admitting it. I hope that's all you need, Detective Flynn?"

"That'll do nicely, thank you." Malachy gave Arnoldo's arm a firm twist. "Arnoldo Messini, you are under arrest for the murder of Friedrich Mann, and the attempted murder of Elsa Von Streng…"

The tenor did not go quietly and in the end, Dempsey threatened to gag him to stop the flow of curses in Italian and English. Chef Maurice disappeared into the kitchen only to reappear carrying a tray of sandwiches, cakes, and snacks. Taking her cue from her dad, Chrissie made tea and coffee and started to distribute them. Elsa accepted a chair gratefully, and managed to sip hot coffee, but she looked paper white and shaken. Teresa watched approvingly as Fintan, hero of the hour, fussed over the conductor, who accepted his ministrations graciously. When he turned away for a moment to fetch her some food, Elsa stared after him with a very intense expression. Yes, Teresa had high hopes there.

She had to accept a fair share of fussing herself, as Mai and the Super Ukers hovered anxiously. She probably should have felt scared when Arnoldo attacked but if she was honest with herself, the over-riding emotion had been relief, that he broke. It was almost as good as the admission of guilt that Elsa had wrung from him. Malachy and Dempsey had departed with their prisoner, but a text from the older detective reported that the forensics had indeed come through for them - they had pinpointed the moment Arnoldo had produced the knife. A couple of seconds, caught on an influencer's camera, and almost deleted by them later. She thanked heavens for their good luck.

Mai and her mother were almost beside themselves with worry about her, Teresa submitted to their fussing more for their sake than her own. Not for the first time, she realised that Mai got her kindness and manners from her parents, Mrs. Khan was such a sweet and motherly woman. When the teenager was finally satisfied that Teresa was fine, she wandered off to chat to the others, leaving Teresa with her mother.

"I must thank you," Mrs. Khan said quietly. "Mai had a big talk with us last night, about this Niamh brat and her bullying."

"Oh, thank heavens! I did hope she would."

"She said you and Lisa helped, we're so grateful. We rang the school this morning, told them she was taking the day off and that we wanted to discuss these issues with them tomorrow."

"Don't take any nonsense from them," Teresa pressed her friend. "They may try to pass it off as just two kids squabbling."

"They can try. But already we've had two or three parents

reach out to us, their girls went home and told them all about it. They said their kids are more than willing to back Mai up."

"Well, isn't that something?" Teresa was pleased to hear it. "The kids are better than we give them credit for - they really are."

"We want Mai to understand that you can't quit, she will face people like that again. But we have her back and if it comes to it, we will insist that Niamh is moved to another class. Believe me, when her father decides that his child needs something he will make sure it happens. They won't know what hit them."

Teresa made Mai's mother promise to fill her after the meeting with the school, then announced that she was ready to go home. Lisa immediately volunteered to walk her to her car, Teresa crossing her fingers for good news about Michael.

"He turned up at the hall earlier," Lisa told her. "My god, the state of him."

"I know. I saw him earlier. You can't say he didn't make an effort."

"He - I mean he looked very well, but I nearly laughed in his face. He looked like he was going for a photo shoot, for some posh hipster magazine."

"And I take it he apologised?"

"He did. I told him I needed time to think about it."

"Oh." Teresa was half-proud of Lisa for not rolling over and accepting Michael's behaviour. But also, half-disappointed because she had hoped so much that they would reconcile. At least it seemed Michael hadn't blurted out some half-baked proposal.

"Ah, don't look like that. Of course I'm going to forgive him! But I don't want him to think it was that easy. I realise now, he took me for granted and I let him. Never again."

"Well, tell me. What did he say?"

Lisa's cheeks went rosy pink and she couldn't hide her smiles. "He said I was his whole world, that he's ashamed of himself for how he acted but most of all for not making more of an effort. He said - well, he said lots of nice things."

"Did you give him any hope?"

"A bit. I'll ring him tomorrow, let him take me out for dinner."

"Oh, dear Lord, not to blooming Lanigan's, I hope!"

"If it's Lannigans, I'll drop a plate of beer battered fish and chips on his head." Lisa hugged the old lady, and added, "But I don't think he'll make that mistake again!"

Epilogue

The Hibernian orchestra filed off the stage of the Concert Hall, to thunderous applause. This was their second encore, and the audience was still enthusiastically calling for more. The new repertoire had appealed to a wider audience than they had enjoyed in years, from the old regulars to young people who were fans of the *Men of Action* comics, dying to hear the new film's theme music in full orchestral glory. Lisa had performed her two solo pieces, the part that Arnoldo would have played going to a newcomer called Kevin O'Reilly, a local lad on the cusp of a glittering career. In Lisa's opinion, he brought an authenticity of emotion to the role that had been missing despite Arnoldo's undeniable talent, and his good-natured attitude as he stepped in at the last minute had endeared him to everyone.

Now, backstage, the players exchanged congratulations, Lisa and Ollessa hugging each other and even Elsa permitting herself a rare display of approval.

"Very well done," she said. "I think that is a decent start."

Elsa's brother and parents were in the front rows of the concert. Her near-miss at the hands of Arnoldo Messini had prompted her to visit them and explain everything. To her amazement, her brother had produced a battered scrapbook, stuffed to overflowing with cuttings from newspapers and magazines, photos downloaded from the web and any scrap of information the family could collect about Elsa Von Streng over the years.

"We knew," her mother said gently, "But we didn't want to ruin anything for you. David was afraid his past would be brought up, and your uncles too, and then it might make problems for you. We're so very proud of you, Emer - Sorry, Elsa!"

Elsa had brought Fintan to visit them, Teresa knew, and it seemed as if the conductor's past, present and future were finally coming together, harmoniously. And Elsa had given Ollessa's husband an exclusive interview, and *Classical Ireland Monthly's* October Issue would feature the headline "Elsa Von Streng, Liberties Girl Made Good!" She had singled out the late, great Cathal O'Brien as a major influence on her life and career.

Teresa applauded the orchestra now, until her hands hurt but even she couldn't match Michael's enthusiasm. Since Lisa had taken him back, the young luthier had been a changed man. He had made every effort to show her how much he cared, and while they had settled back into a comfortable routine, date nights meant a proper restaurant, or a play or a concert, whatever he thought Lisa might enjoy. And Teresa was privy to a little secret, a glittering little secret that was nestled safely in a small velvet box stamped with the name of Dublin's most famous jewellers. Michael wanted to wait until Lisa's solo performance, rather than distract her from her work, but tonight was the night - and Teresa couldn't wait.

Chef Maurice had insisted that the post-concert celebrations be held in his restaurant, promising that Chrissie and the rest of the staff would actually set the tables and bring the food. That was the only way they could persuade Mrs. Khan to accept the invitation. Maurice also made sure that the newspapers came to see the celebrity guests arrive, and using the opportunity to pose for pictures with Mai and her parents. A very tense meeting with the school, with Mai's story backed up by her classmates, had landed Niamh in hot water, there and at home. Maurice just wanted to twist the knife a little, let everyone see that the Khans were his honoured guests. Although Mai told him it wasn't necessary, she added honestly, "But thanks, I hope she sees us on the front page tomorrow and gets *sick!*"

Elsa and Lisa arrived with the rest of their colleagues and Michael hung back until Lisa sought him out, her face pink with happiness.

"You were amazing!" Michael assured her. "You're the star of the whole thing. Never mind the great Elsa Von Streng, they'll all be talking about the incredible Lisa Kennedy tomorrow."

"Ah hush," Lisa grinned, then caught her breath as Michael suddenly dropped to one knee.

From across the room, Teresa O'Brien and the O'Brien Irregulars watched as the young man spoke earnestly, his hand outstretched, the velvet box nestled in the palm of his hand. They leaned forward, as Lisa replied, and Michael stayed where he was, stock still, as if frozen in place.

And then they erupted in relieved and happy cheers as a huge beaming smile broke across Michael' face and Lisa accepted the ring.

"Oh!" Clara burst into happy tears, clutching Peadair's arm. "Doesn't it remind you of our engagement, love?"
"Eh, I blurted it out in a pub on a random Tuesday night, Clara.

I didn't even have a ring at the time. But yeah, other than that, identical…"

Eamonn kissed his wife, Elsa and Fintan exchanged a long look while holding hands, and Mai's parents giggled at each other like teenagers.

Teresa thought of her Cathal and sent up a kiss to heaven. In the end, love was what mattered. Friendship love, romantic love, love of beauty and music and art. It was love that would beat the Arnoldo Messinis and the Niamh Finnegans of the world.

Eventually, people like that had to face the music, while everyone else got to enjoy it. And that, Teresa thought, was enough for her.

Plus, now they had a wedding to plan!

About the Author

Geraldine lives in Dublin, Ireland with her husband, two boys and her mother. Her work is mainly set in Ireland, especially in her beloved Dublin. A lot of her work draws on Irish heritage and society, and in her spare time she teaches Irish mythology, folk lore, and folk magic.

She studied in UCD, worked in Advertising and Publishing and finally returned to her family roots to run a famous music shop in Dublin. She retired in 2021 to devote herself full time to writing and teaching.

Her detective novels include modern mystery novels **The Body Politic** and **The Body Count** (*Caroline Jordan Mystery Series*) She also writes **The Old Bat Chronicles** as Nina Hayes: cozy mysteries with a dollop of Irish magic.

She also writes non-fiction: her book on the Irish tradition of Draíocht Ceoil will be published by Moon Books in April 2026, and her next work will be on early Celtic Christianity in 2027.

She is proud to bring authentic Irish stories to life.

She has a very large and beautiful yarn collection and she loves to hear from readers.

You can connect with me on:

🌐 http://www.celebratingwords.com

f https://www.facebook.com/geraldinemoorkensbyrne

🔗 https://www.facebook.com/NinaHayesAuthor

Subscribe to my newsletter:

✉ https://mailchi.mp/a3703e884df5/author-sign-up

Also by Geraldine Moorkens Byrne

Traditional and Cosy Mysteries, Non-Fiction and more

On The Fiddle!

Mrs. O'Brien runs Ireland's oldest music shop, a landmark in Dublin city. Now, property developers are sniffing around her precious Stephen Street West, threatening residents and local businesses. As all the shop owners band together against the new landlords, murder strikes in the local cafe!

All the evidence points to the owner Dan, and the Gardaí seem satisfied - but Mrs. O'Brien is sure there's more to the story. She's determined to clear his name, aided by her protege Michael Clancy, madcap teen Mai Khan and the Super Ukers Ukulele Band.

But who can she trust, and who is *On the Fiddle!?*

The Kimberly Killing
The Old Bat Chronicles Book 1

Murder and mischief with a dollop of Irish magic make this a fun, escapist cozy mystery!

Artist Eve Caulton is 50, divorced and ready for a new life in idyllic Kimberly Cottage, on Bramble Lane.

But before she has even unpacked, there is a dead body in her living room and she's a chief suspect! Her mother Niamh calls on her gang of feisty older ladies, who bring wisdom, experience, and very special skills to the case. They might be known as "Old Bats" by some, but they will stop at nothing to untangle the secrets of Kimberly Cottage's past and solve the case before it's too late.

The Holly Homicide
The Old Bat Chronicles Book 2

A heartwarming, authentic, magical Irish Mystery!

Eve Caulton is looking forward to a peaceful Christmas in Kimberly Cottage until the Marrinans move into Holly Cottage, with plans that could destroy Bramble Lane. They've also brought trouble with them, not least the unpleasant Dolores McIntyre

When murder strikes, it's the last straw. Eve joins forces once again with the Old Bat herself, Dymphna Moriarty and the unique senior ladies of the area. It'll take the entire community, but the Wise Women won't let Christmas be ruined.

The Wisteria Wedding

The Old Bat Chronicles Book 3

Spring is the perfect time for romance, and the residents of Bramble Lane are looking forward to the wedding of neighbours Margaret and Ronan. To add to the excitement, the Merrion Literary Festival brings famous author Humphrey Sterling to Dublin, to the delight of the senior ladies of the area. Eve is busy helping with wedding preparations - until a terrible crime threatens to derail everything.

With the young couple's happiness under threat, Eve and the Old Bats must work their magic to save the day. Can they solve the crime before the big day - or will there even be a Wisteria Wedding?

Crochet, Canines and Crooks
*Part of the "A Paw-liday Craft Caper" series
(19 books)*

Ellie Maguire has volunteered to teach crochet at St Brigit's Nursing Home, where the residents are in dire need of some Christmas cheer. While she helps them to find their way around a hook and yarn, and her adorable hound Lexi brings laughter and wagging tails, it becomes clear that something is amiss at St Brigit's. Even her friend, Nurse Manager Sunita is worried.

A missing necklace and a night-time intruder puts everyone on edge but Ellie - and Lexi - won't let the residents down! Join the fun with great characters, lots of Irish charm and a fun mystery!

Draíocht Ceoil: The Sound of Magic in Irish Traditions
Within us all is the ability to hear the magic of sound, to use music and words to create a new reality. In Irish traditions this is known as Draíocht Ceoil - 'music magic' - an ancient art deeply rooted in Ireland's mythology and culture, used for generations to harness the power of sound for connecting to natural magical energy. This is the first book of its kind to examine the tradition of Draíocht Ceoil, its ancient roots in the poetic tradition of Old Ireland, and its evolution into a vital part of Irish folk magic practices.

Dreams of Reality

A collection spanning 40 years of published, and award winning poems inspired by the heritage and landscape of Ireland, the literary and poetic forms of Old Irish and the long political and satirical tradition of the Filí. This collection is divided into several parts, **At the Gate** (a reference to the ancient Irish tradition of fasting against an injustice) deals with the poetry of politics and justice. **In the Grove** contains the poetry of spirit and philosophy. **By the Fireside** showcases the poetry of love and personal life.

The final section **Bedside Manners** contains a series of poems written to express the grief and concerns of family carers for those with Alzheimer's and Dementia.